ISOBEL SCOTT MOFFAT, who was born in Scotland, but has lived many years in North Yorkshire, fulfilled an early ambition when the first of her romantic novels was published. Then came the compulsion to 'stretch' a favourite love story; *Mistress of Pemberley* is the result. In homage to Jane Austen.

MISTRESS OF PEMBERLEY

MISTRESS OF PEMBERLEY

Isobel Scott Moffat

ATHENA PRESS
LONDON

MISTRESS OF PEMBERLEY
Copyright © Isobel Scott Moffat 2008

All Rights Reserved

ISBN 13-digit: 978 1 84748 220 4

First Published 2008 by
ATHENA PRESS
Queen's House, 2 Holly Road
Twickenham TW1 4EG
United Kingdom

Printed for Athena Press

Chapter One

E lizabeth sat huddled in the corner of the coach, exhausted as much by the rigours and tensions of the seemingly endless journey as by the sense of guilt which had closed about her like a dark cloud when the news had first been relayed to them. It was not as if there had been the least indication of her mother being unwell, rather the opposite; for when they had seen her immediately before leaving for France, she had appeared in unusually good spirits, to such an extent that even her husband, Lizzie's own father, had been singularly amiable in temper.

Sighing deeply, she closed her eyes, settling further into her corner, thankful for all the padded comfort, still something of a novelty to her. Such luxury had not, after all, been long enjoyed by the Bennet family. Aware of a stool being slipped beneath her feet, hearing a murmur of the beloved voice, she flickered her eyelids towards the tall, dark figure sitting so close, allowed her mouth to curve in an appreciative smile. She had been so very fortunate. Sometimes, waking in the night, for an instant unable to recall where she was, then seeing him so close, the tumble of dark hair against the pillows, she would release the breath she had been holding in her apprehension before gratefully adjusting herself to the curve of his body.

But that very thought brought a sting of tears to her eyes. It was so unjust that her mother, having recently seen, after many troubled, anxious years, two of her daughters finally settled in the most comfortable of situations, should not have been granted a few more years to enjoy... A sob broke from her lips and, at once, she found a linen handkerchief pressed into her hand. His arm came comfortingly about her shoulders; his lips, as he spoke, moved against her brow.

'Hush, my dear, she is at peace now.'

'Yes.' A shuddering sigh. 'But... I do so hope we shall not be late.'

'Well, we have done our best. And I think we shall be in time. We have just passed Headley Crossroads so should arrive within the hour.'

And she relaxed, knowing he spoke only the truth, grateful for his strength and comfort in this sad time, her mind much occupied with memories which were, in such circumstances, invariably those happy ones which increased feelings of tearful longing.

'Elizabeth.' Even as his voice brought her from her reverie, she recognised from the sweeping change of direction which had always distinguished the drive of Longbourn from all other houses in the area, that she was home. Consequently, she was composed as they drew up in front of the house, grateful to be assisted by the coachman on one side and her husband on the other. 'You are ready, my love?'

'Yes, of course, Fitzwilliam.' Her wan face essayed a smile and he nodded approvingly as he saw her straighten her shoulders and raise her head high, as she walked towards the opening door and into her father's arms, uttering only the smallest cry of pain before turning to Jane, the dearest of her sisters, to whom she clung for some time before thinking of the others. Mr Darcy, who, over the last few days, had done much to comfort his wife in her sudden bereavement, became aware of a searching gaze on his face and, half turning, encountered the speculative expression of Mr Collins, who was strolling about with a proprietorial air that Mr Darcy's distant bow did nothing to subdue.

It was mid-afternoon when the mourners returned from the melancholy business of the day, returned to Longbourn for the almost equally dispiriting ritual of offering refreshment to those who had come from a distance – which was virtually everyone, Elizabeth decided, as she surveyed the groups spilling through the hall and into the downstairs apartments. Slowly, she and her sisters, following their father, began what she wished might be the final ceremony: that of greeting the many who had come to console – neighbours and friends. Elizabeth was especially glad to see those who had served the family for many years, and she made it her task to let them know how much she valued their presence at such a time. Then, with a sense of relief, and feeling that for the moment she had done enough, she freed herself from her duties and walked into the large, infrequently used formal dining parlour where all the refreshments were laid out and waiting, a splendid collation enhanced by gleaming china, silver and glass.

Until that moment, she had imagined herself alone, but now, at the far end of the table, she caught sight of Mr Collins, her father's heir (the estate being entailed in the male line), who was now raising a fine glass to the light, studying it intently before, with a light flick of the forefinger and a faint, approving smile, he assured himself of its quality and value. Clearly, he, too, thought himself alone, unobserved, and it was only too easy to visualise what thoughts were running through his mind as he saw himself move one step closer to his inheritance.

'Mr Collins.'

Despite the occasion, she could not resist the spark of mischief for which she was known and which now left him wondering if his ill-judged proprietary gesture had been observed. Instantly, he replaced the glass and turned towards her with a heightened colour not wholly concealed by his deferential bow.

'Mrs Darcy. May I say on behalf of Lady Catherine de Bourgh, as well as of Mrs Collins and myself, how greatly saddened we are by the untimely death of your most esteemed parent. To me, she was always most kind, her welcome warmer than perhaps might have been expected in the circumstances, so warm indeed that I feel I knew her much longer than was, in fact, the case.'

'Thank you, Mr Collins. I did see you at the church but was unable to speak to you then. Mrs Collins is, I understand, not with you.'

'No, regretfully, no. Since her time is so close, I beg you will excuse her.'

'Of course, it would have been foolish, especially—' Swiftly, Elizabeth bit off the implied criticism which so nearly burst from her lips. That her friend was about to have her third child within two and a half years of marriage was no excuse for an impertinent intrusion on her part. Quite regardless of the fact that, after Rose's difficult birth, Charlotte had expressed a weary hope that there would be no further pregnancies for some time, she herself must not express an opinion which might be traced back to her friend. Charlotte had more than enough to contend with in her marriage, for though Mr Collins was seen by outsiders as something of a buffoon, in the domestic role he ruled his kingdom like a petty tyrant. 'And,' she spoke in guilty haste, 'how are the children, Lily and Rose?'

'Oh, splendid. They are both well, although there was some concern last week when we thought Rose might have been in contact with one of the children from the cottages, but as soon as she heard that there was fever about, Lady Catherine, with her own hand—' He paused to afford a moment's astonished admiration for his patron's condescension. '—her own hand, mixed a remedy from a secret recipe which has been in her family for generations and which has kept our little one from harm. Her graciousness has no limits.'

'Indeed.' His companion, who had personal experience of Lady Catherine's graciousness, replied with some feeling then, with a little more thought for her godchild. 'And what, pray, Mr Collins, are the ingredients of this special mixture?'

'A secret recipe, Mrs Darcy,' Mr Collins emphasised in a skittish tone, which nevertheless bore a hint that the Spanish Inquisition itself would not wrest that information from him. 'Most secret, but if I were to guess,' he simpered, 'I would suggest vinegar, ginger and horseradish... But you must not betray me.'

'Naturally. But please tell me, what did Rose herself think of Lady Catherine's special compound?'

'She put up a fight, Mrs Darcy. She, of course, was unaware of whose hand had been involved, but, in time, she will learn.' His mouth closed in a firm line, which inclined Elizabeth to increase her sympathy for the child and to decide that when next she visited the Collinses she would have a few special sweetmeats for the little girls.

While these pleasantries were being exchanged, the other mourners had been entering and assembling about the room, which offered Elizabeth the opportunity to detach herself with a murmur of apology. Besides which, she had had little time to speak with dear Jane, whom she had just seen walk in on the arm of her husband, Mr Bingley. His sister, Miss Bingley, who was presently staying with her brother and his wife at Netherfield, had waylaid Fitzwilliam and backed him into a corner, her whole demeanour suggesting a determination to keep him in conversation. Elizabeth and Fitzwilliam had had time to do little more than exchange the briefest of greetings with the Netherfield company on their arrival, since when there had been no opportunity for that exchange of confidences which had always made her relationship with her sister such a very happy one.

Jane looked pale and somewhat wan which, combined with her husband's solicitous attentions, made Elizabeth certain that her sister's suspicion, briefly confided at their last meeting before the unfortunate journey to France, must now be a certainty.

'Now, Jane...' Crossing the room to where her sister was seated alone, Elizabeth joined her on the sofa, took her hand and leaned towards her so that her words would not be overheard. 'How are you? Am I to congratulate you and Mr Bingley?'

'Lizzie—' A sudden flush washed the white skin; the blue eyes studied their linked hands; her mouth trembled for a moment before she looked up. 'Yes.' A sigh. 'You are to become an aunt. But, for the moment, Mr Bingley and I wish to keep this news to ourselves. So much has happened so quickly...' The brilliance in her eyes indicated that tears were not far off, and Elizabeth felt a sympathetic sting in her own. 'I shall miss her...' The voice was barely steady. '...sorely. And you will understand, Lizzie, that this changes things... I feel that we cannot consider leaving Netherfield at present. We must wait. Papa will need our support.'

'I did think of that, my dear Jane, and, while I am disappointed and have missed you greatly, I know that our father needs you and he will be relieved to have you and Mr Bingley staying so close. We must wait and see what the future brings. And, perhaps later, at some time, you may be able to reconsider your wish to move to Derby. As to your secret, it is safe with me,' her sister assured her fondly, while thinking that it was one which would not long keep, since Jane's entire demeanour seemed to advertise that which was to be kept privy. But she must be reassuring and casual. 'Well, I am almost used to being an aunt now.' She cast a glance towards where their younger sister, Lydia, was holding forth with great and unbecoming gusto to a group which included

Sir William and Lady Lucas, the latter looking exceedingly haughty at such lack of dignity on the day of her friend's funeral and doubtless deciding her own disapproval of the younger Bennet girls had been richly merited.

'Ah, yes,' Jane sighed. Lydia and Mr Wickham were still not wholly restored to the family, and since Mrs Bennet, their greatest champion, was now gone, it was unlikely that they ever would be. 'Their two boys must be a great expense.'

To this Elizabeth made no reply. From the corner of her eye, she saw her husband, having apparently thrown off Miss Bingley, had just re-entered the room with her father and knew they would have spent some time in the library discussing just what must be done to help the Wickham family. The matter had been fully thrashed out even before they had gone to France, and though she, Lizzie, had not wholly agreed with the plan, she knew her husband had made a considerable settlement on them with the strict proviso that it was to appear as if it came from the Bennets. Of course, it went against all his instincts to involve himself further with Mr Wickham, but for the sake of his wife's peace of mind concerning her sister, he was prepared to stifle his own feelings of dislike and betrayal.

As the two men circled the room, stopping once or twice to exchange sentiments with neighbours, Elizabeth was conscious of her husband's eyes searching her out, causing that familiar flutter in her bosom, which so often afflicted her when they were in company. To be truthful, neither had been entirely prepared for the state of bliss into which marriage had led them; certainly, it was far from the appearance of mere contentment that was general among their acquaintances unless, perhaps, like themselves, most preferred to conceal it from the common view.

But even with Jane, her sister and confidante as well as her dearest friend, she suspected things were not quite so... so impassioned. Warm and comfortable certainly, but, when she had hinted at something deeper, more intense, then Jane's faintly puzzled expression had made her change direction and keep her thoughts to herself. She was happy, of course she was, that Jane and Mr Bingley were so content each with the other but rather smug that she and Mr Darcy... yet a tiny shiver instantly tempered the warm feelings, for here was Jane in her condition while she...

A finger brushing against the nape of her neck brought her head round and the wisp of a smile to her lips as she looked up at him, exchanging a secret glance which held so much promise but yet... Her anxiety would not quite be banished. He had given her so much and she... she longed to give him the news for which she was sure he was waiting.

Yet, when she had confided her fears, whispering miserably in the dark hours of the night, he had held her to him, kissing her, gently at first, comforting, reassuring her that all would be well. But, the fear continued to nag, if it should not... if it should be beyond her ability to give him the one thing so important to a man in his position... She wondered if he would be able to forgive.

'Your father,' he interrupted her troubled thoughts, 'has gone back to the library, my dear. I expect he would be glad to see you there presently.'

And she smiled at him, for the moment her fears banished.

Mr Bennet sat in the library, a glass of port on the table beside him, the decanter already half empty but close to hand. He sighed deeply as he considered the conversation he had just had with Mr Darcy. It was hard for a man to be dependent on his son-in-law and, no matter how easy Fitzwilliam had made it for him, the whole business of the Wickhams stuck in his throat. Tossing back the wine, he refilled his glass and, while he sipped, allowed his mind to meander back over the years.

To come to this and all because a pretty, but foolish, young woman had caught his eye some twenty-five years earlier. And since one of his friends had thrown out a general challenge that not one of their group could cut out the swaggering young officer with whom the pretty young creature was seemingly obsessed, he had been hooked. Well, he sighed deeply, young men in their cups had ever found such innocent foolishness irresistible and, where redcoats were concerned, it was more than the twenty-one-year-old Mr Bennet of Longbourn could resist. Even when he had detached her from the dashing young ensign, he felt honour bound to satisfy his pride by acting the gallant a little longer and did not perceive the danger until he was standing in front of the preacher with the eyes of her father and brother boring into his back. He barely had time to reflect on his folly, and certainly lacked the military experience to make a proper tactical withdrawal, before he was aware of his own voice making the appropriate responses.

And thus two lives were brought to ruin, for Mr Bennet could not think of two people who were so ill prepared for marriage, let alone marriage to each other, as he and his wife had been. She, with her heart forever set on redcoats – a trait she had passed on to at least one of her daughters – and giddy for the company of soldiers, with scarcely a serious thought in her head, while he… Well, it was too late for self-pity and, to tell the truth, as a husband he had been no great catch, though through all the years of disillusion, beneath all his impatience, he had harboured feelings of regret for his wife even more than for himself. She might very easily have been deliriously happy married to an officer, giddy with delight at the prospect of her officer eventually achieving the rank of colonel; she might have had that perfect life which he knew he had some part in denying her. He would not, on this day of all days, dwell on the less generous thought he had harboured through the years: that he had very likely saved some young ensign, as callow and gullible as he had been, from a lifetime's frustration – though that condition might very easily have been eased for them by the separations occasioned by his calling. And he, because of the clutch of daughters following one so speedily on the heels of the other in his determination to breed a son, was robbed of the means of assuring a future for any of them. Had even the plainest, poor Mary, who, while inheriting her mother's lack of sense had singularly missed the compensation of those long-flown youthful charms, had the sense to be a boy, then their entire circumstance might have been turned about. For then the estate would have been secured, providing some assistance for any daughter who remained unmarried, and would especially have avoided falling into the hands of that grasping fellow, Collins.

But fortunately – and he must remember to count his blessings – the eldest two girls had done rather better for themselves than might, at one time, have been hoped for, and certainly his dear Lizzie had narrowly avoided disaster. For, had her mother's will prevailed, she could even now have been tied to that preaching nincompoop, Mr Collins, and already breeding petticoats. For a moment, he cherished the image of his *bête noire* suffering the same terrible anxieties as he himself had endured unto the fifth degree. Normally it afforded Mr Bennet some comfort, but today of all days even that could not raise his melancholy mood for long. Besides, such an outcome would mean only that the inheritance would pass further away from his own family, possibly toward some far-flung colonial who had not as much as heard of Longbourn. Yes, a superfluity of girls was a burden for any man to endure, and what might have become of Mrs Wickham but for the intervention of Mr Darcy was hard to say. But for his swift action, Lydia would certainly have been disgraced and the entire family with her. Then, he doubted not that Bingley and Darcy would have fled the district lest their emotions should overcome their sense, and they woke to find themselves entrapped by his notorious tribe.

Now, there were still the youngest two to be considered, and while there might be some hope for Kitty, who, though easily led astray, was not entirely without some of the comelier qualities of Jane, he despaired of poor, silly Mary unless a visiting curate might be persuaded… But no, he must not jest – however privately – on such a matter, rather, try to make some arrangement whereby her other sisters might 'share' her throughout the year when he was no longer here to act as her protector. And with that decision arrived at, he reached out unsteadily for the decanter, feeling he owed himself another glass for having done so much to resolve their future difficulties.

'Papa.' It was Lizzie's touch on his arm which woke him; he started, knocking over his glass as he tried to rise to his feet. 'Sir William and Lady Lucas are leaving. I knew you would wish to say goodbye to them.'

'Yes, my dear. Yes, indeed.' With some resolve he rose, brushed one hand over his slightly disordered hair and pulled down the corners of his coat. 'I am sorry, my dear, I felt so weary that I closed my eyes for a moment and... it may have been a little longer than that.'

'Yes, Papa, I am sure everyone will understand.' She made no reference to the empty decanter, which she had already noted and, since her father was a very moderate drinker, might be considered of little consequence. Who could blame him for seeking some consolation on a day like this? And, being aware of her father's foibles, she was all too ready to assume that there had been regrets, as well as sorrows, to be faced. Lacing her arm through his, she accompanied him through the door and into the hall where departing friends were already assembling. 'Mr Collins is with Charlotte's parents. You will be civil to him, Papa, will you not?'

'To be sure, Lizzie, when am I ever other than civil to a man of the cloth?'

'Papa!' She spoke warningly. 'The poor man cannot help the situation, you know that. It was none of his making.'

'True, my dear. But if only he would be less... triumphant about it. Each time he looks at me, he is seeing me in my shroud, his lips muttering prayers of thanksgiving.'

'Papa!' But she could not control a smile, her mischievous nature irrepressible even on such an inappropriate occasion and difficult to conceal until she touched a handkerchief to her face.

'Think, Lizzie, you might have been Mrs Collins if you had played your cards more cleverly.' And without giving her time to voice some passionate reply, which would remind him that all her mother's tears and persuasions would have had not the slightest effect on her own determination to protect her maiden state from the likes of Mr Collins, he detached himself and began shaking hands in the most gentlemanly way, putting himself out to be so civil to her cousin that the poor man was torn between his habitual gratification and such intense suspicion as to cause his eyes to narrow and to look closely at Elizabeth, who turned away in some confusion.

'Mrs Darcy.' Elizabeth was startled from her own thoughts by the sudden, but instantly recognisable, voice from behind, and she turned, trying to find a mild enquiring expression as she faced Miss Bingley. 'My brother and I have been so upset for all of you.

Dear Jane was quite beside herself, and it has been hard for us to find words of comfort'.

Gravely, Elizabeth nodded her acknowledgement while knowing deep down that such assurances were mere platitudes. It would never be erased from her mind that this woman had been an instrument in all the slights and condescension she had been forced to endure during her involuntary stay at Netherfield when Jane had been suddenly taken ill during her visit. Now, she was aware that Miss Bingley was a more frequent visitor at Netherfield than either Jane or her young – and slightly ineffectual – husband would have wished.

Fitzwilliam, too, did not wholly escape censure on the matter of his conduct at that time. Occasionally, in her teasing, provocative way, she made reference to it, but inevitably her husband begged her to forget the matter and, most of all, to forget his own part in the sorry business. Normally, having had her few moments of diversion, she was only too happy to spare his embarrassment, especially since she knew how deeply he regretted his failure to do anything to protect her from the spiteful behaviour shown by both of Mr Bingley's sisters. While her husband was long forgiven, their behaviour still rankled, although she did have moments of pity for Miss Bingley that she had so signally failed in her objective of becoming the mistress of Pemberley. And it must be a source of further grief to her that what she so much coveted had been achieved, without apparent effort, by someone as unworthy of the honour as Miss Elizabeth Bennet.

'You are very kind, Miss Bingley.'

'And if there is anything I can do to help your poor father, who must be desolate at the loss of his dear wife.'

Such hypocrisy robbed Elizabeth for a moment of the power of speech. She knew exactly the general opinion these people had formed of her mother: every amused glance and condescending look was graved on her mind. Not wholly undeserved, since she and Jane had blushed for their mother a thousand times, and if it had not been for the highly respected position held by her father, his place in society, his gentlemanly manner and intellectual ability, then their family would have been in a sorry state. But, as well, her mother had her own qualities not immediately visible to those outside the family, which she had loved so devotedly and by which she was loved in return – at least by her daughters. Had she not, with the best of motives, schemed and plotted for them, though not always with the discretion which they themselves would have wished? Even now, Elizabeth had simply to allow her mind to drift back a little towards the days immediately before Fitzwilliam's final offer of marriage to feel again the scald of embarrassed shame.

But her companion was clearly waiting for some sort of continuance of their conversation and, even as she was trying to recall the last comment, she found Miss Bingley had taken her arm and was guiding her back into the reception room where a moment later they were both sitting on a sofa with the older woman looking anxiously into her eyes.

'Mrs Darcy.' Her face was very close, close enough for Elizabeth to come to the unworthy conclusion that her companion was older than she had originally believed. Fitzwilliam had suggested that she was the eldest of the family – close to thirty he had hazarded – and now she could fully believe that reckoning. She deplored her feeling of satisfaction, trying instead to concentrate on the confection the other woman was wearing on her head. Miss Bingley had always shown a liking for elaborate turban-style bonnets and this one, in dark shades of purple decorated with a swirling black feather, was typical, especially in the eccentric angle at which it was set upon her head and pulled down over the left eyebrow. 'A style all her own,' as Mr Bennet had so often referred to Lydia's much decorated attempts at millinery.

'Mrs Darcy.' The other woman's repetition of her name, allied to her intimate manner, brought Elizabeth back to the moment. 'I wish to assure you that you need have no concern about your sister in her—' Here she gave a tiny apologetic cough, lowered her voice: '—her present condition.'

'Oh?' Elizabeth was slightly taken aback, having understood that no one… but before she could consider how to proceed, the other went on.

'I know how fond you are of dear Jane, and now that I, too, know her so well I share the same tender feelings for her, believe me. And I want to reassure you that I shall watch her as carefully as you would yourself if you were at hand. But living at Pemberley, so far from your beloved family... I am sure you will welcome regular reports, since I shall be a frequent visitor at Netherfield until she is safely returned to her normal health.'

'You... you are too kind, Miss Bingley.' Elizabeth could think of nothing more to say. It would not do for her to suggest that perhaps Jane and Mr Bingley would welcome rather fewer of these visits. It was his place to control such affairs, though she doubted he had the will to do so. But the Bingley family had, from what she had recently been informed, always been controlled by determined and dominating women.

'And, while I am at Netherfield – and though sadly I cannot promise to be with Mr and Mrs Bingley constantly throughout the next several months – rest assured that I shall do my best to ensure that they... we,' here a smirk, 'do not mean to leave Mr Bennet moping too sadly and too long on his own.'

'Well...' For a moment, Elizabeth could think of nothing which would please her father less than to be subjected to the company of this meddling woman, but since the niceties had to be observed, she nodded approval. 'That would be taken very kindly, Miss Bingley. And as you say, I cannot be forever on the scene, since Pemberley is at some distance, but naturally I do hope that my father will spend some time with us there. He and Mr Darcy are already quite close, and I hope in the future their intimacy will increase.'

'Indeed, that is much to be hoped for in all families, and certainly, if he can spend some time with you and Mr Darcy as well as with my brother and Jane, then we may hope that he will soon revive his spirits.'

'Indeed.' Elizabeth heard out this conversation with feelings she could not quite identify, a sensation of unease, though her companion's manner was more amiable than it had ever been. But, at that very moment, Miss Bingley, giving the impression of sudden emergency, got to her feet and bustled off in search of 'dear Jane' who must, she stated anxiously, be wearied and sorely in need of rest. For a moment or two, Elizabeth pondered the conversation before rising to her feet with a great sigh, which indicated she had reached no very firm conclusion, and going to join her father and her husband, who were saying their farewells to the last of the mourners.

It was while they were driving home the next day in their carriage that Elizabeth, knowing he was aware of Jane's condition, felt free now to recount to her husband the conversation with Miss Bingley. 'I hope it is not her intention to spend too much time with the Bingleys at Netherfield. This is a time when they ought to be together, without a third party always with them.'

'Hmm. You must remember that the brother and sisters have always been very close, although he is the youngest by several years, I believe.'

'Yes, of course.' Remembering her own situation and Fitzwilliam's fondness for his sister, Georgiana, Elizabeth understood she must be careful. It was all very well to be given to expressing her opinions forcefully, but she no longer wished to call her husband so keenly to account as she had done before they were married. The recollection of those early days when she must have tried his feelings to the limit was sufficient to encourage her to slip her hand through his arm in a warm manner, which caused him to link his fingers through hers in return before taking them to his lips.

'It must have been very hard for you, my love, these recent days. Your bearing and dignity have been admirable, but I know that inwardly you have been mourning the loss of someone who was very dear.'

Understanding his own opinion of her mother, Lizzie could not help but find his words affecting, and her voice shook slightly as she thanked him. Since their marriage, his restraint towards the woman he had described as 'much wanting in propriety' had been admirable, and certainly Mrs Bennet herself had reacted by behaving with more decorum than she had shown in her entire life. The words Elizabeth had read in the letter he had handed her in the wood near Rosings had forced her to confront the frequent embarrassment caused to her family by her mother and younger sisters. For as long as she could recall, she had devoutly hoped that others would be less sensitive to such behaviour than she was herself, but his letter had torn away any such comforting delusion. Then, when her first anger had cooled, she had been forced to acknowledge that much of what he had said was the simple truth: that her mother behaved with much less circumspection than might have been expected of the mistress of Longbourn. Recollection of the dance at Netherfield and her loud criticism of Mr Darcy was still capable of inducing a scald of colour, making Lizzie wonder how he, a man in his situation, could have brought himself even to acknowledge his feelings for her.

'Miss Bingley seems to think she will be able to coax my father out of his despondency.' Even as she spoke, she pondered how deeply her mother would be mourned by the man to whom she had been married for so many years. During their brief exchange in the library, she had detected in her father a sense of true regret, but it was impossible to rid herself of the idea that many emotions came to the surface at such times, and he might simply have felt sorrow that they had been so ill matched.

'And what do you think, Elizabeth?' His question interrupted her reverie. 'Do *you* think she might be able to coax him from those desolate thoughts which afflict him?'

'I do not think she will have the least effect on him, Fitzwilliam. But at least, if she does visit him at Longbourn, that will mean Jane and Mr Bingley may have a little more time to themselves. But I am rather pleased,' the thought appearing to have a lightening effect on her rather melancholy spirits, 'that we shall be sufficiently distant to avoid the possibility of being cheered by Miss Caroline Bingley.'

'Oh.' Sensing that her husband was slightly taken aback by her vehemence, she looked up into his face, one brow arched in query as she noticed his disinclination to meet her eyes. 'Oh,' he repeated, gnawing briefly on his lower lip. 'Then, I am sorry, my dear, that I have just issued a pressing invitation that she come and stay with us at Pemberley as soon as may be.'

'Fitzwilliam!' For a moment she contemplated the prospect of a visit from the woman who had tried to wreck her sister's happiness, whose entire manner was condescending, and wondered how she would be able to endure such an ordeal. Then at last she said, 'And for how long did you suggest that Miss Bingley should stay at Pemberley?'

'Oh.' Again he gave the impression of embarrassment, averting his eyes from her upturned face, apparently intent on the passing scenery. 'I think I suggested that, considering the distance, she ought perhaps to make a lengthy visit.' Then, as if taking his courage in both hands, he looked straight at her. 'My dear, I am conscious that you must find Pemberley rather dull and that you will miss the family atmosphere of Longbourn without the companionship of your sisters.'

'No, Fitzwilliam, I do not.' She spoke with much of her old passion. 'I do not,' she repeated, still more firmly, and then, observing something about the brightness of his eyes, seeing the corners of his mouth twitch, she paused for a second, feeling a faint lightening of her spirits. 'Fitzwilliam?' And her own lips began to quiver as she sensed, with a stab of pleasure, that she was at the receiving end of one of his teases.

'Don't look at me like that, Mrs Darcy!' His head bent towards her and she caught the gleam of white teeth. 'Or I shall be forced to kiss you.'

'It will take more than a kiss, Mr Darcy, to restore my humour after what you have told me.'

'Then we must wait until we reach Pemberley, I suppose.'

'And, in the meantime, you will inform Miss Bingley that your wife is in no need of companionship so long as,' and her mouth was now moving against his, 'so long as she has her husband with her.'

'If that is... what you wish, my dear.'

'That is what I demand, Mr Darcy.' And she sat back in her seat, smiling, wondering how she could ever have imagined that this man was so stiff and proud. She suspected – and indeed was touched by the idea – that beneath the proud surface lurked a shyer man than was ever shown to society.

Chapter Two

*I*t was several months before Mr Bennet felt sufficiently recovered from his changed circumstances to fit in a visit to his favourite daughter and son-in-law at Pemberley, but at length they were able to welcome him, with not a few tears on Lizzie's side and repeated 'there theres' and patting of shoulders from her father, which was a comfort to both.

But after an hour or two, things had settled down, and Elizabeth was happy to note that her husband and her father were as much at ease with each other as she could have wished. News from her old home had been reported and discussed from every angle, and it was with interest that she heard of how steadily Mary's music was progressing due to the diligence of a Mistress Castlemain, who had come to reside in the district.

'Yes.' Elizabeth rose from her sewing frame where she had been trying to interest herself in making a new seat for one of the library chairs and carried it to a far corner of the room, where it was abandoned with a sigh of relief. 'I have heard all about this wonderful lady from one of my sister's letters. It appears she is a great favourite with the girls.'

'Indeed. A great hit, and I cannot say how glad I am that they have taken to her, for her influence is just what is needed after...' Here Mr Bennet paused for an instant before continuing in a slightly vexed tone, '...After all, they are now without a mother and need a steadying hand.'

'Of course.' Neither she nor Mr Darcy was in the slightest doubt as to what he had begun to say, but to Elizabeth it was a relief that he had not sought to tarnish her mother's memory. Now that she was gone, it was imperative that they should forgive her small peccadilloes and—

'Naturally,' Mr Darcy agreed smoothly. 'And from what Elizabeth has heard from Kitty, she, too, is benefiting from her good influence.'

'Yes. Kitty is determined to learn French, in which Mrs Castlemain is fluent, and the good soul is perfectly willing to teach her. Though I fear she may find such a prospect beyond her capabilities. None of my children, with the exception of Lizzie, has ever shown the slightest inclination to stretch her mind.'

'Papa!' Elizabeth's tone held some reproach. 'You must not. Truly you must not say things which are so far from the truth. Jane, as well as being the sweetest of creatures, is more than my equal and if the others—'

'Stuff and nonsense, Elizabeth. You are the only one who ever spent more than a few moments in the library at Longbourn, and while I agree that Jane is a sweet girl well enough, I dare say, for a man like Bingley – I doubt that Mr Darcy here would have found her sufficiently spirited.'

Mr Darcy, who had been listening quietly, raised an eyebrow in his wife's direction as if inviting her to argue the last point with her father, which, with a faint toss of her head, she refused to do, preferring to return to the matter of their new neighbour and friend.

'I understand Mrs Castlemain has travelled widely and so commands many languages.'

'Especially Italian and French, I believe. Her late husband was in the diplomatic service and with him she travelled round much of Europe and the Near East. It was while she was at Longbourn for a music lesson that Kitty suddenly discovered this longing which she had so successfully kept hidden these many years: a desire to become proficient first in French, then to move on to Italian, perhaps to study the works of Dante. Upon my soul!' He slapped his hand against his thigh. 'That is the very explanation. It had escaped me until this instant.'

'Papa! You must not be so hard on Kitty and Mary. Be thankful that they have come under the influence of a sensible woman and encourage them.'

'Forgive me, my dear.' Mr Bennet did appear to be slightly chastened at his daughter's reproach. 'Having spent a lifetime in cynical observation, it is a hard indulgence to give up. And you are right to remind me of such things, but the truth is that I am indeed thankful for the kindly administrations of Mrs Castlemain, and not simply for the sakes of Kitty and Mary but on my own behalf as well. If she had been less willing to lodge at Longbourn, then I should have found it difficult to leave the two girls with only the servants. She is such an amiable woman, with a keen interest in events and a quick mind. Besides, she saves me much vexation when Miss Bingley calls unexpectedly.'

'Oh?' There having been little mention of Miss Bingley in the letters which had reached Elizabeth from Longbourn, her anxieties had gradually slipped away over the weeks. 'Miss Bingley is a regular visitor, is she, Papa?'

'Very regular, my dear. Very regular indeed.'

'I should have thought, sir...' Darcy rose from his seat opposite his father-in-law and strolled to the window. Having successfully avoided pursuit by the woman now being discussed, it crossed his mind to question what possible motive she might have for such frequent visits to Longbourn. 'I should have thought Miss Bingley might have been an admirable person to show guidance to your younger daughters. She is, after all, cultured, also with an enquiring mind, which would be of great benefit to two girls as young as Kitty and Mary.' Returning, he took a seat by his wife's side on the sofa, sitting at an angle where he could indulge his tireless interest in the changing emotions of her expression. 'Having her own fortune, she might be inclined to take them to London to see and to be seen by the *beau monde*.'

'Well, we have seen the effects of the *beau monde* on silly young women,' Mr Bennet retorted, with a return of his old taciturnity before continuing in a more measured tone, 'And I would not wish that on any of them, but...' He appeared hesitant about continuing: then, 'When Bingley's sister comes to Longbourn, she shows little interest in the doings of Kitty and Mary; indeed, often it appears she wishes them anywhere but in their own home. In short...' Again he came to an awkward halt and showed little inclination to go further until his daughter nudged him gently.

'In short... Papa?'

'Miss Bingley, Lizzie,' and his words came forth in a rush, as if he could hide his anxieties no longer, 'gives the impression that she has her mind set on becoming your stepmama.'

There was a lengthening silence, which gave Elizabeth time to recall her thoughts on the day of her mother's funeral, her feeling of unease at the promises of help and comfort for the widower and the suggestion that she would be a frequent visitor at Netherfield. Now, with her father's explanation, it all became much clearer. 'Oh.' Her thoughts were voiced without discretion. 'Poor Papa.'

'Indeed, Lizzie. Poor Papa, indeed. For if I should ever be in need of a wife – which I promise you, I never shall be – Miss Bingley will come far down the list of possible contenders for the honour. And another promise I shall make you is that no sooner would she find herself in possession of the spoils than she would be wishing herself back to her former state.'

'Oh, Papa, you must not—'

'No, Lizzie, we must be honest, and I promise I have no wish to make another woman an unsatisfactory husband. One error of such magnitude is sufficient, and though I am uncertain that Miss Bingley is deserving of such consideration, I have not forgotten how she treated you and your sister. But, that apart, I would not have the heart for it. But before we move on from this sad matter, I must express my gratitude to you, Darcy, for this invitation to spend some weeks at Pemberley. The opportunity to disappear from Longbourn at this time was most opportune, and perhaps before my return there will be an influx of more suitable men into the area, and she will give me up in pursuit of more amenable prey.'

At this, Darcy gave a great shout of laughter in which Elizabeth joined, more discreetly, and even Mr Bennet smiled ruefully. But his daughter suspected he must have been seriously concerned and that he well understood how easy it might have been to drift into a situation from which it would have been difficult to extricate himself.

There the matter rested and was not generally referred to for the remainder of Mr Bennet's stay in Derbyshire, though Elizabeth could not resist a little gentle teasing on the subject in the privacy of their own apartments.

'Were you surprised, Fitzwilliam, to hear that Miss Bingley may be pursuing my papa?'

'No.' He strolled from his dressing room into their bed chamber and watched his wife's reflection as she stood before the large mirror, moving her head this way and that as she admired the gleaming movement of the crystal earrings he had bought for her in Paris. 'No,' he repeated as he came forward to lean his elbow on the overmantel, 'by no means.'

'You are saying,' the dark eyes which had been her first attraction for him brimmed with laughter, 'you are not surprised that she appears to be chasing my papa?'

'Perhaps it is as he said: that she is more intent on becoming your mama.'

'Or yours.' She shot the words back at him with that hint of perversity which was part of her charm. 'Has that occurred to you, Fitzwilliam? That having failed in one relationship with you, she would settle for stepmother to one of the great landowners of Derbyshire?'

'Now, my dear Lizzie, you are allowing your fancy to run out of control. There was never any question of Miss Bingley and me being other than very good friends.'

And, for the moment, Elizabeth was content to leave the matter there. She knew when her teasing had reached the limits of good taste and would not push beyond that point. 'Well...' Walking towards him, she dropped a tiny caress on the corner of his mouth, at the same time raising a hand to smooth the dark cloth of his coat. 'I am happy to hear it. Now, shall we go downstairs? I am sure my father is impatient for his dinner, and since there are no other guests...' Turning, they walked towards the door, her hand contained in the crook of his arm. 'I am so looking forward to Georgiana's return from her visit to Rosings, and I am certain my father will be pleased to hear the latest news of Lady Catherine and the Collins family.' And it was her droll sideways look which brought a decided smile to her husband's mouth as they went to join her father, who awaited them in the library.

'So, my dear Miss Georgiana.' Two days later, Mr Bennet was exerting himself to be an entertaining house guest to the young woman who had just returned from the visit to her aunt and, while tired from the journey, had declared herself fit enough to join the family for dinner. 'You are pleased to be back home once more?'

'Indeed, sir,' the young woman replied, with perhaps more emphasis than the simple question merited. 'Very glad indeed. Although my aunt and cousin pressed me to stay, a month from home is as much as I care to venture, and I was anxious to be back with my brother and sister again.'

'We, too, have missed you greatly, Georgiana.' Elizabeth, who could not forget the ordeal of her own short visits to Rosings and Lady Catherine's overbearing manner, spoke with sympathy. 'And we are happy to have you back with us again. But you found your aunt and cousin well, I believe.'

'Quite well. At least that is true of Lady Catherine, less so of her daughter, but then she has never been strong.'

'And what of Mrs Collins? Did you see anything of Charlotte during your visit to Rosings? It is some time since I had the pleasure of a letter from her.'

'I beg your pardon, Elizabeth, I ought to have told you immediately that she sends you her warmest greetings and will address you soon. She has, alas, been far from well since her confinement, but now she insists she feels better. My aunt has been much occupied in gathering herbs and spices, which she brews into the physics she claims will help poor Mrs Collins, and so I feel she must improve.'

'Indeed,' replied her sister-in-law, her voice heavy with irony, which Georgiana was too innocent to note. Then, intercepting a warning glance from her husband, Lizzie continued in a more general way. 'And have they decided on a name for the baby? Time is getting on and her christening is surely overdue.'

'Oh, I heard my aunt say something of the same,' Georgiana seemed not to notice Lizzie's raised eyebrow at the unwelcome comparison with Lady Catherine. 'But Mr Collins, it seems, is so discommoded by the arrival of yet another girl that he has refused to sanction any of the names favoured by his wife.'

'I should have thought Catherine would have been an appropriate choice.' Elizabeth spoke sharply, then smiled towards her husband. 'That is Charlotte's mother's name after all, so she could not be accused of any indelicacy towards Mr Collins's patron.'

'Well, that is one name my wife and I did not consider, although I fully understand Mr Collins's running out of names in the circumstances.' Mr Bennet, who had taken a noticeably cheerful view of the news which had reached them several weeks earlier concerning the arrival of a third Collins daughter, now raised his glass. 'I wish the child well in any event and hope she may bring her parents as much happiness as my daughter Lizzie has done.'

And so they all drank to that noble expression, although Lizzie wondered if she was the only one who suspected her father's motives. It was unworthy of her, she knew that, but it was impossible to banish the thought that Mr Bennet was finding a great deal of consolation in the spectacle of Mr Collins suffering the same frustrations he himself had been obliged to endure. And at the same time, she felt great concern for her friend Charlotte and some fear for her future health, wishing with all her heart that she might have a few years without the responsibility of providing a male heir for Mr Collins.

This was a concern she shared with her husband when they were alone in the darkness of their bedroom, with only the dying embers of the fire playing a few flickering shadows on the silk-lined walls. And Fitzwilliam, so sensitive to her moods and fears, placed his arm about her and drew her close to him. 'What is worrying you, Elizabeth?'

She felt his breath stir a wisp of hair at her forehead and sighed deeply. 'I was thinking of Mrs Collins. I am afraid she will have displeased her husband by giving him another daughter and…'

'And…' His was a gentle voice, for he was sure she was dwelling on her own uncertainties, which they had already discussed.

'And,' the words burst from her, 'here am I, apparently unable to give you even a daughter. Oh, Fitzwilliam, what if I should never—' And the sob would not be repressed.

'My dear.' He held her close so she could feel the loud beating of his heart against the softer echo of her own. 'I have no doubt that we shall one day have a child… children. But, unlike you, I feel no pressure, no impatience for that time to come. I am very content with our life as it is at present, which is as close to perfection as ever I could hope for in this world. When I recall that at one time, not so long ago, I thought you were beyond my grasp, beyond my hopes and desires, then other wishes and longings are of little importance to me. But let me remind you that my parents were five years wed and had given up hope before I was born, while we have been less than half that. Then, many years later, came Georgiana, whose arrival was such a blessing. These things are best left to providence, my dear. And have you thought...' And he whispered something in her ear, audible to none but his wife and which caused her a tiny, shuddering sigh before she lay more comfortably back on the soft pillow where she could watch her husband while they both drifted off into sleep.

Returning to Longbourn after his pleasant visit to Derbyshire, Mr Bennet found himself once more, and slightly unexpectedly, a grandfather. He had no sooner reached home and was sitting in his parlour when Mr Bingley arrived in a state of considerable excitement and disarray to announce himself as the father of twin girls.

'My goodness me.' Mr Bennet regarded his son-in-law over the rim of his spectacles for a moment, then rose and shook him warmly by the hand. 'My goodness.' He busied himself for a moment with decanters and glasses. 'Twin girls, eh? And how is dear Jane?'

'Jane is well, sir.' Which was more than her husband seemed to be, Mr Bennet thought rather sourly, before raising his glass in a toast. More girls, a thought as repetitive as it was unbecoming, but then it scarce mattered, since the Bingley estates were not entailed and doubtless, as they seemed so fecund, there would be boys aplenty, possibly sooner than might be wished by his daughter. Which took his thoughts in a different but slightly adjacent direction. 'And what of your sister, sir? Is she happy to be an aunt twice over? And so unexpectedly soon?'

'My sister, Mr Bennet?' For a moment, Bingley appeared thrown by the question, then his puzzlement cleared. 'Oh, my sister Caroline has gone to Bath. She of course planned to be here with us, but since Jane was brought to bed rather earlier...'

'Oh, good, good.' More than pleased to discover that, during his absence, Miss Bingley had disappeared in the direction of Bath, where she would hopefully be taking the waters and it was possible that it would be some time before she returned to Netherfield, Mr Bennet thus happily discovered on the very day of his return to Longbourn that he might allow his anxieties to ease.

It was later that same day when a discreet tap on his library door signalled the presence of Mrs Castlemain, who was presenting herself in order to report on the encouraging progress of her pupils, and it was when she had gone that a pleasing thought came into his mind, an idea prompted by the lady's comely appearance and pleasant manners, confident yet quiet, which seemed to him just as it should be in a woman of such obvious taste and style.

When her name had first been mentioned by the rural dean as a possible piano tutor for Mary, who, heaven knows, was badly in need of guidance in that area, he had been doubtful, but from the moment of their meeting it had been clear that her influence on both girls would indeed be beneficial. At first, there had been no mention of her connections, but he had since learned that she was full cousin to the Earl of Clare and, though from a penniless branch of the family, it was a reassuring point in her favour. And thus he hit on the stratagem that, in any future visits Miss Bingley might choose to make to Longbourn, he would protect himself by the simple device of inviting Mrs Castlemain, should she be present in the house at the time, to join them in a glass of wine and a slice of Madeira cake. The simplicity of the plan gave him great pleasure and the only difficulty lay in persuading them somehow to be present at the same time. That was something to which he must give attention, but in the meantime he stretched out a hand towards the letters which had arrived while he was away, and his heart sank somewhat when he saw the handwriting of his youngest daughter on the outside of the first.

Dearest Papa,

(Swiftly his eyes passed over the sprawling lines, which vaguely he understood to be reports on the health of the family: the two boys, it seemed, were well.)

My dear Wickham

(this caused him to harrumph impatiently)

>...is coming south, and while he will be unable to do so, I hope it
>will be agreeable to you if John, Charles and I spend some time
>with you at Longbourn. I have told the boys that they are to visit
>their grandpapa and they are wild with excitement and speak of
>little else but you and their aunts. We shall be setting off from
>here in three days' time and...

'Three days' time?' This piece of information caused Mr Bennet
to throw the letter from him, then to reach out for it once more
to check on its date, which was inconveniently missing. 'Three
days' time,' he repeated angrily. 'How very considerate of dear
Lydia to give us so much notice.' And a moment later he was
storming through the house with warnings for the servants who,
like himself, showed no great enthusiasm for the impending visit,
before going upstairs to the schoolroom and bursting in on Mrs
Castlemain, who now was sitting by Kitty's side and reciting with
her from a text a list of irregular verbs.

'Mr Bennet.' Afterwards, he reflected that his interruption of
their studies was by no means unwelcome to either, but at the
moment he was too disturbed to notice. 'What on earth is the
matter?'

'This!' He shook in their direction the letter which he still
held crumpled in his hand. 'This letter, which I have just read
from my youngest daughter, Lydia, or, as she prefers to call
herself, Mrs Wickham,' all his feelings for the man she had
married were contained in the way he spoke the words, 'who is
about to descend on us with her tribe of boys.' The gender of
Lydia's children was clearly no compensation for his own
disappointments. 'Being Lydia, naturally she gives no detail of
arrival dates, so we may expect them today or tomorrow and...'
He lost his words for a moment and gradually regained control of
his feelings, sitting down on one of the seats by the table. 'Please
forgive me, Mistress Castlemain, for disturbing you in such a
way.'

'Can I help you, Mr Bennet?' The good lady had risen from

her seat and was quickly by his side, contemplating his heightened colour with some anxiety. 'Perhaps a glass of water.' A quick glance at her pupil. 'Kitty, dear, if you would be so kind.' And immediately the girl sprang to her feet and they could hear her shoes clattering on the stairs as she made her way down to the kitchen, while the lady sat close to Mr Bennet and spoke in a voice which he found infinitely soothing. 'You mustn't disturb yourself to this extent, sir. I am confident the servants will deal with the additional visitors in their usual fashion, and if I can be of any assistance at all, I am yours to command.'

'Most kind. Most kind.' By this time Mr Bennet was feeling slightly foolish at his overreaction to Lydia's letter and looked up at his companion with a shamefaced smile. 'As you say, we shall all cope admirably. It is rather… The day has been too much for me. Here am I, newly returned from Pemberley, told I am grandfather to twin girls. And as if that were not enough for any man, then to read that Lydia and her two cubs are to descend within… well, within heaven knows when. Thank you, Kitty.' He looked up at his daughter, who had just reappeared with a glass of water, took it and sipped gratefully. 'You are a good girl, and I fear I have allowed my feelings to get the better of me. So,' he rose to his feet, 'I shall leave you to your studies and, once more, my apologies for disturbing you.'

'Not at all.' Mrs Castlemain rose and stepped with him to the door. 'And I did mean what I said, Mr Bennet. If, when Mrs Wickham and her family are here, I can be of the least assistance, I shall be at your service. I shall be only too happy.'

Admirable woman, Mr Bennet thought to himself as he reached his library, closed the door and sat down in his favourite chair, allowing his eyelids to droop with a feeling of relief. He must remember to thank the rural dean when next they met; his recommendation had proved very timely and beneficial to the whole family, and if she might be persuaded to spare a few extra hours when Lydia came with her brood, then he need scarcely be disturbed at all. That thought was a comfort, but it was almost immediately dispelled by recollection of his foolish behaviour, rushing about the house in a panic just like… But he would allow his thoughts to go no further than that: it would be simply too painful to admit to himself the possibility that… No, never would he admit to such a foolish notion that suggested married couples who are together for many years become… No, never.

The following day brought the arrival of Lydia and her boys, and the whole household was grateful that Mrs Castlemain in the ensuing weeks – she had such a way with young people despite never having had her own – spent entire days tiring them out with challenges suited to their ages, which were not great. Their grandpapa's trout lake seemed to be the focus for these games and, since the weather was fine, he scarce saw the boys, which meant that when he did he was able, within reason, to enjoy their company. The same could not be said in relation to Lydia, but then at least he was used to her and she paid little heed to his fretful comments, which was as it ever had been. At least she appeared to be content with her lot as Mrs Wickham – for this he ought to be grateful – and even if her constant reference to the man's virtues was more than a little wearing, since it was common knowledge that he had few, then that was a small price to pay.

In consideration of Mrs Castlemain's anxiety to help, she had been asked to move into the house for the duration of Lydia's visit, and her capabilities had shown themselves in ways other than simply as a distraction for his daughters and grandchildren. Certainly, when he had the thought one day to ride as far as Netherfield, he was able to set off with an easy mind, knowing that Mrs Castlemain was giving Charles and John a drawing lesson in the schoolroom while Lydia and Kitty were engaged in one of their favourite pastimes, refurbishing last season's hats, this time with the additional advantage that Mrs Wickham, who now considered herself an authority on all things fashionable, was a source of constant advice, and the minor irritation of a lecture from Mary on the folly of vanity was brushed aside. 'Lawks, Mary,' he heard her younger sister say as he closed the door of the sewing room, 'I had forgot what a stick you are.'

So his escape from Longbourn afforded him much relief and he had a warm welcome from Jane and Bingley, much admired the two new babies, who were pretty enough to please even such an old cynic as himself, and it was a pleasure to him to observe how delighted both parents seemed to be with the new family. He was persuaded to stay for a late luncheon, during which innumerable toasts were drunk to the health and happiness of all concerned. He even found himself become slightly emotional when young Bingley singled him out specially when a vintage brandy was being broached, and dedicated a toast to the grandfather of his two beautiful daughters.

Thus, it was a slightly bemused Mr Bennet who took the road back to Longbourn as the evening shadows lengthened, and when he eventually reached it the house was surprisingly quiet and he opened the parlour door with some hesitation, half expecting that Kitty or Lydia, or more likely both, would jump out at him, screaming their delight at his reaction. But instead, there sat Mrs Castlemain in a chair by the fire. The lamps were lighted, casting a golden nimbus about her head, which was bent over some piece of sewing which she held in her hand.

'Good gracious, Mrs Castlemain.' As he spoke she raised her head and smiled, made to rise until he waved her back to her seat. 'How very nice and peaceful it is. May a father enquire what has happened to his family? Too much to hope that they have been spirited away and—'

'Too much indeed.' Her response to his little sally was pleasing: as a rule his womenfolk found his humour at best provoking, at worst plain dull, and it was rewarding to see a glimmer of amusement on her features. 'They have been invited over to the Lucases – for cards, I believe – and will not return for some time. And the boys are both fast asleep, being tired out by a morning of painting and an afternoon of sailing boats on the lake.'

'Capital, Mrs Castlemain, capital.' Mr Bennet sighed with pleasure as he lowered himself into his most comfortable chair, more than content at the prospect of a peaceful evening in undemanding company. His eyelids drooped, his head sank onto his chest and the sound of peaceful dozing filled the parlour.

Chapter Three

*M*eantime, back at Pemberley, Lizzie and Darcy's happy tranquillity was in the process of being disturbed by what was their first quarrel, or, at the very least, their first serious disagreement.

'But, Elizabeth, my love…' His manner was calm and gentlemanly as ever, which in some perverse way was the more irritating to his wife. 'But of course I must insist upon it. Lady Catherine is my aunt and she has been coming to Pemberley at about this time since I was a child. Recent years have been exceptions for various reasons, but now she wishes to visit us. You must give way to me on this.'

'And,' she spoke with the passion which would not forget past slights, 'I am to forget that you were to wed her daughter, that she came to Longbourn especially to tell me so, that she—'

'Lizzie.' His voice held that solemn, but amused, quality as ever making her own mouth twitch in sympathy, a reaction which she now subdued with iron control. 'Do you truly think I should ever have married my cousin, Anne? I would have been as like to marry an anchorite nun as poor Anne, who has never been allowed to express an opinion since she left the nursery. But pray, do not forget that as well as being my cousin, she is also cousin to Georgiana. The two young women have ever been friends, and I imagine her visits to Pemberley have long been the highlights in Anne's season. When she is with my sister, she becomes quite… animated might be an exaggeration, but shall we say… lively?'

'But she is always travelling about with her mama, going to Bath and—'

'Not always: occasionally,' he replied forcefully. 'And can you imagine how diverting that is for one such as she, stifled by shyness and inadequacy? No, Elizabeth.' Here he rose from his seat, strolled across the room to look for a moment out over the lake, before swinging back to face her. 'On this my mind is quite made up and you must submit. I am the master of Pemberley and—'

'And am I not the mistress?' The words were out before she could consider their wisdom and inwardly she quivered, although she continued to hold her chin high.

'Indeed.' He took a step close, and, before she could resist, he had placed his arm about her waist, pulling her to him. 'Yes, indeed, you are the mistress of Pemberley, and if your objection were reasonable then I should concede, but... with the position come obligations and duties. I owe these to my family, which includes my aunt and cousin. As, my dear, you do yours.' For a moment the dark eyes glittered down at her, reminding her without a word on the subject of all his indulgence towards her relatives, of her mother's last visit, which had not been without its trials for her husband, but still had ended in a spirit of great felicity. And in the blessing of that memory, she instantly forgot her petty objections.

'You are right, Fitzwilliam. I am sorry.'

'Now,' he held her still closer and dropped a kiss on the corner of her mouth, 'do not play the penitent too loud or I shall forget what brought us here. Do you not know how much I admired you for the way you stood up to Lady Catherine during your visit to Rosings? Few would have had the stomach for it, and she, I suspect, has never met anyone, let alone another woman, who could match her.'

'Fitzwilliam...' As the heat began to touch her skin, she pressed her fingertips to his lips. 'Say no more, I beg. I am shamed to have been so petty. Pray write to your aunt, invite her and Anne for their usual visit and I promise I shall make them both welcome. As you say, her daughter and Georgiana must not be disappointed. By the end of their stay, I shall have Lady Catherine telling the world what a wonderful match her nephew has made; you will be proud of me.'

'Do not be overly ambitious, Elizabeth: do not attempt the impossible.' He smiled down at her. 'And besides...' He paused so long she began to feel anxious. 'Don't you know already that I am proud of you?' For another moment they stared at each other, before Lizzie buried her face on his chest lest he should see the brilliance in her eyes and suspect a tendency to tearfulness.

And indeed, when at last Lady Catherine with her daughter, Anne, arrived at Pemberley, Elizabeth welcomed them with all the civility she could find, and perhaps the older lady, realising that here, in her nephew's wife, she had met her match, seemed a little less haughty than she had been at Rosings, and much less certainly than at their bitter encounter at Longbourn, to which not the least reference was made.

'You have done very well, Mrs Darcy.' On the first evening, having been persuaded by her husband to play something, Elizabeth listened to Lady Catherine's approval with some surprise as she ended and prepared to relinquish her place to Georgiana. 'You have come on well since the last occasion when you played at Rosings. I think I then expressed the opinion that if you would apply yourself, you might benefit, and so it has turned out. Your fingering shows signs of great improvement. Pray, who is instructing you now?'

'In truth, no one, ma'am.' Elizabeth rose from the instrument and, with a smile, motioned Georgiana and Anne to take her place. 'But I do mean to take your advice.' Here she cast a mischievous glance towards her husband, whose eyes had scarce left her face. 'I am sure Miss Darcy would not object to my sharing her tutor with her if it could be arranged.'

'Well said.' Lady Catherine appeared slightly disconcerted by the unexpected mellowing of this young woman with whom she had ever been in a state of undeclared war. 'Indeed.' To Lizzie's relief she transferred her attention to the duet now being played, tapping in time with the beat and frowning at any minor mistakes. 'I think even dear Georgiana would do much better if she were to practise more. We ought all to do so. Georgiana!' She raised her voice, the better to attract the attention of the pianist. 'I am sure it would do you much good if you were to undertake an extra hour of scales each day; it would improve your touch greatly.'

'Lady Catherine.' Greatly daring, Elizabeth took her place at the far end of the sofa occupied by the formidable matriarch. 'I must ask you.' She lowered her voice slightly, as if to keep matters between themselves. 'I did not wish to speak of this to Anne or Georgiana before seeking your permission, but my aunt and uncle, Mr and Mrs Gardiner, have taken a house in the area for a month and are accompanied by their children and two friends, and I wonder... They have invited me to spend a day with them during that time, and it occurs to me that Anne and Georgiana might enjoy the company of my young cousins, if you would permit it.'

'Mr and Mrs Gardiner?' Lady Catherine frowned, and the fan with which she had been beating time to the music closed with an ominous snap. 'This is the uncle who is in trade?' She spoke in a voice of such surprised distaste that Elizabeth felt her anger rise, controlling it only with difficulty.

'Yes, indeed he is a very successful merchant with connections in many parts of the world. We are very proud of him.'

'Proud of him?' the lady repeated in a tone of outrage. 'And it is with his family you wish my daughter and my niece to... to consort?'

'Consort?' Elizabeth considered. 'Not perhaps to consort, exactly: simply to meet. Their elder daughter is only a year or two younger than Anne, and the friends are of about the same age. All are extremely musical and I feel sure would have much in common.' Sensing the pressure mounting, she turned towards her husband for support, but he merely sat there, looking at her with that faintly irritating smile on his lips. 'Fitzwilliam says we may have the carriage to take us there; we can spend a few hours with them and shall be back at Pemberley later in the day. They would then have much to relate after passing some time in the company of young people of their own age, and you, Lady Catherine, would have the chance,' here she lowered her voice conspiratorially, 'to speak with your nephew without distraction. There are one or two matters concerning family affairs which I know he wishes to discuss with you. In confidence.' Having finished her prepared speech, she sat for a moment, scarcely daring to breathe.

'Well.' For a few moments, Elizabeth was aware that a refusal – Lady Catherine's normally preferred response to any idea other than her own – hovered on her lips, but then her eyes turned to her nephew, surveying him for some time. 'Family affairs?' She shot the words at him and waited.

'Yes, Aunt. There are one or two matters on which I would value your advice. You have such an understanding of things which happened in the past and can thus offer me guidance – if you feel you can spare the time, of course.'

'In that case, I cannot refuse. And it is a great pity you had not come to me for advice when you were having trouble with that wretched fellow—'

'Yes, Lady Catherine.' Darcy cast a sudden glance towards his sister, who was fortunately fully engaged in a discussion with her cousin, but as he continued his voice held a warning edge. 'But that is all in the past now; other matters are more pressing, and it would be useful if you could spare a day to go round the estate without having any concern about Anne. And Elizabeth will, I know, make a very careful chaperone.'

'Hmm.' It was clear enough that the lady was considering how a young woman who had herself been so inadequately chaperoned could have learnt the skills of such a calling, but, before the question could be posed, Darcy had turned to his wife with a smile.

'I think my aunt agrees, my dear. She and I will decide how to rearrange things here while you take the young ladies to visit Mr and Mrs Gardiner at Lambton. And you will not forget to tell Mr Gardiner that he is welcome to Pemberley at any time if he should feel the need for some sport. Dawson has been complaining of the pigeons, which are attacking his crops, and in fact I may find time to arrange a shooting party while Mr Gardiner is still here.'

So it was that three days later Elizabeth set out for the house which her uncle and aunt had taken for the holiday, and, the instant they decanted from the carriage, Anne and Georgiana were taken away by the older girls while Elizabeth was led into the parlour where she was offered tea and the welcome opportunity to discuss all the family events since she had last met her aunt and uncle.

'And tell me, Lizzie,' Mrs Gardiner smiled as she passed over the cup, 'how do you like being mistress of Pemberley?'

'I like it greatly, Aunt.' Conscious of the colour in her cheeks,

Elizabeth looked down as she stirred the steaming brew. 'Mr Darcy and I are very content with each other.'

'So, it has all worked out perfectly. I am so pleased, my dear, and think you have both chosen wisely.'

'I am not certain his aunt would agree with that,' Lizzie smiled. 'But I feel she now accepts what she cannot alter. She was loath to allow poor Anne a day's freedom, so we had to hatch a plot which demanded her presence at Pemberley and thus allow us to escape.'

'It will do some good. We have advised our young ones that they are to be gentle – occasionally they tend to grow a little boisterous – but when we told them that Anne and Georgiana were virtually lone siblings, that touched their hearts, for they think it a penance to be without the company of the family.'

'And so,' this appeared a suitable moment for Mr Gardiner to interrupt, 'it seems dear Jane does not mean to have a single child. What excitement that two little girls should arrive together!'

'Indeed, Uncle. It has caused a great flurry.' Elizabeth, not for the first time, was conscious that her companions must also be considering her own situation, and felt her colour rise again. 'My papa, having shown no great interest in his own daughters, is now becoming besotted with his granddaughters.'

'Well, that I can understand, my dear. Your papa has no responsibility for the Bingley family, whereas with his own…' Mrs Gardiner allowed her words to trail off, giving Elizabeth a moment or two to compose herself. Then, 'Have you heard any more from Lady Catherine about Mrs Collins?'

'No. So far not one word, but I do mean this evening to bring the matter up. When last she wrote, Charlotte was unwell, and of course her mother, Lady Lucas, is presently at Hunsford, so at least Charlotte will be having a rest from her household duties and her mother's presence will be a great comfort to her and the children.'

So the day drifted by with family gossip. An afternoon entertainment was being arranged in great secrecy by the young people and their governess – entrance to the schoolroom was guarded as if by Cerberus himself, heavily disguised as a young Gardiner – and it was while the afternoon performance was about to reach its climax that the door quietly opened and Elizabeth felt someone take a seat behind her, then Darcy's touch on her skin.

'I have been weary without you.' The whispered words stirred the hair on her neck and it was by the greatest act of self-control that she was able to resist her impulse to turn and put her arms about him. And so conscious was she of her husband's closeness that Lizzie quite lost the thread of the performance, which contained much declamation with elaborate little twirls on the pianoforte at which Anne, somewhat surprisingly, showed herself to be more than capable.

And it was later, when the adults were seated in the parlour taking tea, while the young people cleared all the props from the schoolroom, that Darcy remarked on how impressed he had been at the results of the impromptu concert. 'And I was particularly taken by the animation shown by my cousin. I do not think I have ever seen Anne laughing. Smiling, yes. From time to time.' It was clear to his listeners that he was endeavouring, with little success, to fix such a moment in his mind. 'But I declare I scarce knew her.'

'It can hardly be otherwise, Mr Darcy.' Mrs Gardiner spoke in her usual douce, kindly way. 'She sadly lacks the friendship of others of her age and station. Experience has taught me that in the company of their peers, young people flourish. Deprived of that stimulation, they find it exceedingly hard when, later in life, they are thrown into the hurly burly of social contact.'

'Yes, I am certain you are right, Mrs Gardiner.' His smile readily excused her of any allusion to his own past situation, one which had eased so much in the time since he had first visited Netherfield. 'And that leads me to suggest that perhaps you would all come to Pemberley one day, before you leave Derbyshire; then we and the young people can continue the acquaintance. There, perhaps, they can go on with their theatricals, Mr Gardiner and I can walk round the fields with the guns, and I promise that my wife shall look after you, Mrs Gardiner.' His smile towards the latter was almost conspiratorial. 'I am certain she would value your assistance in dealing with my aunt.'

And so it was arranged. The Gardiners and their extended brood arrived several days later at Pemberley, the two younger of the boys preferring for the first hour to fish with nets in the lake while the older children, under the supervision of Mrs Annesley, Georgiana and Anne, began to organise a show with which to amuse the adults later in the day.

And so this left Elizabeth and her aunt, after the men had departed for their sport, to do their best with Lady Catherine de Bourgh, who had reverted to her supercilious manner of previous occasions.

'So, Mrs Gardiner, you have a large family, I see.'

'We have three children, Lady Catherine. The other two are friends.'

'A great responsibility in such times; it must be a considerable drain with boys to educate.'

'Not at present, and I dare say that is a challenge we shall meet when the time comes but—'

'Mr Gardiner is in trade, Mrs Darcy informs me.'

'Yes. Successfully so.' Mrs Gardiner exchanged an amused look with her niece, who appeared to find little diversion in Lady Catherine's behaviour. 'But, as to my sons' education, at present the cost is nothing, since I myself teach them with the assistance of a governess.'

'You, Mrs Gardiner?' Her tone implied both disdain and scepticism. 'You teach your own children?'

'Indeed, Lady Catherine. I should not care to entrust their early education to anyone else.'

'My aunt,' Lizzie could hide her irritation no longer, 'is well qualified by being the daughter of one of our finest classical scholars. She travelled widely with him and was immersed from an early age in the philosophy of the ancients.'

'Indeed?' There was a long moment of silence during which a warning glance from her aunt reminded the mistress of the house of her position as hostess and, in a moment, Lizzie saw the humour of the situation and her mischievous side took over.

'Yes, indeed, Lady Catherine. Mrs Gardiner's parents engaged in very intellectual company. I understand they moved in circles which included the Shelleys and—'

'The Shelleys!' Lady Catherine could not have been more shocked if Byron himself had been mentioned.

'I think,' Mrs Gardiner interrupted soothingly, 'they met but once, and since they were by no means of the same mind as the Shelleys, there was no move to develop any kind of intimacy.' Then, with an abrupt change of subject she continued, 'Tell me, Lady Catherine, have you taken the waters this year? I myself have been invited to accompany Lady Cummings to Bath before the end of the season.'

'Lady Cummings?' Mention of such a distinguished person caused Lady Catherine's eyebrows to reach her hairline. 'You are acquainted with Lady Cummings?'

'She is my cousin and we have always been friends as well. That is why I find it pleasing to observe that Georgiana and Anne are so much at ease with each other. Since neither has a sister, then a cousin can be a great comfort.'

'Yes, indeed.' Now feeling slightly ashamed of having baited the older woman so readily, Lizzie put on her warmest smile. 'I cannot myself imagine what it is to be without a sister.' She ignored the loud sniff from the chair opposite. 'And I wish to put in a plea that Anne might delay her journey home and remain with us a little longer.'

'But I have told you, Mrs Darcy, that I am bound by a pressing engagement on the fifteenth and must return to Rosings in advance of that date. I cannot possibly change such arrangements and—'

'Lady Catherine, I would not presume to ask that of you: I know how important it is for you to honour your engagements. But if perhaps Anne might remain with us... Truly, I think the fresh air here in Derbyshire is good for her; there is more colour in her cheeks and—'

'It is out of the question, Mrs Darcy. How would the child manage without me? She has never in her whole life known what it is to be without her mother's guidance and I do not think it would do. No.' With that as her final word, she rose majestically to her feet and walked to the door. 'And since I see my nephew returning across the park, I beg you will excuse me while I go to meet him.'

'So...' When they were alone, Mrs Gardiner glanced at Lizzie. 'Poor Anne. It seems she must return to Rosings with her mama.'

'Yes, it seems so. And it is my fault,' Lizzie burst out, 'simply because I could not resist teasing her.'

'Well, that may have been injudicious, Lizzie, but it is very hard to resist when she is so haughty. But perhaps it might have been more sensible to avoid giving the impression that my family were part of that radical hotchpotch. It was scarcely an idea which would recommend itself to someone of Lady Catherine's opinions.'

'Yes.' Despite her regrets, Elizabeth could not resist a giggle. 'But did you observe her expression, Aunt?'

'Yes, I could scarce preserve my own countenance, Lizzie. You ought not to tease her so, but I suppose it is impossible for you to change your nature.'

'Quite impossible,' she agreed amiably. 'Only on this occasion I was wrong. But for that, she might have agreed to let poor Anne stay a little longer, without her mama. Can you imagine, Aunt, what it might mean for a girl who has been dominated by such an overwhelming presence for her entire life? It would be like freeing a bird from a cage.'

'Yes, Lizzie. But you do realise that caged birds can seldom exist outside. Are you certain that Anne would even know how to stretch her wings?'

'I am not certain, Aunt. But I feel if she does not soon have the opportunity, then we may for ever regret it. It is true, I dare say, that we at Netherfield were given too much freedom – that was very evident in Lydia's behaviour.' It was a moment or two before she continued in an increasingly reflective tone. 'But there must be some middle course for such as Georgiana and Anne. Each would benefit from the other's company, and if Anne cannot have a little freedom I truly fear for her future. I shall speak to Fitzwilliam; perhaps he shall be able to persuade Lady Catherine that Anne might benefit from a few extra days with us.'

'And in that case, Lizzie, it might be better if you try to demonstrate that you would be the most perfect influence on her daughter, rather than remind the lady of your past differences.' Which mild remonstration left the mistress of Pemberley for a moment silent before she and her companion collapsed in a burst of mirth which Lady de Bourgh would have considered as perverse as it was unseemly.

In the event, life at Pemberley soon returned to its usual tranquil felicity with all the visitors departing with the exception of Anne de Bourgh, her mother having acceded reluctantly to her nephew's plea and at the last moment possible. In fact, Elizabeth saw little of the two young ladies during the day, since Fitzwilliam, as part of his persuasions, had drawn up a plan whereby they and Mrs Annesley – once Georgiana's governess and now her irreproachable companion – were to be escorted on a tour of the galleries and places of historic interest. All very improving when described to Lady Catherine, who was, perhaps, still mulling over and being impressed by what she had heard of Mrs Gardiner's connections. But to the two young ladies themselves, these excursions were seen more as exciting diversions than as occasions for learning and led to much amused chatter at the dinner table in which, Darcy and his wife were interested to observe, Anne joined, at first with some diffidence, then with increasing animation, which brought forth an entirely new aspect to her previously repressed, colourless personality.

From time to time, Elizabeth accompanied them on their expeditions but normally thought it best to leave them under the supervision of Mrs Annesley. It was also arranged that they have some additional musical instruction, which both added to the pleasures of their evenings and resulted in improvements she thought would impress Lady Catherine. In general, Elizabeth was hopeful that, the ice having been broken, Anne would be allowed future visits without her mother, persuading herself that Lady Catherine would also come to recognise the benefits of short breaks from each other's company. On this point, her husband was less sanguine, having experienced his aunt's dominating ways throughout his life. He felt it was a power she would be reluctant to relinquish, but he, too, was pleased at the change, however slight, in his cousin and encouraged his wife in her efforts.

But the highlight of Anne's extended visit was an invitation to a ball given by some neighbours who had been living abroad since the Darcy marriage and who, having now returned home, wished to celebrate with their friends. Naturally, such a prospect caused much excitement, and for the previous week the corridors of Pemberley rang with chatter as patterns were studied, admired for a moment, then discarded in favour of something different, thus reducing the milliner, who had been summoned from town, to a state of despair. But at last, final decisions were made and the two young ladies were pleased and excited with the results.

Fortunately Elizabeth, having decided which of the new gowns she had bought in Paris would suit the occasion, was in no rush on her own account, but there were slippers to be bought for Georgiana and Anne, and silks and ribbons for trimming, all of which kept them pretty well occupied until the day of the ball.

Georgiana, too, had a wardrobe filled with pretty things which had scarcely been worn and she was generous in allowing her cousin to choose what she liked before herself deciding what she would wear, Anne having brought nothing with her for so grand an occasion. This omission was something of a relief to Elizabeth, who, since her travels in France, had much more ambitious ideas of fashion than previously, when she had been simply Lizzie Bennet of Longbourn. She was of the firm conviction that if Anne could be dressed in a more flattering style, if her hair could be arranged more becomingly and a little colour persuaded into her cheeks, it would add to the confidence she had gained since her mother had quit the party. In fact, at the back of Elizabeth's mind, a plot was hatching, one she had not yet confided to her husband, that before the end of the season they ought to repeat that interrupted journey to France, taking Georgiana and Anne with them. She would love the opportunity to provide both with some pretty dresses: Georgiana, who was at last blooming again after her setback with Wickham, and Anne, who sadly needed considerably more encouragement.

But in the meantime the ball at Astley Abbey was all they could talk of and it was in a spirit of great excitement that they gathered in the long gallery half an hour before the carriage was to pick them up. The satin gown Elizabeth was wearing brought her husband to an abrupt halt as he walked into her bedroom to collect her that evening. The glowing shades, merging from gold to bronze, picked up the colours from the lamps and firelight, and she felt her heart beating fiercely against her bodice as he at last stepped forward and raised her fingers to his lips. His eyes never left hers and his free arm circled her waist in a subtly persuasive movement. 'Must we go out this evening, Mrs Darcy?'

'I… fear we must, Mr Darcy.'

Smiling, he released her and offered his arm as they went downstairs. 'Then may I tell you how lovely you look? I shall be the envy of every man at the ball.'

'Oh, I hope not, Fitzwilliam. I am looking forward to seeing our two young ladies capturing a few glances, too. You and I are too old to be excited by such things as balls and must give way to the young,' she said demurely.

But Mrs Darcy, being the most recently married woman present, found herself in great demand when the music started, so her husband had no chance of standing up with her until the third dance. It was very much a reprise of that first occasion at Netherfield; thus the opportunity of teasing him as she had done then was as irresistible.

'Now it is your turn to say something, Mr Darcy. Perhaps you could remark on the weather, or say how proud you are of your sister, who is behaving with such decorum.'

'I can think of little else but my wife, madam. I feel sure she will disapprove of my paying attention to other young women.'

'Indeed, sir? Then I can scarce understand why you are standing up with me.'

'It is because of your eyes, madam. They hold the colour of your gown with astonishing accuracy.'

'Sir. You should not say—' But there the movement of the dance split them and they moved apart with smiling reluctance.

But, as the evening progressed, Elizabeth discovered it was no easy task to find partners for two such shy and retiring young women as those she had brought with her. Fitzwilliam had taken both onto the floor and had presented them to such of his acquaintances as were available, but the evening was growing late before two presentable young men appeared in the arched entrance to the ballroom and walked towards a group standing close by.

'Mrs Darcy.' Her hostess, Mrs Arbuthnot, was immediately at her elbow, smiling in a friendly manner. 'May I present my son, John, and his friend, Mr Fife, who have just returned from a walking holiday in the Black Forest.'

Graciously, Elizabeth Bennet bowed and could not for a moment but wonder if she were turning into her mama, such were the soaring hopes which afflicted her and which were immediately dismissed before they could take hold. Her two charges were brought forward, presented and, without her even having to make the suggestion, she watched the two young men lead Georgiana and Anne to join the set which was even then being arranged. When, a moment later, her husband touched her hand, together they walked off to one side where they were happy to sit watching the dancers, talking easily, comfortably to each other.

'Georgiana looks amazingly pretty this evening, Elizabeth. That shade of rose pink suits her exceedingly.'

'Yes, she looks charming. And her hair is so pretty with her mother's pearls twisted through the tresses. And Anne, too, is much improved, is she not?'

'Yes.' On this matter he was less confident. 'You have done wonders with her, my dear. But she will never have Georgiana's complexion, nor her smile. But still, I do believe with a little more persuasion from you, she will do still better.' His gaze returned to his sister. 'But her partner – Georgiana's, I mean – he is the young Arbuthnot, is he not, and seems much taken.'

'Do not,' here she gave him a little reprimand with her fan, 'start matchmaking, Fitzwilliam; it is even more unseemly in a man than...' She allowed her voice to trail away, though her meaning was clear enough.

'I would not think of it, my dear, but would you not say he seems much smitten?'

'Do not forget he has for some weeks been walking in the Black Forest and allowance must be made for that. Doubtless he has been much cut off from society during his time abroad.'

'Aye.' He slanted a sardonic glance in her direction, which she affected not to see. 'I do not doubt he has had little company but that of the elf king and water sprites. And who is that standing up with Anne?'

'That is a friend, who has also been in travelling on the continent.'

'He has an... interesting face, though he is small.'

'What the French call pleasantly ugly, I believe. And they are both small. Strange that Anne so lacks height when her mother is tall.'

'Her father was lacking in stature, too. They were an odd assorted couple. I think...' His voice shook slightly, causing Elizabeth to look at him with suspicion. Since he seemed practised in her own game, she was never certain that she was being teased. 'I think,' he repeated, 'that Lady Catherine decided he would do, and he then gave up the chase in face of the *force majeure* so... the match was made. Hers was the fortune and he spent the rest of his life trying to please her.'

Poor man! Elizabeth thought, but did not say, though, when she did find her voice, the words might have been more carefully chosen. 'Well, he might have lived a little longer simply in order to protect his child.'

'I doubt he had much choice in his going, my dear. But tell me; I have been meaning to ask. I heard you and Lady Catherine speaking of the Collinses on the day of her departure. Your friend Mrs Collins is, I hope, well.'

'Yes,' Lizzie sighed. 'Well enough, but I can scarce bear to think of anyone, and certainly not my dear Charlotte, being happy with such a man.'

'We cannot arrange such things for others, Lizzie; sometimes we fail even ourselves in this. You and I have been very fortunate, but not everyone can be so, and did you not tell me that Charlotte was content?'

'She told me so: that she is very content.' But Elizabeth's voice was full of doubts.

'Well, for that you must respect her. And who knows, my dear: Mr Collins may improve with the passage of time. And if his wife should present him with a son, he will doubtless be so delighted at his cleverness that she will be forgiven the daughters.'

'Oh, Fitzwilliam.' Such a reminder was most unwelcome at that moment, arousing as it did all her apprehensions. 'How I wish—'

'I do not.' Rising, he stood in front of her for a few seconds before bowing his head. 'I promise you, I do not. And, at this moment, it would make me very happy if my wife would consent to dance with me.'

And his manner was so light and sincere that she had little difficulty in accepting his assurances and allowing herself to be persuaded onto the floor.

Chapter Four

'What is the matter, Elizabeth?'
        She and her husband were taking breakfast alone, and her stifled gasp as her eyes quickly scanned the letter which she had just received engaged his attention. But before replying, his wife gave a little cry, pressing her fingers to her mouth.

'Elizabeth?' he queried again, in some concern.

'It is this news from Netherfield…'

'There is nothing amiss with the children, I hope.'

'No, nothing like that: the children are well. But— Oh, Fitz-william! You recall I told you that my father had employed a woman as chaperone to Mary and Kitty?'

'Yes. He spoke of her himself when he was here: an estimable woman, the widow of a diplomat, did he not say? He appeared mightily pleased with her and—'

'Well, it now appears she is fast becoming more than a chaper-one. Miss Bingley – Caroline, I mean – has been to call on my father and each time has found him *tête-à-tête* with this Mrs… Mrs Castlemain, in what appears to be a more intimate setting than might be expected.'

'My dear.' With a sigh, Darcy put down the handful of papers he had been studying. 'Are you certain that Caroline Bingley has not made too much of this? It did occur to us that perhaps she herself might have designs on your father and—'

'Yes. Even he spoke of it when he was here, but…' Since then, she had decided it was one of the asides her father used from time to time to tease and torment his family, but added to Miss Bingley's manner at Mrs Bennet's funeral and Lizzie's own sense of unease at that time, the matter began to take on a different aspect.

'As I have reason to know, my dear Mrs Darcy, Miss Bingley is set upon finding herself a husband.'

'But… my father?' The prospect was little to her taste. 'He is very much…' Her voice trailed off.

'Older, were you about to say, my dear? But your papa is not yet fifty, and many young women and still more who are no longer quite so young – would be happy to have an admirer such as Mr Bennet. He is so clearly a gentleman.'

'But…' Elizabeth refused to see her father in the role of suitor; it was of all things distasteful to her. 'It is… nonsense.'

'You are most probably right, my dear. And it may simply be that your father, feeling himself pursued from one direction, seeks safety in another, so long as he remembers that threats can come from all quarters. And, in fact, I should not be the least surprised if that is what he has in mind: he has thought it expedient to find other unattached ladies to form a screen about him. I doubt that he will welcome the attentions of Miss Bingley.' He considered his wife's agitated features before continuing. 'Though he could, if he had such an inclination, make a worse match. She has thirty thousand pounds, as I believe I mentioned before.'

'Money ought not to come into such things. And it is most unseemly with my poor mother dead so short a time.'

'It is more than twelve months.' He spoke comfortingly and rose, placing a hand on her shoulder. 'And while I know you would not welcome having a stranger in your mother's place, there might be some benefits to the whole family.'

'I cannot speak of it, for I can see none.'

'Consider, Lizzie.' He took his seat once more. 'A kindly woman, who might set a very good example to Kitty and Mary, would that be such a disaster? I feel even your mother would not have objected to such a happening.'

For a moment, his wife retained a thoughtful silence as she recalled that unhappy time at Netherfield when Mr Collins had descended on the Bennets with his unwelcome advances, which, when refused, sent her mother into a state of the vapours. Mrs Bennet had foreseen herself widowed and her children dispossessed, and Mr Bennet, with a clumsy attempt at comfort, had suggested that she might go before he did. Of course, it was her father's teasing way of dealing with difficulties, and now that she was distanced from such woes, she could spare a sad little smile for them.

'I hope,' and her voice shook with her emotions, 'I hope you are wrong, Mr Darcy, for I do not believe I could ever bear to see another woman in my mother's place.'

'Then let us trust, my dear, that it does not happen. But as I said, your father is by no means an old man; he may yet live twenty more years, and should he feel inclined to seek some female society, then I hope you would not condemn too harshly. If two unattached people find companionship together, I can see no reason for objection. Now tell me; how are the children and have they at last chosen names for them? Does your sister say when the baptism is to take place?'

'Yes.' Hastily, Elizabeth riffled through the pages and read out, 'Emily Rose Bingley and Catherine Jane, but no, she makes no mention of the baptism. Will you excuse me, Fitzwilliam? I feel I must go at once and write.'

'Then take my advice, Elizabeth, and before you do so, walk twice round the lake. He pushed back his chair and rose. 'In fact, I shall come with you. I have often found that letters written while in a state of anxiety come back to haunt one. Try to calm yourself, my dear, and, in doing so, you will find that you calm your sister.'

So it was, and afterwards Elizabeth realised how timely her husband's advice had been. Being herself so passionate, she was much inclined to stoke her emotions until they reached fever point, and replying at such a time would have been folly. Thus it was mid-morning when she sat down in a much calmer mood to answer her sister's letter, a reply in which rationality was paramount. She even found herself using some of her husband's words as if they were her own, and the letter was despatched in the hope that it would arrive at Netherfield the following day.

It was a mere two days later that Darcy made a proposal which delighted her so much that she ran across the room and threw her arms about his neck. 'Fitzwilliam, you are the best and kindest of men and—'

'Miss Bennet, what can have brought on such a sudden change of mind? I thought you had quite made up your mind that I was haughty and proud and that I was the last man in the world you—'

'If you say another word, Mr Darcy, I swear I shall—'

'Yes?' He held her at arm's length, the dark eyes glinting with mischief. 'Yes, you will what, Mrs Darcy?'

'I have eaten those words so often that I shall eat them no more. But thank you, Fitzwilliam. I shall be beside myself to see my father and sisters again, as well as Mr Bingley and the two little girls. What a clever man you are to think of such a thing.'

'Well, you'd best go up and decide what you will take for your journey to Netherfield. We shall travel first of all to Rosings with Georgiana, who has been pressed to stay for some days; then we drive back to Netherfield to visit the Bingleys, from where you can visit Longbourn as often as you wish.'

'But...' She appeared to hesitate.

'What is it? Are the arrangements not entirely to your liking?'

'It has just occurred to me: you do not suppose there is a faint chance that my father will feel slighted that we do not mean to stay with him?'

'I do not think your father will be so petty. But if, when we reach Hertfordshire, you find that he would welcome us to Longbourn, then it will be the simplest of moves. I have the feeling that perhaps he might still more welcome the fact that he can see as much as he wishes of his favourite daughter without the responsibility of turning the whole establishment upside down in the process.'

The journey went much as Darcy had planned. Having lodged two nights on the road, they reached Rosings mid-morning and, after some refreshment, left Georgiana with her aunt and cousin while they continued their journey to Netherfield.

'Poor Anne.' Elizabeth spoke regretfully when they were on their way. 'She is quite subdued again and would scarce answer when I asked if she had heard anything of Mr Fife.'

'I fear Lady Catherine would not welcome such a question, my dear.'

'Mmm. Well, Anne blushed scarlet when his name was mentioned, but when I wrote to her mother I did tell her about the ball at Astley Abbey and explained that both girls had engaged the attention of partners. I cannot see the harm in it.'

'The reverse, rather,' her husband agreed with a sigh. 'But I am uncertain that Lady Catherine would consent to any serious connection.'

'Well, that is indeed a pity and it saddens me to see her so downcast, but, at least with Georgiana visiting, things may improve.'

I am surprised at you, Lizzie.' As he spoke, her husband reached out for her hand. 'I would not have thought you would take such a kindly view of the Rosings family after all that has happened.'

'Oh, now I can find it in my heart to forgive your aunt,' she replied lightly. 'It must pain her to have lost what she had so set her heart on. But most of my sympathy is for her daughter, since I cannot imagine such a life as she leads. I know I should have been much the poorer without my sisters: all the tensions and silly rivalries have made us what we are. And now, despite poor Lydia, I would not have things other.' Intercepting her husband's quizzical glance, she became more heated. 'I speak the truth, Fitzwilliam. Of course I wish Lydia had been more restrained and that she had not ended married to Wickham. And I fear for her future with such a man, but... on the whole, I am grateful to have been brought up in such a lively atmosphere and that is my main concern for Anne. Oh, we must soon plan a journey to Paris and take the two young ladies and—'

'And what if Lady Catherine should agree to your plan pro—'

'Then I shall be eternally grateful and—'

'—provided that she, too, can come with us and enjoy the delights of the French capital.'

'Oh.' For one frightening moment she considered a possibility which had not previously occurred to her. Then, rightly gauging her husband's demeanour, she joined in his laughter. 'Then I should have to feign an illness.'

'In which case, she would decide that we might make the journey without you, Elizabeth. I believe you have each met your match. But I do not think there is the slightest chance that she would wish to make such a journey, though I am by no means convinced that she will agree to part with Anne. Rosings is a devilish dull place for everyone at the best of times, but it must be still duller for my aunt without her daughter. So prepare yourself for a disappointment, my dear.'

But this concern was soon dismissed in all the excitement of reaching Netherfield and seeing again her dear sister and Mr Bingley as a prelude to being introduced to the two latest members of the family, who were sleeping peacefully side by side in identical cradles trimmed with pink ribbons.

'Are they not perfect, Elizabeth?' Mr Bingley had taken on a graver air in respect of his new position as head of a family, and even Darcy was affected. Elizabeth could not suppress a tiny pang as he exclaimed on this or that aspect: the minute perfection of their fingernails was mentioned by him more than once. He was captivated by them.

'Well, Lizzie.' Jane was pouring tea for her visitors before there was any allusion to the subject which had brought them from Derbyshire at such short notice. 'Have you heard from Papa since you wrote to me?'

'No, not a word, but then there has scarce been time. I wrote to let him know that we were to spend a few days here, but naturally I made no reference to our concerns.'

'Have you seen Mr Bennet recently, Jane?' Darcy rose from his seat and walked over to the window, in doing so reminding his wife of the first occasion she had stayed at the house. 'I imagine he comes to visit fairly often.'

'He did.' Jane looked a little distressed. 'At first. After... after Mama died. And we drove over to Longbourn regularly. And that is why it is so strange, that his visits become less and less frequent.'

'But...' Elizabeth knew her husband was choosing his words with care, anxious to avoid giving offence. 'But is that not how it ought to be, Jane? At first he was in a new situation: his whole way of life had changed. But gradually he adapted, as we all must do in the circumstances.'

'Yes, that is so.' Bingley added his assurance. 'And that is what I have told you, Jane, is it not?'

'Yes. We have spoken of it endlessly. But it was when Caroline visited Longbourn that we first began to suspect the reason.'

'And the lady, this Mrs Castlemain,' asked Elizabeth. 'Have you had the opportunity of meeting her, Jane?'

'Yes. I have met her on more than one occasion, Elizabeth, and

I liked her. That is what makes it so difficult. She is the perfect person to be in charge of the girls and, while Mary is much less giddy than Kitty, both of them need a firm hand, though in different directions. Mrs Castlemain was very kind, coming to stay at Longbourn when Papa visited Pemberley. She has studied music and, as a result, Mary is being more consistent and self-critical, and Kitty is certainly less foolish, though that may simply be that Lydia's influence has faded. No, really, there is nothing I can say to the lady's disadvantage except...' Her voice trailed off as she balked at expressing her fears.

'But,' again it was Darcy who spoke, 'have you any grounds for suspecting that she has designs on your father?'

'No. Not exactly.'

'None at all as far as I can judge,' Bingley spoke stoutly. 'And for the life of me I cannot see what the fuss is about. She is a gentlewoman and it would not perhaps be a disaster if they should—' Catching sight of his wife's downcast expression, he stopped abruptly. 'But I do not think that is the way of it. Not at all. In any event,' he brightened up, as if more than ready to cast aside the problem, 'you may be able to judge for yourselves, since your dear papa is to dine with us this evening, and I daresay you, Miss Lizzie, and you, Darcy, will be glad of an hour to refresh yourselves before then, so I shall ring for Dewar to show you to your apartments.'

'So, Elizabeth.' Darcy came through from the dressing room, shrugging himself into his coat. 'Have your fears settled? Are you no longer convinced that Mr Bennet is about to rush off to Scotland with Mrs Castlemain?'

His wife smiled. 'I never saw him in that role, and I confess I am a little less concerned, but some anxiety remains.'

'You heard what Bingley said: that she is a gentlewoman and—'

'I am not convinced that Bingley is such a true judge of character as—'

'What?' He appeared shocked by such a statement. 'In spite of the fact that he selected the sweetest and dearest—'

'Hush! I was about to pay you a compliment, if you will allow it. I would value your opinion of these matters much more than Bingley's. He is altogether too artless and candid for—'

'And this is a compliment, Elizabeth?'

'It was meant as such, for I could not respect one such as Bingley as greatly as… others. Would you have chosen differently if Bingley had told you to do so?'

'I doubt that I would.'

'But he did, and that, I feel, is the difference between you. He is a good, kind man and makes my sister very content, but I could not respect him as much as a man who makes his own decisions, however difficult, and stays with them.

'Mmm. I shall try to look on that as a compliment, my dear.' Taking her hand, he raised it to his mouth before offering his arm. 'Now, shall we go down? I think I observed the Longbourn carriage turn into the drive and I expect Mr Bennet is waiting downstairs. I do not think you will disappoint him, Elizabeth.'

And indeed, their meeting was a happy occasion, only temporarily endangered by emotions which all were determined to keep under control. There was a considerable amount of local gossip to be exchanged, with news that Lady Lucas had last week returned from Hunsford, Charlotte now being on the mend; that the small millinery shop in Meryton, the one where Lydia and Kitty had wasted – according to their father's summary – so much time, was now in the hands of a woman who had spent some years in Paris. 'So, I expect,' Mr Bennet wound up in a tone of weary resignation, 'soon we shall be unable to see across the church. Last Sunday, Mrs Craven's confection practically blacked out the north window and gave much mirth to the choirboys, a welcome diversion, perhaps, considering the tedium of the service.'

The evening passed pleasantly enough and a return invitation was issued for the following day, when all were engaged to dine at Longbourn. 'The girls are anxious to see you, Lizzie,' said Mr Bennet as he donned his hat. 'And it may be that Mrs Castlemain can be prevailed upon to join us. Jane and Mr Bingley have already made her acquaintance and I think you will consider her a good influence on my two silly girls. She has,' now he spoke particularly to his eldest daughter, 'returned to her own cottage, so I shall have to send out the carriage for her, but if you and

Charles could be prevailed upon to take her back with you afterwards it is scarce half a mile out of your way and would save a journey...'

'Of course, sir.' Bingley, as always, was obliging. 'It would be a pleasure.'

When they had seen Mr Bennet from the premises and had returned to the drawing room, Darcy spoke reflectively. 'So it does not appear as if your father is in the grip of a great passion, Elizabeth.'

'I did not imagine he would be,' she declared with a faint blush and an apologetic look towards her sister.

'I think it is all a storm in a teacup and that we ought to consider things calmly.' As he spoke, Darcy walked about the room before taking a seat next to his wife. 'But I wonder why you, Jane, feel so anxious. Perhaps...'

'Oh, I thought nothing of it until Caroline suggested that perhaps Mrs Castlemain was setting her cap at Papa.'

'Oh?' The other two appeared not to notice the swift exchange of looks between their visitors, and Jane continued before either could make further comment.

'She had been so good, going over most days to see him and our sisters. I think she felt that she could help both Mary and Kitty. As you know, she has travelled widely in society and...'

'Yes.' Since his wife appeared momentarily overcome, Bingley took over, his kindly countenance clouded with concern. 'I should not have thought my sister would be so conscientious in this matter, but she was indeed concerned when she saw how things were going at Longbourn and reported them to us somewhat reluctantly, since she did not wish to upset dear Jane.' And he reached out to touch his wife's hand comfortingly.

'Well...' Throughout their exchanges, Elizabeth had been struck by her sister's changed attitude to Caroline Bingley. All past slights and unkindness were apparently forgotten: the time when visiting them in London that she had been quite deliberately kept apart from the man she loved and... A second's reflection, and she drew back from any criticism of her dear Jane, for had not her own husband collaborated in this past ungentlemanly treatment? And been long forgiven. Also, his relative, Lady

Catherine, who had been so insulting, Lizzie now found she could treat with a degree of civility and… 'Well, there is little more we can say on the matter, and perhaps tomorrow's meeting will show that all our fears are mistaken.' Rising, she smiled at her sister and held out her hand. 'So shall we treat our husbands to some music, Jane? I have been told by Lady Catherine de Bourgh, no less, that I am much improved since I went to Pemberley and shall be glad of your opinion.'

The following day brought back a host of memories as the sisters walked through woods and along paths familiar to them since childhood, and inevitably their conversation included memories of their mother, happy ones which gave some comfort to both, though neither was unaware of what had been her more regrettable qualities, ones which had come very near to ruining their happiness.

'Poor Mama,' Jane sighed deeply. 'If only she might have enjoyed our success a little longer.'

'Yes.' Lizzie squeezed her sister's hand. 'But let us be thankful that she was given time to share our good fortune. And she would have been so proud of her two little granddaughters. It is sad that they will not know the indulgence of a grandmamma, but I think Papa is as lief to spoil them as Mama would have been.'

'And poor Papa, too, Lizzie. I think, in spite of all, he must have missed her sorely.'

'Indeed.' But Elizabeth was less convinced than her sister, though she had never doubted that her father would have regrets. 'But we cannot pretend, Jane, that their marriage was perfect: they were ill suited and one can but wonder that they ever came together in the first instance. I am sure our father, with his experience of matrimony, will never wish to repeat the experience. But let us not be too gloomy and wait until this evening when we go to Longbourn. I am impatient to see my sisters and it will be interesting to meet Mrs Castlemain. I am certain we will find we have been too imaginative and that Papa is simply glad to be rid of some of the responsibility of looking after the two daughters who are as yet unmarried.'

There was much excitement when the carriage at last drew up in front of their old home, where they found their father, smiling happily, and Kitty and Mary by his side, waiting to greet them. Elizabeth presented to the girls the gifts she had brought, and was thanked excessively by Kitty for the pretty necklace and by Mary for the Indian shawl before they moved into the drawing room, where the lady who had been so much in their minds and conversation rose on their entering.

Mrs Castlemain was of medium height, with pretty hair curling about an intelligent face lit by brilliant dark eyes and a ready smile, which showed good teeth. Her dress had a degree of elegance without being overly stylish, and her manner was exceedingly pleasing, restrained but not shy, and it was immediately noticeable that the two younger Bennet girls deferred to her more than they had ever done to any family member.

When they were sitting at table, Mr Bennet appeared to be enjoying the occasion, and, since she noticed no particular partiality towards Mrs Castlemain, Elizabeth found that her fears quickly slipped away. After they had eaten, Mary was persuaded to the pianoforte where the improvement of her technique was immediately noticeable; likewise many of the harsher notes of her voice had been smoothed away, which Elizabeth felt could be due only to the influence of Mrs Castlemain. It was so agreeable that even Fitzwilliam congratulated her as she rose from the instrument, a fact which gave his wife as much pleasure as that shown on Mary's blushing face.

'Well done, Mary,' added Elizabeth, perhaps – as she admitted to herself later – relieved that raucous performances were a thing of the past. 'Your technique has improved immensely.'

Mary took a place on the sofa. 'Mrs Castlemain has spent a deal of time helping me, Lizzie.' She cast a glance towards where that lady was sitting, listening to a conversation between Jane, Bingley and Mr Bennet. 'And,' she continued, her voice growing more confidential, 'she has wrought much improvement in Kitty, who is less giddy than she has been in the past. It is almost a pleasure to be in her company now.' She had not entirely abandoned her former pompous manner, Lizzie noted. 'And she scarce talks of officers. In truth, I am inclined to think it was much down to Lydia's influence and, since she is now in the north, she may take at least some of the credit for that.' A slight smile was another indication of a freer attitude, which was very pleasing, and the evening passed in a remarkably easy way. It was only when they were taking their departure that Elizabeth felt a sharp pang for her mother as they travelled to the village where Mrs Castlemain lived, finding it difficult to keep her countenance, her mind being so flooded with sorrow for her mother's premature departure from this life. And when farewells had been made to Mrs Castlemain, they travelled back to Netherfield in silence, each seemingly occupied by private thoughts.

But on their arrival, habit led them to the small parlour where the gentlemen comforted themselves with glasses of brandy while Jane and Elizabeth were consoled with hot chocolate. 'Well…' It was Bingley who first broached the subject so much occupying their minds. 'It appears Mrs Castlemain is a perfectly admirable woman, I would say. What say you, Darcy?'

'Yes. It appears so.'

'Appears? So you do not wholly agree with me?'

'I do, but… things are not always as they appear. What I will say about the lady is that she is a most intelligent person, the kind of woman I would not hesitate to employ as a chaperone for Georgiana.'

Elizabeth felt her face grow heated and dared not look at Jane, who, like her, would interpret this as a criticism of their mother, for most assuredly the late Mrs Bennet would have been the very last woman who would ever have been considered for such a post.

'I think we are all agreed on that,' she said, and if there was a note of reprimand in her tone, she did not know if her husband had taken it to himself. 'Everything we have heard of Mrs Castlemain has been confirmed by our meeting her, but that is not the concern: we want to know if our father has any desire to change her position to that of mistress of Longbourn and, as to that, I confess I am as much in the dark as before. Like you, Fitzwilliam, I welcome her as a guide and chaperone for my sisters and am thankful for the good influence which is already noticeable in that sphere. If the matter rests there, then I shall have no more to say, but…' Replacing her cup with a tiny bump,

Elizabeth rose, and when she spoke her voice was not entirely steady. 'If you will excuse me, Jane, Charles, I think I shall go to bed.'

The men rose and Charles held open the door, his eyes noticing the brilliance of hers but making no comment beyond wishing her a good night, and Jane also left the room with her sister, walking with her upstairs to the door of her bedchamber, their arms about each other's waists.

'Sleep well, my dear Lizzie.' Gently, Jane embraced her. 'I understand your feelings exactly, and it is right, of course. We shall always miss Mama for her kindly intentions towards us and it is hard, indeed it is, to contemplate some other woman in her place.'

'But,' Elizabeth said sadly, 'I suspect you were about to add something to that opinion... Only, if such an idea is in Papa's mind, then... perhaps Mrs Castlemain would not be such a bad choice?'

'Perhaps,' her sister agreed. 'That is what Charles thinks, and I confess it is hard to disagree. After all, our father may yet live many years, and if she could make him happier...'

'Happier than ever our mother was able to do: is that your meaning, Jane?'

'Well...' Jane was gentle and hesitant as ever. 'We ourselves have often speculated, have we not, that they were ill matched, and it seems that Mrs Castlemain and Papa might have a more agreeable understanding. They share similar interests, which surely was not the case with Mama.'

'No. That is true.' For a moment, Elizabeth toyed with the idea of enquiring if Miss Bingley, who had first drawn attention to the situation, had shown any personal interest, but she did not. Her sister was so trusting – innocent was a word which sat easily with her – and it would be pointless, unfair even, to introduce another strand into what was already an unsatisfactory problem. 'And we are most likely concerned over something which has not even occurred to Papa. Or to Mrs Castlemain, either.' She smiled at her sister and kissed her cheek. 'Let us go to bed and sleep, dear Jane. Whatever fears we have are surely groundless and would astonish our father if he had the slightest idea.'

And so they parted, but as Elizabeth sat in front of the glass, brushing her long hair, a tiny frown drew her brows together as she acknowledged that the evening at Longbourn had done absolutely nothing to subdue her fears, and that was mostly due to Mrs Castlemain herself. She would not even allow herself to consider how admirable that woman would be as mistress of Longbourn, but it was impossible to block out the treacherous idea that their lives would have been so much easier if their mother had in some way resembled...

The door from the dressing room opened and Fitzwilliam came towards her, reaching out as always for the brushes with which he began stroking her hair in his usual soothing manner, while regarding her in the looking glass.

'So,' he began. His eyes had a power which never failed to make her wonder that she had once disliked him, an idea that now made her lips curl in amusement. 'So, my dear, now that we are alone, tell me what you think of the situation at Longbourn? You approved of the lady, I am sure.'

'Who could do otherwise? She is a perfectly acceptable person and no one could disapprove.'

'But?' he said, in much the same way as she had to her sister minutes earlier. 'I suspect a but is coming?'

'But... I do not know. I imagine it is mainly a reluctance to imagine that anyone can be so soon replaced as...' Tears stung her eyes and she bit her lips.

'I understand, my dear Lizzie.' Sitting beside her, he put down the brushes and extended a comforting arm. 'But simply think this: your father may enjoy the company of a comely, intelligent woman; he may be lonely, though I dare say he would not confess to such, but it is possible to be lonely, even in such a busy house as Longbourn. And, if it should be so, consider: if he were to choose another wife, how much more acceptable for it to be someone we can admire rather than someone we... do not much care for.'

Something in his tone made Lizzie look at him more closely. 'Fitzwilliam? Are you referring to Caroline Bingley?'

'Not directly. But, from what Bingley told me, Caroline was carrying her role of concerned neighbour to excess. He is too simple a man to have thought much of it, but her visits to Longbourn were daily and lengthy. She spent time with Kitty and Mary, who did not welcome her manner, and so... I wonder if your father introduced Mrs Castlemain, as we at first thought likely, in a spirit of self-defence. In which event, he may find he has to search out another lady if this one should also prove too attentive.'

'Oh, Fitzwilliam.' His manner brought a smile to Elizabeth's lips. 'I feel there is something in what you say and I may be worrying unnecessarily. Now, let us go to bed; I am wearied with so many family concerns. Thank you my love.'

Together they rose and instinctively she raised her mouth to his, grateful that he had such patience with the concerns and indiscretions which continued to affect the Bennet family.

Chapter Five

O n their return to Pemberley, Elizabeth was occupied with some domestic decisions and allowed her concerns for her father to drift to the back of her mind, while her husband was also much engaged with the business of the estate and some of the changes which he considered to be beneficial. But his wife's thoughts had been returning to her earlier plan of taking Georgiana and Anne de Bourgh to Paris on a visit, and when she submitted this idea to her husband, he first of all sighed very deeply, before conceding that, while he thought it a capital idea, she herself must undertake the planning, including an initial approach to his aunt.

'But, Fitzwilliam, it would be received with so much more approval if you were to issue the invitation.'

'Nonsense, my dear, it is one of your charges. If I were to do so,' his smile indicated that his words were not to be taken wholly at face value, 'my aunt would mock me for undertaking the duties of a wife.'

'But you have in the past always issued invitations, is it not so?'

'That,' he said, rising from his chair and crossing to where she sat at her writing desk to drop a swift kiss on her furrowed brow, 'was before I had the pleasure of a wife to relieve me of so many tedious tasks. No.' He strode to the door and stood there for a moment. 'I feel such an invitation would be much more effective coming from you, and I believe Lady Catherine would lack the courage of a refusal.' And with that and a faintly mocking glance, he opened the door and disappeared from sight.

And so it was that Elizabeth, with much frowning, pursing of lips and chewing of fingers, began the letter of appeal to her great adversary, starting with the assurance that Lady Catherine's nephew, in recognition of the valued advice he had received from her on her recent visit, was putting certain improvements in hand, with a sense of advantage already being achieved. Elizabeth hated herself for adopting an attitude which seemed both cowed and craven, but, if it would bring the desired response, she supposed it must be worth the humiliation. After several more flowery references to Anne's friendship with Georgiana, she wondered if Lady Catherine would consider sparing her daughter so she might accompany them on a short visit they were planning to the French capital. It would be so good, as she was confident that Lady Catherine herself would agree, for both young ladies to be exposed to the beauties of art and architecture, and, since they already had some knowledge of the language, such an opportunity would increase their understanding in many directions. Nothing, she assured Lady Catherine, had been said to Georgiana about the hope of the trip being further enhanced by the possibility of their being joined by her cousin, and Elizabeth looked forward to having Lady Catherine's permission et cetera, et cetera. And so the letter was despatched.

The first response was discouraging, since it contained a straightforward refusal on the grounds that Anne's health was much too delicate to permit such an arduous journey, and, while agreeing it was true that her daughter had benefited from the recent company of Georgiana, there were matters of propriety to be considered. Regarding this as a scarcely veiled reference to her own background, Elizabeth bit her lip and spent the rest of the day composing in her mind a series of responses which would leave her adversary gasping with vexation, but then, so it seemed to her, she heard her sister Jane whispering in her ear, advising caution. This was sufficient to switch her to a different plan of attack, and before she had time to reconsider she had taken up her pen again, expressing deep regrets that Anne's health had so badly deteriorated since they had last seen her and wondering if a visit to one of the spa towns – Vichy came particularly to mind – would be of any help in persuading Lady Catherine to reach another decision. It was such a pity, she wrote, if the dear girl were to be deprived of the pleasure of such an expedition, which, as well as providing food for the mind, might also result in some physical improvement. She concluded by sending all good wishes to Lady Catherine, reiterating that they were very much hoping their plan would eventually result in her approval.

It was but a few days later when the reply arrived, which resulted in Elizabeth exclaiming with pleasure as her eyes skimmed the first few lines; then, looking across the table, she encountered her husband's enquiring expression.

'It is,' she said, and her smile grew quite broad, 'a letter from your esteemed aunt.' She had not relinquished the teasing air which in the past had given such a particular pleasure to the then Miss Eliza Bennet. 'And she says,' she continued, picking up the sheet of paper and reading aloud in a voice which exaggerated the older lady's most condescending manner, '"since I do not wish to disappoint my dear niece, then I may withdraw my objections, though with some misgivings. Since last we corresponded, Anne's health is slightly improved and she feels she could undertake such a journey and, having every confidence in the protection Mr Darcy will show the two young ladies in his care, I am prepared to give it some further consideration. Visiting a foreign medical establishment will not be necessary since we have complete confidence in Sir Compton Lomax, who has attended my daughter from birth. As he also cares for the highest in the land, I feel we have no need of others, who probably do not even speak our language. Please let me have a timetable and itinerary before I give my final decision".'

'Well,' Elizabeth offered the letter to her husband who took it, hastily scanning the lines. 'What do you think of that, Fitzwilliam?'

'I think my first feeling is of surprise, for I have hardly ever known the lady to alter her decisions, once made. And I should like to know what you said to persuade such a change in her.'

'I was very docile, Fitzwilliam: you would have been proud of me. I recalled my sister's reproof some time ago.' Thinking of how Jane had so properly reprimanded her at the time of all the misunderstandings involving Wickham, Lizzie felt her skin grow warm. 'And now I am determined to be less…'

'Dogmatic?' he offered helpfully when she hesitated. 'Imperious?' he considered with a frown. 'Yes, that is the better word. You are determined to be less imperious and I for one am glad of it.'

'I am trying to reform,' she replied with mock humility. 'And I think in the case of Lady Catherine, I have had some success.'

'I doubt that she would agree with you, my dear – certainly if she had heard herself ridiculed as you read aloud from her letter.'

'I am sorry, Fitzwilliam, but… it is hard to resist.'

'So long as you remember to resist when we have her daughter with us. And even Georgiana would not necessarily find it amusing to hear her godmother cast as buffoon.'

Sensing that her husband himself had not found her efforts entirely amusing, Elizabeth was reminded not to push too heavily against formal barriers. Not everyone had her sense of the ridiculous, and the last thing she wanted was for Darcy to become impatient in the same way her father had done with her mother.

'I am truly sorry, Fitzwilliam; it was thoughtless of me and I deserve your disapproval. I know how tolerant you have been on… on so many occasions. Since our marriage, you have never by word or manner shown any disrespect for my parents, and that must have posed many difficulties for you. And for my part, I ought to be able to show the same tolerance for your aunt.'

'Yes, my dear,' His manner had an air of weary restraint. 'But now I shall leave you to compose your reply. I see Lady Catherine requires an itinerary and you will find details of that in the library.'

And so it was done. Elizabeth wrote what must have been an acceptable précis of their expected route and arrangements, receiving in return Lady Catherine's agreement, by no means wholehearted, but still it enabled them to go ahead with their plans for a journey to Paris.

When they arrived at Rosings some ten days later to collect their cousin, having spent two nights on the way, Elizabeth, on alighting from the carriage, was genuinely touched to see the warmth with which the two young cousins greeted each other after their separation. It was a reminder of her own good fortune, being brought up in a family where loneliness was a word none understood, and she decided that the moment they returned to Derbyshire she would set about organising a ball for Georgiana as a means of encouraging visits from some of the younger people in the area. And, if this journey to Paris should be a success, then she might persuade Lady Catherine to allow Anne to join them there.

Anne did indeed, as her mama had indicated, look less lively than when she had left Pemberley. Always sallow, her skin had taken on a still paler hue, but how could it be otherwise when she lived almost entirely deprived of fresh air and of company, apart from that offered by her mother and their companion? So this was an occasion for Elizabeth to be particularly deferential to the mistress of Rosings, who appeared rather gratified that such a rebellious young woman had been brought to heel and was at last showing signs of being, perhaps, a worthy mistress of Pemberley. Mr Darcy was less impressed, as his raised eyebrow showed when he observed his wife being especially gracious, resulting in Elizabeth doing her best to avoid his knowing expression at such times.

At length, they were free to quit Rosings, but not without many instructions for their safety and comfort being repeatedly pressed upon them by Lady Catherine, and so, as they turned from the drive, Elizabeth sensed she was not the only one who inwardly sighed with relief. Their journey to France was long, but with so many new sights and experiences the time passed easily; the crossing was blessedly calm and, in a surprisingly short time, they were alighting outside their temporary home in the centre of that most beautiful of cities.

It was only later, when they were in their private apartments, her maid, Dorcas, putting the finishing touches to Elizabeth's toilette (she, Darcy's valet and the other servants having travelled ahead of them), that her husband spoke of her changed attitude to his aunt.

'Yes.' Elizabeth touched her hair approvingly. 'Thank you, Dorcas. And if you would be kind enough to go and help the young ladies…' And when the door had closed, she raised a coquettish glance towards the dark figure sitting in a red velvet chair and regarding her though the glass. 'My changed attitude? But I thought that was what you wanted, Fitzwilliam? That I should be less… imperious. Didn't you say?'

'Aye. I am pleased to note that at last you are paying some heed to what your husband wants in his wife.'

All at once her tendency to jest vanished and she felt foolish and immature. 'That,' she said, biting her lip as she half turned away, 'has become my first aim in life, Fitzwilliam. I thought you understood that my most fervent wish is to please you in all things.'

'Elizabeth.' Rising, he crossed towards her and put his fingers beneath her chin, turning her face gently up to his. 'You have taught me many things, and one of these is to take life more lightly. Now, I enjoy being provoked, and I think I have, in turn, learned to provoke. I enjoy both experiences, which are still quite novel to me, and you must not mind when I tease you a little. It is done in the most loving way.'

'Oh, Fitzwilliam.' Turning, she pressed herself into his arms, which closed about her. 'You make me so ashamed. How I wish I could aspire to your goodness and—'

'Is this the same Miss Bennet who threw so many bitter accusations at me such a short time ago?'

'It is the same.' Now she was smiling, just blinking aside a tear from the luminous eyes. 'The same Elizabeth, but now the mistress of Pemberley and...' Leaning forward, she whispered against his cheek, 'married to Mr Darcy. Can you believe it?'

'I am glad of it but, like you, can scarce believe it.' He dropped a kiss on her brow. 'Now, Georgiana and Anne will be waiting.' He offered his arm. 'Shall we go to their suite and then we may all go down to dinner together? While we are here we must try to persuade my cousin to eat a little more. If she could gain a few pounds in weight, I am confident she would feel, and look, much better, and surely Paris is the place to do such a thing.'

The days in Paris simply flew past, the young ladies appearing thrilled with all they saw and experienced, and for Elizabeth, too, there was much to be seen that her previous short visit had not allowed, making her excitement almost as great as that of her younger companions. Darcy, with his considerable knowledge of France, was a competent and concerned guide of the great art galleries, while on fine days they picnicked in the royal hunting parks, lunched on a *bâteau* on the Seine, sat entranced at the opera and, on a more mundane level, laughed at each other as, moustachioed, they drank chocolate at a favourite pavement café.

'It has been a perfect journey,' Elizabeth told her husband on their last evening before going down to dinner. 'You have been tolerance itself in accommodating two young ladies in addition to your wife. Such patience! I cannot imagine any other man showing so much consideration.'

'It was by no means difficult. My main objective is to give pleasure to you, for thereby I contrive my own happiness. But it also pleases me to see Georgiana so happy. She admires you very much: do you realise that, Elizabeth?'

'As I do her. I would so like to wipe from her memory what happened in the past and—'

'That would not necessarily be the best thing to do, my dear. She has learned from that unhappy episode, learned that a smooth tongue and a charming manner are not always to be trusted.'

'Well, as to that, older and wiser heads than Georgiana's have been turned by such accomplished rascals, have they not?'

'Happily that is over, and I suspect even now they are waiting for us, probably in need of dinner, since we have starved since luncheon…'

'Except for hot chocolate and gâteau on the journey back from the Bois. And I think your hopes for Anne have been achieved, since I observed she has gained a little weight, but, truth to tell, I am certain she will always be small and slight. But she looks so much more alive, though I am uncertain that Lady Catherine will approve so much animation in her daughter.'

'She may yet surprise us all. But now, let us go downstairs.'

With some celebration and not a little laughter, they had eaten what was to be their last dinner in Paris and, since there was no entertainment planned for that evening, they settled down in the parlour, Darcy with a book that he had found in a discreet little *bibliotheque* just off the Faubourg. Georgiana and Anne were sitting by the pianoforte, wondering aloud if anyone could tell them what had happened to the piece of music they had been playing recently, when there was some sort of commotion in the hallway, the striking of footsteps on the tiled floor and then Dorcas, who as well as lady's maid was helping in other less specific ways, came into the room.

'If you please, sir,' she addressed Darcy, who looked up from his book, 'two young gentlemen wish to see you. It is Mr John Arbuthnot, sir, and a friend.'

'Mr Arbuthnot?' Darcy's tone held surprise. He closed his book carefully, laid it on the table beside him and rose, while Elizabeth's expression echoed her husband's astonishment, and the subdued laughter which had its centre about the pianoforte ceased entirely, as all heads turned towards the door. 'Very well, Dorcas, show Mr Arbuthnot and his friend in.'

An instant later, the two young men entered, the one, Mr Arbuthnot, tall and handsome, and the other, Mr Fife, much shorter in stature and, if not exactly regular in features, then certainly not ill-looking, and, as Elizabeth recalled the moment they appeared, a young man of strong opinions and with a wry sense of humour.

'Mr Darcy. Mrs Darcy.' They spoke one after the other, each bowing smartly.

'Mr Arbuthnot. Mr Fife.' Welcoming them, Mr Darcy indicated that they should sit, which they proceeded to do with some swishing aside of coat tails. 'You have met my sister, Georgiana, and my cousin, Anne, I believe.'

'Indeed, sir.' Both rose and bowed towards the pianoforte where the two young ladies were sitting. 'Miss Darcy, Miss de Bourgh.' Their greetings were returned, albeit in subdued murmurs.

'Forgive our intrusion, sir.' John Arbuthnot was, for the moment, spokesman. 'We have been travelling and just this day returned to Paris, where a letter from my mother awaited with the astonishing news that you and Mrs Darcy were also in town. We immediately decided that nothing would do but that we should at once pay our respects to you, sir. And, you, ladies.' With this last word, his eyes slid past Mrs Darcy and towards the two young women, who bowed their heads becomingly, though Elizabeth observed with some amusement that both were blushing slightly and looked shy and excited, as was perfectly natural.

For some time the two young men sat discussing their journey with their hosts and also making enquiries about how the Darcys had travelled from Derbyshire, showing an interest in all aspects and offering advice gained from their own experience.

Mr Fife grew quite animated about the grandeur of the Eifel, which they had explored the previous week, giving an entertaining account of the days they had spent in Geneva, while Elizabeth could not help smiling to herself as she noticed his frequent glances towards Georgiana and Anne, which encouraged her to ask the ladies if they would defer their playing and come forward to join the company.

But there again, Mr Fife showed himself to be quite masterful, for at once he rose and, crossing to the pianoforte, he asked that they should not disturb themselves, that both he and Mr Arbuthnot were much involved with music, that they sang in their college choir and that, if they were not disturbing the family, they would be delighted to hear the young ladies play. 'With your permission, ma'am.' This last was addressed to his hostess.

'With pleasure,' Elizabeth replied happily. 'There is little we enjoy more when at home in the evenings than music, and though we may not reach the levels which we have experienced so much during our stay here – I mean, of course, at the opera and the concerts we have been fortunate enough to attend – I am confident Georgiana and Anne will acquit themselves with honour.'

And so the two began to play one of their favourite duets, to which all present listened with considerable attention. Elizabeth was conscious of her husband's eyes on hers and was reminded in a stab of real pleasure of that first time that she, along with Mr and Mrs Gardiner, had visited Pemberley, and how she had helped Georgiana with her music. And, as she did then, she returned his attention with a provocative little upward flick of her lashes, amused to see how the corners of his mouth curved upwards as if in recognition, before returning her attention to the players.

By this time, both young men had quit the older pair, with one, Mr Fife, turning pages while Mr Arbuthnot had his eyes on Georgiana, who was blushing and looking pleased, yet slightly ill at ease, which made Elizabeth feel she ought to intervene lest either Georgiana or Anne should feel alarm. Unhurriedly she rose, moving across the room and lingering beside a bookcase where, earlier that day, she had seen for the first time some choral music. Picking up a few sheets, she advanced towards the instrument just as the end of a piece was reached. When the polite applause had faded, she handed over the loose sheets with the suggestion that perhaps, as they were so fond of singing, the young men would oblige them, which both appeared more than happy to do. In fact, one might have hazarded that they were waiting for just such an invitation. So Elizabeth returned to her place beside her husband, listening to the subdued discussion which was taking place as papers were rustled and keys discussed, and then it was that Mr Arbuthnot took Anne's place beside Georgiana on the long stool, as together they began to play the introduction.

The two young men then sang together, their voices both strong and musical, while Anne, her eyes fixed on the sheets of music, dutifully turned pages as required. When they came to the end of the piece, Darcy and Elizabeth showed their appreciation, and the latter, at least, experienced a pang of regret that they were so soon to leave for home when the company of two such acceptable young men might have added considerably to their pleasure.

Later, at the end of the evening, she and her husband were in their bedchamber, he sitting watching her at her toilette, she looking at him through the glass. 'The evening went well, I think.' She spoke lightly but with an enquiring note in her voice.

'Mmm.' He appeared less certain than she would have thought, and then he continued. 'But you must not set yourself up as matchmaker, Lizzie. I quite forbid it, since we both know how disastrous such intervention can be.'

At once, Elizabeth recalled the hideous embarrassment visited on the whole family by her mother's behaviour in that direction and felt her colour rise. 'You need have no concerns on that score, Fitzwilliam. I have not forgot the lessons of the recent past and would not dream of manipulating anyone's emotions.'

'Do not be too downcast, Lizzie: it suits you ill. And besides, I was not entirely serious. I, too, was amused by the behaviour of the two young men.'

'And of Georgiana and Anne.'

'And of Georgiana and Anne,' he agreed, 'both of whom appeared pleased and a little excited by the evening's diversions. But,' his manner became more serious as he replaced the hairbrush on the dressing table, 'do you suppose their arrival was as fortuitous as they said?'

'I cannot see why you should doubt them. They both appear to be honest young men and—'

'Aye,' he agreed reluctantly. 'Arbuthnot, I am sure of. He is the eldest son of a good, though not, I think, particularly rich family, but the other young man, the Scotsman, we know nothing of him. And did you observe, my dear, that of the two young women it was Anne who gave the appearance of animation more than Georgiana, though I do not deny that my sister also enjoyed the unexpected diversion. You see, although Anne has improved remarkably under your and Georgiana's influence, I have never thought of her as likely to marry, perhaps because of her delicate constitution and frame, which seemed unlikely to attract the right sort of man. But, on the other hand, she is a considerable heiress and is therefore vulnerable, a prey for fortune hunters. Remember, I have much experience of the breed, and though I would not say Mr Fife is cast in that mould, I shall be, to the end of my life, wary where young women of fortune are concerned.'

'What a bugbear money is. Those with few expectations, such as myself, must look to marry advantageously, while young women who have some fortune must look to increase it.'

'I thought, perhaps, the system had worked well enough for you and for your sister, Jane. Do not tell me you have regrets.'

'You know I have not. I swear, if the situations with you and Mr Collins had been reversed, I would be most happily settled with you at Hunsford and should never have thought of Pemberley, but...' Under his sceptical scrutiny, she lowered her eyes and coloured slightly. 'But I am glad that they were not.'

'You are telling me,' her husband quizzed, 'that you would not have married Mr Collins even if he were the first lord in the land?'

'I promise you,' she replied, with great feeling and conviction, 'there are no circumstances in which I should have accepted Mr Collins. To save my life, I should not have become his wife, especially...' She broke off her protestation, again colouring prettily.

'Yes? Especially? Do not keep me in suspense, my dear Lizzie.'

'Especially now that I know... Oh!' she burst out in great emotion. 'Poor Charlotte! How I pity her and—'

'Hush, my dear.' Rising, Darcy wrapped his arms about her, drawing her close. 'Do not dwell on it. You have no need to fear any such involvement with Mr Collins. And you have told me, and I myself have seen with my own eyes, that Charlotte is perfectly content with her choice. I cannot see that she regrets marrying Mr Collins.'

'No,' his wife agreed from the stifling folds of his dressing jacket. 'But can't you see, Fitzwilliam, that is what makes it all so... very sad?'

At this, her husband burst out laughing. 'I cannot see it. Each is content with the other, and I dare say Charlotte may pity you, married to the proudest man in the north of England with all the responsibility of a great house.'

'That is not so. You know it is not and, as for dear Charlotte, she was never one of your critics. Always she admonished me if I spoke harshly of you and the Netherfield people.'

'Then I must be more attentive when next we call on her. She has much to endure, I fear, with only the Rosings family for company. And I am certain Lady de Bourgh would have much to say on the subject of a certain young man, should he pursue her daughter to Kent. I doubt that she has the least intention of ever allowing Anne the freedom to meet any man.'

'No. For she thought she had the perfect husband already chosen.'

'Do not let us go down that route again.' He sighed deeply. 'You know that idea was solely in her own mind.'

'Well, now that you have escaped her clutches, perhaps she will turn her eyes in the direction of your cousin.'

'My cousin?' Leaning back, he held her away, affording the opportunity to study her features. 'My cousin? Surely you do not mean Fitzwilliam?'

'Why not? It would seem an obvious step. His fortune is less than yours, but in every other respect he would appear the perfect match for Lady Catherine's daughter.'

Darcy laughed. 'But then you mistake my cousin's character, Elizabeth: he is not the man to allow his wife to be chosen for him. And besides, though he is fond of Anne, he sees her as little more than a child and would certainly never embark on such a union. And, as I am certain you must know, his inclinations lie towards a more challenging wife, one who will not shrink when asked a question, who will on occasion be inclined to disagree with popular opinion, and whom do you imagine would fit such a description, Elizabeth?'

For a moment, lying back in his arms, she stared up at him, and then, when the drift of his words came to her, she lowered her eyes in confusion. 'I don't know what you are saying, my dear. I cannot think who you mean.'

'Don't play with me, madam. You know perfectly well that not only did your extraordinary candour captivate me, but you very nearly enslaved my own cousin, and but for my timely intervention you might now have been Mrs Fitzwilliam.'

'Nonsense.' She toyed with a button on his shirt. 'Besides, Colonel Fitzwilliam could not have taken a wife without a fortune. And that is one of the reasons why I thought a match between him and your cousin, Anne, would have suited both sides.'

'Take my word, Elizabeth: there is no chance that Fitzwilliam will think to marry Anne, and, since that subject is exhausted, let us go to bed. There, we can further discuss the prospects of Anne with Mr Fife, and let us not forget Georgiana and young Arbuthnot. In that at least, I see some merit, and think how happy it would be to have my sister living within a few miles of Pemberley. Now that I have considered the matter, it seems to me that nothing could be more happily settled.' And with that, they snuffed out the candles and went to bed.

Their Paris expedition having apparently been so entirely successful, it might have seemed especially perverse that, on the return journey, Elizabeth found herself so uneasy as to elicit concerned enquiries from her husband. Each of these she dismissed with some reference to a piece of fish, which she alone had eaten the previous day and, thereafter, the perfectly calm channel was accused of a touch of *mal de mer*. At this juncture, it seemed impossible for her to explain to Darcy that it was his behaviour which had raised suspicions of the worst sort. Suspicions which, if stated and subsequently exposed as unfounded, would assuredly undermine the trust which she believed was the basis of all true relationships. And especially, she was convinced, the basis of the closeness of that twixt Fitzwilliam Darcy and Elizabeth Bennet.

The incident which was causing so much torment and a pain verging on disillusion had happened on the very morning of the day they were to leave Paris. Darcy, on the pretext – the more she considered that word, the more appropriate it later seemed – of some urgent but unspecified business suggested, since the young ladies were engaged with a drawing master, Elizabeth might seize the opportunity and laze a little longer in bed.

In her innocence, and grateful for such consideration, she ordered a second cup of chocolate and lay sipping, dreamily imagining that it would indeed be in keeping with her husband's generous nature to go off and purchase that pretty bracelet she had so admired in a shop window the day before yesterday. Or the ring or…

This took her thoughts in a different but not unconnected direction to the nearby row of little boutiques with their elegant displays. Such temptations ought not to be resisted, and there was the added benefit that she might find some additional little trinkets to take back to her sisters and the little Collins girls. Close by she had seen a *parfumerie*, which she was sure would provide something unusual to excite those who had never left the shores of England.

Thus within the hour she set off, having left details of her plans. Feeling quite adventurous, Mrs Darcy strolled forth into the warm sunshine, pausing for a moment to raise her parasol and, with the aid of an obliging shop window, to adjust the veil of her bonnet to a more coquettish, Parisian angle. Her smile was more sister Lydia than Mrs Fitzwilliam Darcy as she turned away, quickly reaching her goal, where she spent a glorious hour buying all sorts of little gifts and spending a considerable amount of money.

At last, tired but entirely satisfied with the morning's business, Elizabeth decided her final indulgence would be a delicious cup of coffee before returning with her booty to make final preparations for their journey. The small café, unobtrusive on the outside, was, inside, surprisingly elegant, and she chose a table towards the rear with a view over a delightfully extensive garden, which led on to a small park. Having given her order, she leaned forward in an attempt to identify some bushes fringing a small lake where water fowl glided, her mind intent on the changes her husband was currently considering for Pemberley.

At the far end, a woman with a small boy – five or six years old, she imagined – threw some bread onto the water, laughing at the speed with which the birds darted forward. Elizabeth was so absorbed that she did not at first notice the tall dark figure who emerged from the screen of foliage. The man was very warmly welcomed by the young woman; the child jumped up, reaching out a hand. And it was with a shiver of something close to apprehension that she realised the newcomer was none other than her own husband.

The coffee in front of Mrs Darcy grew cold as she watched, and afterwards she could not justify her failure to rise, to go out into the garden, smiling, waiting for an introduction. But... She sat stock still, unwilling to believe the evidence of her own eyes while the scene in front of her was played out.

Serious, consoling, affectionate: certainly Darcy was all of those, and – for some reason this gave Elizabeth an especially sharp pain – easy and teasing towards the child. It was only later she considered and identified the source of this feeling. She saw Darcy cover the woman's hand with his; a few tears might have been shed; there was a glimpse of white linen and then... then they were gone, swallowed up by the swaying bushes, as if they had never been.

It was not until they were within sight of the White Cliffs that Elizabeth decided she must put her fears and suspicions to rest. Her first inclination, almost a determination, was to have things out with her husband, to confess that she had been a witness, however unwitting and unwilling, to her husband's secret rendezvous in Paris, and to invite, even to demand, an explanation. But after lengthy and serious contemplation, she convinced herself that any forced answer from him could easily lead to further grief and disillusion. And on his side, perhaps even more than on hers – something she did not care to contemplate. In any event, she was sufficiently worldly to know that many men, kind and responsible men, devoted husbands, had, in their youth, made mistakes later regretted, and she had little doubt that Mr Darcy had faced up to whatever responsibilities he had to the young woman and to his… to the boy.

But deep beneath all else was the anxiety that, if she should probe too deeply, she might have to face the certainty, the confirmation of her fears, and then, indeed, it was likely she, Elizabeth Darcy, who would suffer most grievously. In that moment, she determined all recollection of what she had seen would be wiped from her memory.

Their return to Derbyshire being smoothly completed and Georgiana having been invited to spend another two weeks at Rosings, life for the Darcys resumed its normal pleasant pattern. Once or twice a week they dined with friends either at Pemberley or at one or other of the houses of their neighbours, and it was at one of the latter that they met the parents of young Mr Arbuthnot and had much news to exchange of their meeting in Paris.

'Yes,' Mr Arbuthnot, who was Elizabeth's partner at dinner explained, 'John gave us a detailed account of their visit to you on the evening before your departure and said how very welcoming you were. They were, I assure you, delighted to have the opportunity of furthering their acquaintance with your family, and Mr Fife is, I think, somewhat taken by your husband's cousin. Apparently she reminds him of a very dear sister, who died at the age of twelve.'

'Oh, I see. I quite thought it was the music which drew them together.' Elizabeth did not know how to respond to such a bold statement.

'That as well, of course. Both he and my son are devoted to music and that was the reason for their travelling to the great opera houses of Italy, Germany and France. But they enjoy it at a more homely level as well, being happy sitting around the pianoforte singing the simplest of melodies.'

'We enjoyed listening to them.'

'I believe you, too, are gifted in that direction, Mrs Darcy.'

'I? No. A complete amateur, I confess. I play well enough in the presence of my own family, those who will endlessly indulge me but... I am an indifferent performer. Tell me: Mr Fife is from Scotland, is he not? Have he and your son been friends for some time?'

'For many years, Mrs Darcy. They first met as boys at school and formed a close friendship despite many differences of temperament before going to Oxford together. I always think Mr Fife exerts a good influence on John, who is inclined to be impetuous from time to time.'

'He is a young man and ought not to be forever serious.'

'Indeed. That is the time to be carefree: responsibility comes soon enough. And all too soon he will find himself weighed down with the cares of the estate, since I have determined to hand over much of the business to him. I confess,' he smiled at her with a droll face, 'I begin to feel my age, Mrs Darcy, and my wife and I wish to have more freedom to follow our own interests.'

'You are too young to be feeling your age, sir,' Elizabeth answered, adopting his own light hearted manner. 'And what interests do you wish to fulfil when you have the freedom to do so?'

'My wife, Mrs Darcy, is an accomplished watercolourist and loves nothing more than travelling to the highlands of Scotland, which sits very happily with my own obsession of fishing for salmon.'

'Indeed? I had no idea your wife was so gifted. Once upon a time, our governess tried very hard to find in us, we two elder girls, some aptitude for art; with Jane she was more successful than with me. So I admire anyone who has such a talent. About salmon fishing I am entirely ignorant, but from time to time my husband does have fishing parties on the lake at Pemberley.'

'I have enjoyed his hospitality there on occasion, though it is a different sport, fishing in the rushing waters of a highland burn.'

'I can see it must be and have heard the Scottish fish are very wily.'

'That is so, but even when the catch is very light we all enjoy the sport, and then, in the evening, it is pleasant to return to the lodge, which we take for the season, and join the ladies, who have surfeited themselves on the grandeur of the scenery, have spent the day walking, reading or, in my wife's case, with her paints and easel. But tell me of your impressions of Paris? Was it your first visit? It is many years since we visited the city; since all the troubles, I have deemed it safer to travel elsewhere.'

And so they embarked on an animated discussion of the city which Elizabeth described as the fairest she had ever seen and one to which she longed to return as soon as may be. This carried them to the end of the meal, and afterwards, when the company repaired to the large gallery, she talked amiably with other local families with whom she had recently become acquainted, keen to further her knowledge of the district and all that was happening there.

It was as they were driving home in the carriage that her husband remarked that she had given every appearance of pleasure throughout the evening, an opinion with which she agreed wholeheartedly.

'But of course I did, Fitzwilliam. It would be churlish indeed to have been other than very happy in such company. On every side there was civility, and I am surprised that all are so informed on matters of taste and fashion.' At this her husband's eyebrows were raised, but since his arm was about her, with her face resting on his shoulder, she had no means of seeing and continued, unaware of his amusement. 'Oh, and I have been told there are, from time to time, concerts in the nearby towns, and I hope we shall be able to attend those when it is convenient.'

'That is good,' her husband conceded gravely. 'I am pleased that the Arbuthnots and their friends have not disappointed and that perhaps we can match the excitements of Meryton. Not for the world would I wish you to feel deprived, my dear.'

'Mmm.' Recognising his tone at last and determined to play him at his own game, she smiled quietly to herself. 'I knew you would agree with me, Fitzwilliam. You are such a good, kind man.'

'Yes,' he answered dryly as the carriage turned into the drive of Pemberley. 'I shall always try to agree with you, Lizzie. It is my mission in life. And now,' he disengaged himself as they came to a halt, 'let us try to behave as if I have some authority in my own house, otherwise I shall be the butt of jokes below stairs.'

It was shortly after that when Mr John Arbuthnot and his friend Mr Fife, now returned from their travels, called at Pemberley, and their disappointment on finding that Miss Georgiana and Miss Anne were not in residence was very ill concealed.

'I quite thought,' said Mr Arbuthnot, with no notion of his feelings being so clearly etched on his features, 'indeed I am certain that my father said the young ladies were to have returned.'

'No. I am sorry; I must have been careless when an enquiry was made.'

'And Miss de Bourgh? Is she to accompany Miss Darcy when she returns to Pemberley?'

'Nothing of that sort has been suggested.' Mr Darcy, who had been called from his estate duties to welcome the callers, rose from his seat and strode to the window where he checked that some of his alterations to the lake were being supervised by his agent. 'You understand that my aunt, Lady Catherine, who is very close to her daughter, is loath to allow her to leave Rosings. The journey to Paris was a very great…' Turning round, he added the only word which to him appeared appropriate: '…concession. She seldom concedes on such matters.' He smiled at his visitors and, though Elizabeth knew well enough that he was anxious to attend the outside work, his present great interest, he returned to his seat.

'Yes.' Despite her own feelings on the matter of the overbearing Lady Catherine de Bourgh, Elizabeth saw it as her duty to support what her husband had said. 'It is touching to see a mother and daughter in such sympathy, a result, I imagine, of Anne's father having died so young and…' There was little complimentary she could say on this matter, so she changed the subject abruptly, conscious as she did so of the disappointment on the face of Mr Fife, which almost exactly mirrored that on Mr Arbuthnot's countenance. 'And tell me about the other sights you observed on your travels. You returned by way of the Belgian capital, I understand. Please tell me what you thought of the architecture, which I have heard described as very fine. And the music. Were you able to attend a concert or the opera?'

But no matter how she endeavoured to keep the conversation alive, the young men appeared despondent and soon took their departure. She followed her husband upstairs to watch him change his coat into the rougher one he used when busy about the park, anxious to share with him the ideas which were bubbling through her mind.

'Fitzwilliam,' she said, sitting on the divan in his dressing room and watching with a degree of pleasure as he discarded one coat and shrugged himself into the other, 'I am determined that we write to Rosings at once and suggest...' Here she paused, determined to choose her words with care. '...suggest that it is time for Georgiana to return and that perhaps she might also bring her cousin with her.'

'Lady Catherine would never agree,' he stated shortly and took a step towards the door.

'But... don't go. My dear, does it not seem touching to you that two eminently suitable young men should go to the trouble—'

'Trouble?' he interrupted. 'The trouble of keeping me from my duties to chatter about... about what, I do not know.'

'They wished to talk about Georgiana and Anne; surely you were aware...'

'Indeed I was aware, Lizzie. I was aware that having grown used to all the liveliness of life in Paris and Brussels, now they are finding Derbyshire slightly dull and seek the company of two young ladies to relieve their ennui. Do not build a double romance from such meagre beginnings, my dear. And I have already warned you of the folly of matchmaking.'

Elizabeth ignored that final remark, though she acknowledged its truth. 'You think that is all it was, Fitzwilliam?' She spoke rather sadly, which sponsored a swift embrace from her husband. 'That they are two rather bored young men in search of diversion?'

'It is a state not unknown in young men of all stations and I do not wish to see Georgiana's heart broken a second time.'

'No, of course not and nor do I. I have too much experience of that condition and would not wish it—'

'And have I not?' If his tone was indignant, his look was tender. 'Having offered an honourable marriage to be told by the object of my affections that I was utterly and completely—'

'Hush.' Lizzie pressed her fingertips against his lips. 'I will not hear it again and have apologised a thousand times in words and in deeds. You are none of the things I accused you of...' She stood back from him with a smile which held a hint of provocation. 'And in any event, you cannot say that the outcome of that was very unhappy.'

'No, I cannot say it has been unhappy. I am simply being very careful where my sister Georgiana's feelings are concerned. If things are to work out happily, they will do so on their own account without any help from the outside.'

'But surely you would not wish to impede matters of the heart.'

'No, Lizzie,' he said wearily. 'That I shall never do. But now I must be away: Dawkins awaits a decision on—'

'But you will think, Fitzwilliam, on what I have said.'

'My dear, I scarce think of anything other.'

And, before she could say a further word, the door had closed between them, and it was not until a few moments later, when her mind had revolved in a most agitated way, that she was able to put all concerns of Georgiana and Mr John Arbuthnot from her and go downstairs to compose a letter to her sister, Jane, and thereafter one to her father, in which she forbore to mention the name of Mrs Castlemain. She congratulated herself that at last she was determined to take note of her husband's words and refrain from interfering in the private affairs of others. Fitzwilliam's words, light and teasing though they had been, were yet further reminders of the dangers of falling into the same habits as her mother. Such habits, which had brought so much embarrassment and humiliation in their wake, must surely put her on her guard against any inclination to matchmaking.

Chapter Six

*N*evertheless, she could not but acknowledge a feeling of great satisfaction when, just two days later and unexpectedly, a carriage bowled along the Pemberley drive bearing the de Bourgh device on the door and disgorged the two young ladies who had been the source of so much recent thought and discussion.

'Mrs Darcy, ma'am.' A maid hurried into the morning room where she was trying to compose a letter to her sister, Mrs Wickham, who had written with a scarcely veiled appeal for accommodation for herself, her husband and family, enabling them to break their journey from Newcastle to Netherfield where they were to spend a few days.

> Dear Lydia,
>
> Thank you for your letter of the twelfth. I was pleased to learn that all is well with you, despite young Charles having been ill with a chill from which I hope he is now fully recovered. Fortunately, here, we are all in the best…

Which was where she had paused and was nibbling the end of the quill as May burst in, giving her the opportunity to break off from a weary task.

'Yes, May.' With relief she rose from her chair, looking towards the door where the girl stood. 'What is the matter?' She was conscious of May's difficulties and always tried to persuade her from her extreme shyness.

'If you please, ma'am, it is Miss Georgiana and the other young lady. They are come back, ma'am.'

'Nonsense, May.' The words actually hovered on her lips but were fortunately staunched by the appearance of the first-named lady herself, who came striding into the room, undoing the ribbons on her bonnet as she did so and immediately embracing her sister, who then found herself looking into the eyes of Anne de Bourgh. 'May…' When she had greeted the other, Mrs Darcy immediately became the chatelaine of Pemberley – 'May, please arrange some refreshment for the young ladies, we shall have it in the parlour' – and then proceeded to lead the way down the long corridor and across the hall into the small room, elegant but by no means grand, where she and her husband spent most of their time together.

'Now, tell me,' said Lizzie, when she had seen the new arrivals seated and divested of their outer garments, and she herself sat facing them, her expression still puzzled at their unheralded arrival, 'what brings you back to Derbyshire in so sudden a fashion? It is…' For some inexplicable reason, dire pictures came into her mind; she was alive to all the dangers of modern life that might afflict those at Hunsford and Netherfield. The children especially the children… 'It is not bad news? Tell me it is not.'

'It *is* bad news,' Georgiana retorted lightly, 'but happily not for either of us. No, you see, Elizabeth, the village at Hunsford has been stricken with measles. Indeed, your friend Charlotte's eldest has been infected and at one time her life was despaired of.'

'Oh!' Lizzie pressed her finger to her mouth. 'Oh, my poor Charlotte. And poor Lily. Tell me that the worst is over.'

'For her – Lily I mean – it so appears, but there are concerns about the other children.'

'Oh?' Elizabeth was subdued by the sudden news and could say no more for the moment, her mind quite taken up by her friend's anxieties.

'And also, cousin,' said Anne, taking up the narrative, 'two of our maids have felt unwell, and Mama was so very concerned that we might take the infection, since I have certainly never succumbed to such an illness and Georgiana was so uncertain she decided the best means of safety for us was to come to Pemberley. I have in my baggage a letter from her for Mr Darcy, which explains everything. I hope that meets with your approval.'

'Yes.' Momentarily distracted by the arrival of a large tray bearing all that was necessary to refresh the travellers, Lizzie poured and offered tea and some small sweetmeats, before sitting back in her chair, holding her saucer in a hand not entirely steady.

'Yes, of course, Anne. Lady Catherine was entirely correct in getting you both safely out of harm's way and… I am sorry.' She replaced her saucer with a bang. 'I am still thinking of Charlotte and those little girls. But come,' she tried to smile, 'we must attempt to discover from Mr Darcy whether or not his sister has had measles. There must be an account somewhere. Does not Rose, your old nurse, live in one of the cottages? She will know, to be sure. But quite apart from the measles, I am more than pleased to see you for your own sakes. You must tell me all about what has been happening at Rosings since we left you there. What have you been doing and who has visited?'

'We have had a very pleasant time, Elizabeth.' Georgiana's assurance was in a minor key, which told her sister-in-law that life at Rosings had been exceedingly dull, while Anne's summary of long walks and visits from Mr Collins more or less completed the picture.

'Well, we must see what we can do to make your time here agreeable.' Already a scheme was forming in Lizzie's mind, one which she determined to keep to herself for the moment. 'We must wait a few days, of course, to confirm that both of you have escaped the infection, and I beg that at the first sign of anything untoward you will tell me, so the surgeon can be called. It is an unpleasant illness even in its mildest forms and we do not want it to spread if it can be avoided. But,' she added, forcing a more cheerful note into her voice, 'I find you both looking very well after your stay in Kent. So many country walks have brought the colour into your cheeks.'

Which was nothing short of the truth, she told herself, when the young ladies had been despatched to their chambers and she was trying to discover in which direction her husband was last seen. Having had no success in that, she fetched her cloak and bonnet and set off in the hope that she might meet him in the grounds.

Anne was the surprise to her. The change – improvement, one might say – was truly astonishing, for, while she would never be handsome, or even pretty, her skin had taken on a rose-like bloom and her hair had been set in a style that was more becoming. Her stature was so small and slight, it was hard to believe she would ever be viewed as a suitable wife, yet there were men who might find something to admire and cherish, something fragile and dainty, which would arouse that protective streak which is present in most good men and…

'Mrs Darcy.' So involved had she been in her thoughts and yes, in her plotting, she was unaware that for the last few minutes she had been walking on a collision course towards the master of Pemberley, so when he spoke she was brought roughly from her reverie.

'Sir, you startled me.'

'I might say the same of you, madam. When last I saw you, you were, I think, replying to a letter from Mrs Wickham.'

'Indeed.' But his reminder brought a great sense of relief, which she was, as yet, determined to keep from him. 'I was trying to compose a letter which, without being unduly rude and—'

'Have you said we may go to Ireland on a journey and shall be from home for some time?'

'No, I cannot say that, Fitzwilliam.' She turned in the direction of the house, slipping her hand inside his arm. 'It would be an untruth.'

'We can soon make it the truth.' He spoke with an edge of determination.

'No, that would not do.'

'I am very tolerant of your sisters, Lizzie, but…'

'As I am of your sister, whom I love as if she were my own. And I am also tolerant of your aunt and your cousin.'

'That is scarce the point, my dear, I—'

'It is the very point, sir, since both your sister and your cousin have this day arrived post-haste from Rosings.'

'Elizabeth?' The face he turned towards her was frowning. 'What nonsense is this? If you are plaguing me I shall—'

'I am not plaguing you, Darcy: I am telling the truth. The girls have been told to leave Rosings.'

'Damn. Told to leave Rosings?'

'Measles has affected the district, and since Anne has not had the illness – and about Georgiana there is some doubt – Lady Catherine decided the safest plan was for them to quit Hunsford at once and to come to Pemberley. They arrived but an hour ago. That is what I came to tell you,' she ended piously.

'You could have made a shorter tale of it.'

'You would interrupt...'

'You do plague me.' He swung her round to face him, tilting her chin so they were gazing into each other's eyes. He watched her expression lose its amusement in growing softness; she saw his tenderness change to something deeper as he repeated, 'You *do* plague me.' This time his tone was touched by wonder. 'And... I cannot think why it should please me so.' His mouth came close to hers and she bent into an embrace, in the course of which she lost her bonnet.

'Fitzwilliam, they will see us from the house.'

'They may.' He released her. 'But they know you are no longer the virtuous Miss Bennet, and surely a man may kiss his own wife if he wishes.'

Smiling at each other, they walked quickly back along the path towards the house, and it was only as they reached the door that he paused, detaining her with his hand.

'Lizzie.' His tone was serious. 'That matter which we spoke of the other day: you will not see this as the opportunity you have been awaiting.'

For a moment she appeared puzzled, and then her face cleared. 'Oh, that? No, of course not, Fitzwilliam.'

He was still unconvinced and stopped her when she would have walked into the hall. 'No matchmaking, Lizzie.'

'Of course not, Mr Darcy. I always try to behave as you wish me to do.'

'Very well, Elizabeth. I trust you. Now, let us go and have a word with the young ladies.'

After the happy reunion of the brother with his sister and then with his cousin, Anne, there followed a slightly excited account from the travellers of the happenings in Kent, which increased with the telling until it reached the level of major drama: how the sickness was first diagnosed in the row of workers' cottages on the fringe of Rosings Park; how it had raced like wildfire through the youngest children, several with serious, though not fatal, consequences. Then, while Lady Catherine dithered, one of the maids had gone down with what was thought to be the illness, whereupon the lady suddenly made up her mind.

'Your mama did not think to come with you, Anne?' Darcy

enquired, as he strolled across the room.

'No. Mama suffered the illness as a child and it seems it rarely strikes twice, and then rather mildly. No, she was concerned for us.'

'Well, it was a sensible precaution, certainly in your case, Anne, for I am almost certain Georgiana had the illness as a child and so ought, by your reckoning, to be safe. That is something which we must check upon later. But I have heard that in adults it can take a more grievous form, so it is well that you are both out of harm's way. Though,' he turned to the door as if anxious to be about the estate again, 'I do not know what we shall do with you two young ladies.' His glance towards his wife was conspiratorial. 'Derbyshire is rather dull nowadays. Mrs Darcy and I have scarce seen a caller for the past two weeks, so we shall be forced to rely on each other for diversion. We shall look to you, Anne and Georgiana, to raise our spirits with your music, and I daresay we can rouse up Colonel Lacey to take a hand of cards with us should all else fail.' With that, the door closed behind him.

'Colonel Lacey?' The face Georgiana turned towards her sister-in-law was wide-eyed with dismay. 'I understood he died some time back.'

'I have never heard the name myself.' With difficulty, Elizabeth composed her features. 'So I cannot say. Perhaps he was only… rather ill.'

'No, I believe he died, though I cannot be sure, since I feel I have never met the gentleman.'

'Well, we shall ask more when Fitzwilliam returns. But now let us go and tell Mrs Annesley that you have returned, though doubtless that news has already been reported to her. She has been enquiring about you for some days and I am sure will be more than happy to have you both back at Pemberley. I feel she has missed the expeditions you shared with her last month, and doubtless even now she is thinking of diversions to keep you engaged.'

It was a mere two days later, when Georgiana and Anne were sitting with Mrs Annesley, making a belated start on some needlework which had caught their attention in Paris, that

Elizabeth, having abandoned all pretence of interest in sewing and still in the throes of replying to Mrs Wickham's letter, raised her eyes to the window, seeking inspiration, and saw two horsemen riding at a gentle trot across the park. It was so reminiscent of earlier days, when Mr Bingley had first come to Netherfield with his friend, that parallels were instant and so unavoidable that she felt her face flush with the challenge of it.

A second glance, however, showed that her husband was also approaching the house from a slightly different direction, that he intercepted the riders, whom he then engaged in what appeared to be an amiable conversation, and that the two men, now close enough to be identified as Mr John Arbuthnot and Mr Fife, dismounted. The trio then walked together, the horses being led away by the stable boy towards the rear courtyard.

It was with the most rigid exercise of self-control that Elizabeth continued to sit quietly, when her instinct was to cross to where her companions were engaged with their needles, to make minute and unnecessary little adjustments to hair, to collars – she could see that Georgiana's was slightly wrinkled at the back – and to encourage the two young ladies to sit up straighter, to smile so, and, in short, to encourage them to behave as her mother had so often done in the past. That realisation shocked her, and it was with relief that she heard the sound of her husband's and other voices and the tread of manly booted feet on the floor, before the door was opened to the wholly innocent and astonished eyes of the two young ladies. Mrs Annesley dealt with the situation in her usual efficient and discreet manner and, with a murmured excuse, withdrew, while Lizzie reflected with private satisfaction that had she, at the last minute, interfered, then the sight that met the eyes of the visitors would scarcely have been more pleasing than the one she was free to observe from her position by the window.

Two innocent young heads, so fully absorbed in the intricacies of stitching; delicate slender necks, which must surely excite male interest; the gentle murmur of conversation, stilled, caught and held by the opening of the door; the enquiring eyes, then… faint confusion, lowered eyes and a bloom of delicate colour in the cheeks: she could scarce have done it better had she been setting the stage in a romantic melodrama. And all without a word from her.

'You saw us arrive, I think, Lizzie?' Darcy challenged later that day, in the privacy of their apartments.

'Yes, I confess. I was astonished when I saw the two young men riding across the park towards the house. I could scarce believe it was a coincidence, but could they possibly have known about Georgiana and Anne having returned?'

'Mmm.' Darcy's face was averted. 'Well, such news travels fast in the country, the servants chatter and...'

'A happy event, nonetheless. And I think all parties were content, although poor Mrs Annesley may have regretted having her sewing class disrupted.'

'And you, my dear: were you happy to have to postpone your letter once again?'

'Not happy, Fitzwilliam, for I still have to deal with that, which, but for the interruption, might have been already completed. But it suddenly occurred to me that in Georgiana's return I have the perfect solution to my problem. Of course, the Wickhams cannot risk bringing their children to Pemberley where they might be at danger of contracting the measles infection. It would be the height of folly to take such a risk with their health. Surely even Lydia can see the sense of that.'

'Mmm. That will serve this time, but I do not think Wickham will be easily dislodged; your sister is writing under his pressure and—'

'I am sorry, Fitzwilliam. The man is without shame, and truly I feel sad that I have brought so much trouble with me...'

'Lizzie. Lizzie. We cannot choose our relations as we do our friends; I am as much aware of that as anyone. Only... I cannot help but think that George Wickham will be a trouble to us for many years. I had thought...'

'Yes? You had thought what, my dear?'

'I had thought I might give the Wickhams the use of a cottage at the far side of the estate. It is, in fact, quite a large house and would be fully suitable but...'

'But?' she prompted, touched by his consideration.

'But,' he continued in a harsher tone, 'I almost at once realised it would not do. There would be the chance – and believe me, I know he would be capable of availing himself of any opportunity – of meeting Georgiana. And I will not have her hurt again. I will not have it. Especially now when she is beginning to bloom again.'

'No, of course not, Fitzwilliam. The risk would be too great.'

He sighed. 'But I have since had another thought of a house, which is part of the estate in Lincolnshire. There they could reside on their journeyings north and south. It has been shut up for many years, but there is a caretaker in a nearby cottage who could be instructed as to when it would be required. In fact, it would be no bad thing to have the house aired and lived in from time to time. That would give them some advantage and there need be no further requests for accommodation here. Besides which, Lincoln is sufficiently distant to offer Georgiana adequate protection.'

'That would do very well, indeed, Fitzwilliam, and I am grateful. Now, if I go downstairs to complete the letter, do I have your permission to offer your suggestion to Lydia?'

'Of course. Then we must await their answer, but if Wickham has any sense at all he will accept that we have reached the end of our association. If Lydia and the children wish to come here from time to time, then I shall have no objection, but even that... I fear the name will strike Georgiana with all kinds of unhappy recollections.'

So the letter was at last completed and despatched, which gave Elizabeth the freedom she required to devote her time and energies to the entertainment of her two young protégées. This was by no means arduous, since Mr John Arbuthnot and Mr Peter Fife became regular visitors, and after having the senior Arbuthnots, together with the young men, to dinner at Pemberley, the relationship between the families moved to a more familiar level – something which surprised Darcy, as he emphasised to his wife.

'It is quite strange. Here am I, having lived for all of my life within a few miles of Astley Abbey, and still we have been almost strangers. Yet now things are moving at such a pace.'

'Am I not right in thinking that Mr and Mrs Arbuthnot have spent some years abroad on their estates in the West Indies?

Surely that would explain the situation.'

'Yes,' Fitzwilliam considered. 'I think there was something more, a misunderstanding between the families some time past, a betrothal which was broken on one side or the other. It is strange how such things can sour relationships over the generations.'

'Well.' Elizabeth hesitated, having no wish to be accused once more of acting marriage broker. 'I do believe – and I must say it despite what you may think of me – I do sense a growing ease between John Arbuthnot and Georgiana. And not entirely on one side.'

'Yes. That is what I have observed, Lizzie, and...'

'And?' his wife prompted.

'And...' he replied, with irritating slowness, 'and while I do not want her to rush into anything, it seems to me that she is so much lighter in her response, that perhaps at last she is over what has happened in the past. But... she is still very young.'

'Not so very much younger than I was when we first met, Fitzwilliam.'

'Ah, but you were older in experience, Lizzie. Georgiana's upbringing has been so much more sheltered than yours.'

Slightly nettled by the implications of his words, his wife replied with a touch of her old spirit. 'Overly sheltered, some might say. Young women ought to be prepared for life as it is.'

Darcy frowned and glared before his face relaxed. 'I was not being critical of you, Lizzie. Or of your family. You must be aware that it was your courage which added so much to your attractions, your ardour in defending what you believed in that I found unusual and intriguing. But we are not all made the same way, and Georgiana was, from infancy, a shy, nervous child, and perhaps that is why she has been sheltered in the way she has. I am not saying it was right, but if it was wrong, then it was done from the best of motives. The very fact that she was persuaded by Wickham does cast some doubt on the wisdom of keeping her so innocent, so trusting. Well, we have all paid the price of that. And consider; it can happen to the more worldly as well.'

'You are right.' She was a little chastened. 'Lydia, though apparently so much more worldly, was as easily seduced.' A faintly cynical smile curled her lips. 'Though I fancy even

Wickham will have lived to regret that particular folly. It will not suit him to be held back by a woman who is by no means wealthy and with few expectations.'

There was a moment's silence while they both considered the situation, before Darcy took up the original subject once more.

'So, Lizzie. Do you think Georgiana's feelings are seriously engaged?'

'I think they may be. As you say, she is more animated when he is in the company and, even when he is not, there is an air about her, that mysterious expression which comes across the features of a young woman on the verge of love. My only reservation is, are his feelings as likely to be serious as hers? I could not bear for her to suffer as...' About to mention her sister, Jane, she changed her mind. '...As she did before. If that were to happen, then I fear she would never risk another attachment, and that would be very sad, would it not?'

'Would it, Lizzie? I would rather she did not marry at all than that she should choose unwisely.'

'But you cannot choose for her, Fitzwilliam.' Elizabeth determined to hide her impatience. 'We can choose only for ourselves. Take guidance from all who care, that is understood, but...' She smiled him out of his gloom. 'If you had taken advice from your relatives, if I had obeyed my mother's express command, then... would you be happier? Do you suppose I would?' The smile on his lips encouraged her to repeat the oft told tale. 'I was told that if I did not marry Mr Collins, my mama would never speak to me again, while Papa... well, you know what he said. The torments of the young who are in love, even though they are unaware of it at the time, are indeed a considerable trial. And I truly do not want to see Georgiana suffer through any hindrance put in their way if they should truly love each other.'

'Yes, you have made your case most successfully, my dear. I shall try to remember all you have said, should there be any development.'

Chapter Seven

*T*he following day brought a letter from Jane, all the family news providing a welcome diversion from the immediate concerns at Pemberley, and Elizabeth, secreting herself in her cosy sitting room, settled down happily with the closely written pages, prepared to enjoy all the local events. This, naturally enough, began with an account of the latest developments of the most wonderful children, who were, according to their mother, already beginning to talk and would soon be running about in the nursery. On a slightly less exuberant note, she went on to describe her mixed feelings at the prospect of Caroline Bingley returning for one of her regular visits, since she had decided that, for the foreseeable future she had seen quite enough of Bath and longed for the country air of Netherfield. There had been hopes of a young man, mentioned more than once in previous letters from that city, where she, with Mr and Mrs Hurst, had been taking the waters, but in the most recent communication his name was noticeably missing. 'Heigh, ho.' Jane ended that paragraph in a comment which spoke louder than words.

Things at Longbourn had settled down, Elizabeth read – which she already knew, since her father wrote regularly and amusingly of all that was happening in the family home. He made little mention of Mrs Castlemain except for the frequently expressed appreciation of her influence on his two 'increasingly less silly' girls. And Jane's letter appeared to convey the impression that the panic about the lady's intentions, or even perhaps his, had faded somewhat, and they all felt more relaxed about her position at Longbourn.

Having read it through, Elizabeth sighed with pleasure, settled further in her chair and skimmed over the words again, savouring for the second time the anecdotes and trivial details so important in any family, at the end of which she sighed more deeply, this time with a sense of longing, a feeling not experienced since her marriage, an acknowledgement that she truly missed her sisters, particularly Jane, and longed to see them again.

But this being an inappropriate moment to indulge such feelings, she stirred herself, recollecting some of the duties which required attention, and arrived downstairs just in time to see Mr John Arbuthnot and Mr Peter Fife being ushered into the house by her husband.

'Mrs Darcy.' Both young men saluted her with swift, formal bows. 'Forgive our intrusion unannounced.' It was Arbuthnot who spoke first; normally he appeared to take the lead on such occasions, his friend being of a slightly more retiring disposition. 'Mr Fife has had some bad news from Scotland and has come to make his farewells to all of our friends here at Pemberley.'

'Mr Fife.' As she spoke, Elizabeth led them into the reception room while her husband gave orders for some refreshments to be brought. 'I am so sorry. If there is anything we can do…'

'Thank you, ma'am.' Again the young man so addressed bowed. 'It is an elderly cousin of my father, who has taken a serious turn. He has been ill for some months, thus the situation has been long foreseen but I must be with my family at such a time.'

Meanwhile a tray and glasses had been brought in, and the young men were sipping Madeira wine and eating cake when, having been summoned, Anne and Georgiana appeared, with their usual shy demeanour, though Elizabeth was glad to see that her sister-in-law was less so than formerly, and was equally intrigued to note that her eyes went at once to Mr Arbuthnot, who likewise showed some pleasure.

'Is this not a sad occasion,' Elizabeth said to Anne, who, she judged, would be the more affected by the news, 'that Mr Fife is obliged by sickness in his family to return at once to Scotland?'

Anne blushed and murmured some expression of regret, before accepting a glass of wine and seating herself in a chair close to Mr Fife, listening while the conversation became involved with travel arrangements. Elizabeth observed with increasing approval that though she kept her head down, Anne was by no means reluctant to be engaged in quiet asides with her companion.

It was an observation which she shared with her husband

later, after the departure of the visitors amid many expressions of regret, and gratitude for the pleasant hours spent in the company of the family at Pemberley – and hopes that the resurrection of their pleasant musical evenings need not be too long deferred.

'Did you observe, Fitzwilliam, that your cousin Anne and Mr Fife appeared exceedingly at ease with each other? It is almost as if…' And here, realising where her thoughts were leading, she broke off.

'Yes, Mrs Darcy, you were about to say?'

'I was about to say,' she would not be silenced in her own home but raised her chin in a gesture of mild defiance, 'as if they had reached some degree of… sympathy.'

But this time she was not to be subject to an unfair accusation, since her husband replied slowly, considering. 'Mmm. Yes, I, too, was aware of something. But surely…' Breaking off, he frowned. 'But I cannot see it. She is such a shy, almost reclusive young woman. Would any man—'

'He has the considerable advantage, Fitzwilliam,' interrupted his wife, again deciding to be bold, 'of not having met the young lady's mama.'

'Lizzie!' he remonstrated, but in a tone which hinted at amusement and so encouraged her to elaborate.

'Lady de Bourgh would frighten off most suitors, and a fellow like Mr Fife might tremble before such an intimidating presence as your aunt.'

'About that, I am less certain than you, Elizabeth. A determined young man would not necessarily buckle at the first hurdle and perhaps… You have always hinted that you think my aunt is unlikely to approve any connection for her daughter, but should the right alliance offer, then you might find her entirely amenable.'

'The right alliance?' His wife considered. 'I think it would have to be something rather grander than Mr Fife can offer to persuade the lady. And whom would she bait if her daughter were to escape Rosings?'

'Since that is her principal diversion, she would find someone. After all, she has Mr Collins close at hand, and there are others who depend upon her. But, as I say, if she could find some advantage in it, a marriage for Anne would not be impossible.'

'Poor Anne. To be married off where there is no feeling – which is what I believe awaits those who must marry solely for advantage.'

'It is a common enough state, Lizzie, and works out well in many cases.'

At this, Elizabeth held her peace, since it was an opinion on which she felt they could never agree. Then her husband continued.

'But, in the case of Mr Fife, which is the one we are discussing, it may be there is some advantage there, after all.'

'I do not know. I have heard nothing direct of the family, but the Arbuthnots, without actually saying so, appear to give the impression that his expectations are modest.'

'That may have been so, Elizabeth. But the uncle who is gravely ill is the last of a distinguished family without direct descendants, and I understand with a considerable fortune, including estates in the Lothians. So, there may be more to Mr Peter Fife than appears on the surface.'

'Well!' With such a surprising opinion, Mrs Darcy scarce knew how to reply – an unusual situation for such as she, who was well known for being opinionated on many diverse subjects. 'You surprise me, Fitzwilliam.'

'I have not been withholding anything from you, my dear; it is simply what I picked up from a remark of John Arbuthnot just as they were leaving. He told me in a quiet word that his friend had long been a favourite with the old man and, though there was nothing further, I cannot but help the conclusion that Mr Fife may well turn out to be something of a catch for... for some young woman.'

'Indeed!' Lizzie was astounded. Mr Fife being the more retiring of the two young men, she had, without considering that side of matters too intently, gained the impression of his always being in the shadow of the other, something which could have been ascribed to his lack of expectations, but in this case clearly was an assumption without foundation. If her husband's words were to be proved correct, then Mr Fife, if he should have any attachment to Anne, would be right to assume that his suit would be welcomed, even –

and she allowed herself a wry smile – even if he had not yet encountered the formidable Lady Catherine. On the other hand, caution bade her consider another possibility of his altered state: if he should turn out to be the heir of a rich man, then Anne might suddenly find herself but one of several candidates for the newly coveted role of Mrs Fife. If this were so, then the advantage of having been intimates with him and his friend could quickly be dissipated as news of his good fortune spread abroad.

'My dear,' she began carefully, 'do you wish me to enquire, very discreetly, as to the state of Anne's feelings? If there is even the beginning of an understanding between the two young people, perhaps it would be wise to advise your aunt.'

'Hmm. I have been thinking of the same thing myself, but I do not want to cause a great hullabaloo at Rosings. Should I give the merest hint of what is in the offing, it might ruin things completely for Anne. That is, if you are right in supposing her affections are engaged.'

'I think they may well be, but she is such a reserved creature I know not if she has confided even in Georgiana and certainly do not mean to encourage broken confidences. The two have become very close. Each time I interrupt when they are alone together, without the company of Mrs Annesley, there is a great amount of whispering, much composing of demeanour before they turn to me, faces quite wiped free of guilt and displaying nothing but the most bland innocence.'

'You are an expert in such things, of course.'

'Of course,' his wife agreed mildly. 'Born of much practice. Jane and I played those parts a hundred times.'

'I see,' he responded dryly. 'I shall not embarrass you by asking which of your admirers was the subject of so much conniving.'

'I cannot lie.' Her hand was placed delicately in the region of her heart. 'It was my cousin, Mr Collins.'

'Hmm. I always suspected that but for his lack of fortune his advances might have been more acceptable and—'

'How dare you, Fitzwilliam!' And, taking a small cushion from a chair, she pretended to launch an assault on her husband, which might have had serious consequences but for the arrival of one of the maids who had come to make up the fire.

And by one of those coincidences which attend such matters, a letter from Lady Catherine was received the next day, stating that she wished to summon her daughter back to Rosings at once, since no further cases of measles had been reported, the one supposed to have been suffered by a housemaid turning into something no more troublesome than a severe case of urticaria, which the silly girl had contracted by eating shellfish during a visit to her nearby family – thoughtless behaviour causing considerable inconvenience to the entire household.

'There, my dear.' Having read the letter, Fitzwilliam handed it across to his wife. 'It looks as if we must arrange for Anne to leave as soon as may be. A pity, as Georgiana will miss her companion, and it scarce allows any time for you to make enquiries of the sort we mentioned yesterday.'

'A great pity.' Quickly Elizabeth scanned the page, idly turned it over and read further before raising questioning eyes to her husband. 'What on earth can this last sentence mean?' Lowering her head she read slowly, '"It is of the utmost importance that Anne should come back at once; I am most anxious for her to meet someone who is visiting the district".'

'I cannot imagine.' Her husband rose from his chair and, leaning over his wife's shoulder, perused the final words more closely. 'I confess I did not see that. But there are so few visitors to Rosings, certainly no one apart from my cousin, and I cannot believe it is him.'

'No.' Elizabeth was thoughtful, her mind relentlessly fixed in one direction, one which she did not feel inclined to reveal to her husband at this point. 'If it had been Colonel Fitzwilliam, I am certain she would have mentioned his name.' She paused. 'Do you propose to accompany Anne on her journey?'

'I think I must,' he sighed. 'It is most inconvenient when there is so much to do in the park, but I dare say Dawkins could be left in charge without any serious concerns. He knows my mind as clearly as I know it.'

'I was about to suggest, my dear…' Elizabeth chose her words with care. 'If it should be inconvenient, then why don't I take Anne back to Rosings? Then, on my return, I could spend a few days at Longbourn and visit my family.'

'A capital idea, Elizabeth.'

'And if she wished to come, I could take Georgiana with me. She might enjoy the company of my sisters.'

'Yes,' her husband agreed, without true conviction. 'That might serve. But… I have reconsidered and, with slight alterations to our plan, it may be that the work could take care of itself for a few days. We could be back within the week, and a better plan might be for us – with Georgiana if she wishes to fall in with our plan – to settle you at Longbourn, return Anne to her mother and then we could stay a few days on our return and enjoy each other's company throughout.'

This was a scheme which recommended itself to Lizzie in that, while giving her some time alone with her family, it also meant that she was not deprived of her husband's companionship for what might have seemed an inordinate length of time. They had been apart little since their marriage, and she had come to depend on him, not merely for his understanding and good advice but also for the continuing pleasure she found in his company.

'The only flaw in that plan of your not accompanying us to Rosings,' her husband continued, 'is that you would be deprived of the opportunity of visiting your friend, Mrs Collins, and viewing the new infant, whom I think you have not yet seen.'

'That is true.' Silently she weighed the consequences before deciding. 'But, on the whole, Fitzwilliam, I think I shall forego that pleasure, happy though I would be to see my dear Charlotte again. It may even happen that she and the children will be paying a visit to her parents.'

'Whatever you wish, Lizzie. Well, I think I must go and find Anne and break the news to her that she is returning to Rosings rather earlier than we had hoped.'

And when she was alone, Elizabeth sat staring through the window, her thoughts miles from the scene of activity resulting from the alterations to the water courses flowing into the lake. She knew she had been less than honest with her husband. The fact was that, in spite of all her protests to the contrary, she was envious of her friend Charlotte Collins. Or at least, envious of one particular aspect of her life: her friend's apparent fertility. Whereas she… If only she could give her husband a child, she

would be the happiest woman in England, but in the meantime…
to be envious of any woman married to Mr Collins! Quickly she
brushed a hand across her eyes, fixed a smile on her face and
walked to the door. She must follow her husband to the girls'
apartments and supervise the packing; at least in that sphere she
did not mean to allow any complaint on the part of Lady de
Bourgh.

They had almost reached Longbourn before there was any sign of
animation on Anne's features, and Elizabeth, despite having
endeavoured throughout the journey to raise the young woman's
spirits, found it easy to imagine that she was about to slide back
into her previous melancholy state. Darcy was sitting in the
opposite corner, his eyes closed so she thought he might be
asleep. With a faint sigh, which disguised her own weariness, she
leaned forward and took the young woman's hand. 'Are you
missing Georgiana, my dear Anne?' The other young woman had
declined to join them, since a sudden attack of toothache
indicated a visit to a surgeon, and she feared the movement of the
carriage on a long journey would increase her discomfort and
make her a handicap to the party.

Anne nodded, apparently too overcome to reply, but then, in a
broken voice, she agreed. 'That and… other things.'

'Other things?' Mrs Darcy smiled, raising an encouraging
eyebrow, wondering if she were to have the opportunity of
mentioning the matter which had been so much in her mind. 'Is
it… that you are sad to have left behind… those young people for
whom you feel some friendship?' She would not state it more
definitely than that, especially since Darcy had moved restlessly in
his seat.

'No, it is not that, cousin. At least…'

'You may confide in me, Anne; I shall be entirely discreet.'

'It is only a feeling I have. You see, Mama has introduced me
to a certain man, and I have the feeling, though she has said
nothing on the subject, that…' Abruptly she stopped talking and
shook her head before continuing more carefully. 'But I must not.
I am mistaken, for she would not. Pray forgive me, Mrs Darcy. I
have always been nervous,' she explained with touching simplic-

ity, 'and though I love Mama dearly, she will ever decide what is best for me. I am sure she is right, for she has so much more experience of the world than I. In fact, until you and Mr Darcy were so kind as to take me to Paris with you, I had seen little of life and, since then, I feel my understanding has been greatly enhanced and...' Her voice trailed off in a miserably low tone, just as Lizzie saw they had passed the crossroads and were almost home.

'Well, Anne, we shall make further arrangements just as soon as we may. And in the meantime, we shall stop at Longbourn where my sisters and my father will welcome you warmly. Although they are, according to their father, silly girls, I think their company will be enough to raise your spirits before you complete your journey. Here we are,' she said happily, as the carriage began to slow, and the corner of the beloved house came into sight. 'There is Kitty, wearing blue, and Mary immediately behind, and... oh, and Papa. Oh, how good it is to see them again!' As she spoke in a cheerful matter-of-fact voice, she saw her husband stir. His eyes opened and she had the distinct impression that he had heard every word Anne had spoken and was as puzzled as she as to their significance.

Despite Anne's low feelings about her return to Rosings, she benefited from the short visit to the Bennet home and in particular showed some amusement at the constant chatter of Kitty and Mary, who now appeared to be much more tolerant of each other, a circumstance which Elizabeth ascribed to the continuing influence of Mrs Castlemain, plus – though she was reluctant to come to such a conclusion – the fading effects of Lydia's disruptive ways.

In fact, it was a pleasant company who sat at table together, with the old servants bustling out and in, bearing what her father assured them were all Mrs Darcy's favourite dishes, which they had insisted in providing. Much local gossip was exchanged, as well as the welcome news that Mrs Bingley would join them for tea in the afternoon, and it was hoped that Mr Darcy and Anne would be able to wait until then.

'I am doubtful about that, Mr Bennet.' Darcy's plan was to deliver his cousin to her mother, then to return to Longbourn before nightfall, which left little time. 'But certainly I shall see Mrs Bingley and the rest of the family before we return to Pemberley. Bingley is at home, I trust.'

'No. That he is not, sir. He has been obliged to travel to Bath to collect his sister, who has been taken ill. He left yesterday, but I am certain they will have returned before you and Lizzie must leave us again.'

'So,' his daughter considered, 'I did not know Caroline Bingley was ill. In her last letter, Jane told me that they were expecting her on a visit. At that time no untoward reference was made as to her health.'

'Well, that is the way of it. I am not myself in favour of so much travelling from one side of the country to the other to take the waters. For those who enjoy good health, it seems scarcely necessary, and I have never heard Miss Bingley voice any complaint. Now, if it had been her brother-in-law...' Here, he appeared to recollect where his words were leading, gave a great cough and changed the subject abruptly. It was so well understood in the family that Mr Hurst might easily suffer from liver complaint or the gout, but the source of his difficulties was scarce mentioned.

The interlude at Longbourn had been a precious respite for Anne, and when she left with her cousin to complete her journey she was more composed, though a little emotional when she made her farewells to Mrs Darcy.

'I am grateful to you, cousin, for your kindness,' she said, her voice trembling slightly, 'and hope we may meet again soon.'

'My dear.' Elizabeth was touched and genuinely concerned for the young woman. 'It is not hard to be kind to one such as you, and you know you will ever be welcome at Pemberley, whenever your mama can spare you.'

And so she departed with her cousin, leaving Elizabeth uneasy, wondering what awaited such a vulnerable young woman who would inevitably return to her formerly repressed state.

But her attention was soon diverted from such concerns by the arrival of her beloved sister, accompanied by her two daughters, who promised, in due time, to be as pretty and as good as their mama. The reunion of the two was warm; they enjoyed a walk round the grounds, arm in arm in their previous manner, and when they turned towards the house the same habit took them to a seat beneath one of the great trees which were such a feature of Longbourn. Jane gave an almighty sigh as they sat, a sigh which ended on a faint sob.

'Jane?' Elizabeth spoke anxiously, turning to face her sister.

'Oh, it is nothing, Lizzie.' Though she smiled, there was sufficient brightness in the eyes to cause concern. 'Just, I had a moment's longings, that we might together go inside the house and hear Mama's voice, raised in her almost constant worrying tone, that you should go to Papa in his library and I should try to comfort Mama and keep Mary, Lydia and Kitty from squabbling in the annoying way they once had...'

'Jane. My dear...'

'I know. I am being very foolish. It is not as if those days were free of care, for assuredly they were not. It is time that lends the past such a mellow glow and... Oh, I am indeed being foolish.'

'You are not.' Lizzie hesitated, something in itself strange, since she and Jane had ever been able to share their innermost thoughts and feelings. 'You are not unhappy? Tell me you are not, for I could not bear it to be so.'

'No, I am perfectly happy, Lizzie. Mr Bingley is the kindest and most indulgent of husbands, a devoted father to our children. No, it was simply the pleasure of seeing you again and thinking of days past. I have missed Mama, of course I have. We have all missed her grievously. Even Papa, I dare say, though he would be loath to confess it.'

'Yes, of course.' Elizabeth was relieved to hear such a firm disclaimer and at once acknowledged how her sister's yearnings for things past was something she, from time to time, shared, though perhaps to a lesser degree. 'Is not this part of life, my dear Jane? Have we not always looked back with feelings of regret for times that cannot come again and long for them simply because they are for ever beyond our reach? But we must remember how much we have now: you with Charles and two adorable little girls; I with Mr Darcy.' She decided to lighten the moment with a sally. 'Can you recall how we thought him proud and arrogant, while in truth, as I have known for so long, he is kind and generous? Let us think how our lives might have been! Think, Jane: you might have been wife to Mr Collins. Then I was next in line for that position. Think of such a possibility and bless the sensible men who are now our husbands! As for Mama, we must be grateful that she lived to see our success.'

'Yes.' Jane smiled, her spirits reviving slightly. Then, in a parody of her mother's way, she added, 'Three daughters married within the year! Yes, of course, at the end she was triumphant.'

'Sadly,' continued Elizabeth, determined to make a sally of it, 'I feel she was as happy about Lydia and her Mr Wickham as she was about your marriage, Jane, and certainly of mine, for she did not understand how much she owed to Mr Darcy and his efforts.'

'Yes. We all owe much to him. And to you, Lizzie, for Mr Darcy would not have had the need to make a move but for his affection for you. Then what would have become of us?'

'It may be that I shall never be able to repay him, Jane,' said the younger sister mysteriously, before hurrying on. 'But what of Papa? Have your anxieties concerning Mrs Castlemain finally died away? Is he safe from scheming women, would you say?'

'I think so,' Jane answered with some uncertainty. 'I think she spends less time at Longbourn now and certainly has no need to live there. It appears the arrangement suits all parties, and most likely I was mistaken in thinking as I did.'

'And Caroline?' As she spoke, Elizabeth regretted the impulse which made her introduce the name into such a conversation. Surely her sister would make a connection, though it had not previously been openly stated. It was a moment for a speedy distraction. 'It is not the thought of her visit which has brought on these melancholy thoughts?'

'Perhaps it is,' her sister conceded. 'When I consider how ill she behaved towards me when I was in London, there are times when I do not want her at Netherfield. But, nonetheless, she is Charles's sister and he is such a trusting man he would not understand.'

Elizabeth pondered these words for a moment before replying. She, too, had a guilty secret which had been kept from her sister, who had no idea that Darcy had colluded in that unhappy time. 'Try to put it from your mind, my dear Jane. She is, I daresay, an unhappy woman. You did mention, did you not, some hopes that have been dashed, and as time goes on…' Her sigh made further words unnecessary and the message was not lost on her sister.

'You are right, Lizzie. And I begin to realise that some of my dejection is that I miss greatly our daily exchanges and wish we were not at such a distance. Letters are not an entirely satisfactory substitute and there are many days when the comfort of a few words with you would be such a solace. But you have made me see things more clearly, and I can say with confidence that of all the Bingleys, my dear Charles is the only one who is truly happy. Both Caroline and Mrs Hurst are discontented, despite the ease of their existence. The latter I can understand, since she is to be pitied in her marriage, while Caroline… Well, if she could find a suitable young man…'

'I have just had an idea, but first let us return to the house, Jane. I, too, miss our closeness and long to spend as much time as I can with my nieces before we leave again for Pemberley, and I cannot imagine why I have not thought of this before. But why do not you and Bingley, along with the children, come north to Derbyshire before the weather changes? You might even recon-sider your previous idea and think of a permanent move to the north. I am astonished we have not contrived this before, since you have not yet seen that country, which is so entirely different from Hertfordshire, grander and more dramatic. I am certain a change would raise your spirits and you might even…' Here she reverted to the mischievous tone of her earlier years. 'You could easily leave Miss Bingley in charge at Netherfield for the length of your journey. Don't you think that a capital fancy?'

And, smiling conspiratorially, they returned arm in arm to the house.

Despite Lizzie having expected her husband to return from Kent that very evening, he did not arrive, obliging her to retire to bed disappointed by his absence. It was mid-afternoon the following day before his carriage appeared at the end of the drive, allowing his wife just enough time to be at the door to welcome him.

'My dear.' Since no others of the family were about, he drew her into the shadow of the porch and embraced her. 'I have missed you sorely.'

'I, too.' His kiss was returned with ardour. 'It was lonely without you.' And together they proceeded to the parlour, where her father was seated by the fire dozing, despite the book which was supported by his hands.

'Bless my soul!' Mr Bennet returned to life with a little start. 'Darcy, my dear fellow. You are back, then? My Lizzie will be pleased, for she was wholly out of sorts last night since you did not appear.'

'Yes. It was my intention to return last evening, but Lady Catherine wanted my advice on a complex matter, which was not resolved till late. And since the horses and the coachmen had been driving all day, I thought it best to rest overnight.'

'Your aunt is well, I hope.'

'What? Oh yes, perfectly well.' But his countenance was telling a different story, at least to his wife.

'Will you have some refreshment, Fitzwilliam? Tea, perhaps. Or a glass of wine.'

'Tea would be perfect, Lizzie. And perhaps a slice of Emma's Genoa cake.' Darcy and his wife exchanged smiles, since she had many times told him how the cook at Longbourn made the most exceptional Genoa cake of which she was extremely proud. Lizzie quit the room briefly to make the arrangements, returning just a few minutes later followed by a beaming maid bearing a silver tray with all that was required to take them through to supper.

When they had eaten and held an amusing discussion about the latest stormy crossings in the channel which had cut off the continent, Lizzie and her husband withdrew, for she could sense that his thoughts were elsewhere and she accurately judged this was entirely to do with the situation at Rosings.

'Now, my dear.' She helped him remove his coat, saw him settled on a comfortable chair in their bedchamber and perched on a stool close enough for her to be comfortable. 'You have had an exhausting day, that I can see. If you wish to tell me of it…'

'Yes, Lizzie. Such a day. I left Anne having an attack of the vapours, and I fear all your good work in coaxing a little liveliness in her has come to naught.'

'I hope you are wrong, Fitzwilliam – for her sake more than my own. She was such a timid little mouse when first I met her; I should hate to see her with all her spirit once again quenched.'

'It may not come to that, Lizzie. But, I confess, I think your original idea of some kind of feeling for Mr Fife may be right. Such was her violent reaction to her mother's plans for her.'

'What... what can you mean, Mr Darcy? I am quite in the dark.'

His smile was strained. 'Oh, Lizzie, how I wished last evening that you had accompanied us all the way to Rosings. I was much in need of your support, and it is still my contention that you are the only person living whose words would have any effect on Lady Catherine.'

'My words? I think you are mistaken, Fitzwilliam. Your aunt long ago formed an opinion of me which I fear is set in stone, so I doubt she would pay the slightest heed to anything I had to say on any subject, especially on one closely concerning her only child. And remember: I still have no idea of the matter being discussed and why the poor girl was obliged to return so suddenly.'

'No, forgive me, Lizzie. The truth is that my aunt has marriage plans for her daughter. She is determined she will marry a near neighbour, who is, she believes, immensely rich and of the highest degree of society, thereby assuring for herself her daughter's continuing proximity, as well as the reflected glory of the rank.'

'Oh?' For a moment, Lizzie considered what she had heard before venturing a tentative opinion. 'And am I to understand that the arrangements find little favour with her daughter?'

'That is one way of expressing it.'

'There are others?

'Others? Yes. The poor girl exhibited more emotion than she had shown in the whole of her life, I dare say. She collapsed on the floor sobbing, refused to get up and servants had to be summoned to transport her to her bedchamber.'

'Oh, the poor child. But since her mother has been shown her total aversion to the proposed alliance, surely that is the end of the matter.'

'By no means. You, as much as anyone, must know what the lady is like when she has made up her mind. I confess that even I, who have known her since childhood, was shocked by her harshness to her daughter. She is determined to have her way and gave instructions Anne was to be confined to her room until she had agreed to the match.'

'Oh. Oh.' Lizzie's sigh was heavy and distressed. 'And is there any hope of Anne coming round to her mother's way of thinking? Perhaps if she were to consider it at greater length she might find the prospect acceptable. You might advise her, Fitzwilliam…'

'I should not, with any sense of honour, be able to support Lady Catherine's plans for her child. Lizzie, this man, Baron Blackstone, is a notorious roué with an especial taste for young women. Reports have it that every young female whom he employs is at risk. I am uncertain if Anne is aware of his unsavoury reputation, and I doubt if she would understand, but she does know that he is old enough to be her father and that he has grandchildren who are almost as old as she is.'

'Fitzwilliam.' Lizzie was shocked and distressed. 'This cannot be! That a loving mother – and I have always supposed Lady Catherine to be that if nothing else – should behave thus to her only child! We cannot allow it.'

'Lizzie, I have pleaded half the night with her and she can see nothing amiss in her plans. She as good as told me—'

But before he could say any more, Darcy broke off, knowing that any repetition of his aunt's words would be grossly offensive to his wife and, fortunately, Lizzie was too preoccupied with her own anxiety for Anne to notice at that moment.

'Why?' she demanded in a voice of despair. 'Why did I not write and say she was unwell? That she had a fever and ought to remain at Pemberley until she was well again?'

'Because we could none of us foresee what was in the offing. Certainly if I had known…'

'What about Colonel Fitzwilliam? Surely he would be equally outraged at such plans and would defend his cousin.'

'Fitzwilliam is on the high seas, Lizzie, and will be away some time, so we cannot enlist his help.'

To her husband's concern and to her own surprise, Lizzie felt a tear roll down her cheek. She brushed it aside instantly. 'Then we must consider what is to be done, Fitzwilliam. For I am determined that Anne shall not be married without her whole-hearted consent.'

'Your feelings do you credit, my dear, especially in view of your own experience with my aunt, but, truly, I cannot see what is to be done.'

'Darcy,' said Elizabeth, the anger which had provoked the tears clearly in her voice, 'can you imagine what marriage to such a man would mean to an innocent like Anne, for I cannot bear to consider it. With one where her heart was truly engaged, it might present difficulties enough, but—'

'Elizabeth.' Darcy placed a comforting arm about his wife's waist and drew her close to him. 'You must not allow your feelings to be influenced by what has happened recently. We have both acknowledged a closeness developing between Anne and Mr Fife, but he has gone – back to Scotland, where doubtless he is much engaged in all manner of family duties. Truly, I feel we must put that from our minds.'

'I am not concerned with that, Fitzwilliam, truly I am not, but,' and she bit fiercely on her lower lip, 'I am putting myself in Anne's situation. It is not so long ago that such a prospect faced me: I was being persuaded by my mother that I should accept Mr Collins. Thankfully, I am made of sterner stuff than Anne.'

'Indeed,' said her husband dryly, releasing her and rising to walk over to the window. 'Of much sterner stuff.'

'And I had my father's support, while poor Anne must feel totally abandoned.'

'Well, I agree with you, my dear; I endorse every word. But let us sleep on it. We must consider carefully; there is no way we can rush in and kidnap my cousin; that would serve no one. But I do have some contacts who know where the Baron passes his time, and they are making enquiries on my behalf. It has occurred to me that Anne is a considerable heiress; that may be a large part of her appeal for a man who is a well-known gambler and rake. Give me a day or two, Lizzie, and I promise you: we shall not return home without having done something to save Anne from the clutches of such as he.'

And that is how their time at Netherfield progressed. In the evenings they were joined by the Bingleys, Jane's husband having returned from Bath with his sister, who also joined them, appearing quite subdued when compared with her former combative self. So several pleasant evenings were spent between the two estates, once at Netherfield, where Mary and Kitty were invited to join the party and appeared to some advantage now that Mary had reduced her tendency to sermonise and Kitty was less hoydenish than previously. Both evenings spent at Longbourn, the second in particular, were bright and pleasant, since Caroline Bingley, apparently in the throes of regaining her spirits, appeared to set herself out to be particularly agreeable.

Chapter Eight

*T*he following morning the Darcys were to take their departure and had decided, in view of the relative closeness of Meryton to Hunsford, that they would return home directly after visiting their relatives at Rosings.

'I wonder, Fitzwilliam, if you would prefer that I should visit Mrs Collins and allow you to travel on to Rosings alone. I am concerned that Lady Catherine may see my presence as an intrusion into her affairs; I would not for the world make matters worse for Anne.'

'I am certain you will not, Lizzie, and I would value your support in what might prove to be a difficult interview. I have some facts at my fingertips which were not available to me until last night. I shall not trouble you with them at this moment, but they will interest you, I have no doubt.'

'So, that was the message you received shortly after the Bingleys arrived?'

'Just so, and I had little time then to consider everything, but I rose early this morning and I feel I have a fair picture, which makes me much more hopeful of the outcome. But about Mrs Collins – and I know you are anxious to see her – we shall make time for that later, Elizabeth, and if we are too late to advance our journey, then we shall spend a night in London. I suppose another day or two will not matter, especially if our interview with my aunt is successful.'

It was strange to be travelling the length of the drive to Rosings for the first time and, despite her normal self-possession, Lizzie could not help but be excited and apprehensive. Previously, when she had spent time with the Collinses, they had walked to Rosings, as had fitted their station, approaching from a different angle. Then, as she alighted from the coach, she caught sight of Lady Catherine at one of the windows, which caused a tiny, nervous flutter in the pit of her stomach and made her long to turn and run down the drive to escape.

But instead, recalling who she was, she raised her head and was supported by her husband's touch on her elbow and his whispered words of encouragement as they climbed the steps and were admitted into the great hall.

'I did not expect you, Mr Darcy. Mrs Darcy.' Lady Catherine's acknowledgement of the woman who had misappropriated her nephew could scarce have been more distant, indicating that the slight thaw during her visit to Derbyshire had not been sustained.

'Lady Catherine.' Elizabeth bowed, determined to be calm and calming in what would surely be a difficult situation.

'Lady Catherine.' For the moment she was happy to hear her husband take control of the situation. 'I felt we could not return to Pemberley without some further discussion of the matter which so closely affects my cousin, Anne.'

'This does not concern you, Darcy. Since my original plan was frustrated,' and though she did not allow her glance to fall on Mrs Darcy, there was little doubt who would for ever be held responsible for that, 'you are not involved. It is a matter solely for me to decide.'

'Of course, my dear aunt. But not entirely your decision, I suggest. There is one even more closely involved, and that is Anne herself. I had hoped that she might be able to join us in this discussion.'

'It is not a matter for a young girl to discuss. I am her mother and know what is in her best interest.'

'And she does not?' In spite of her decision to leave most of the talking to her husband, Lizzie could not control the words which burst from her lips in an accusing manner.

For a moment, Lady Catherine glared. Then, 'We are discussing the future happiness of a gently reared young girl: not some village miss with neither breeding nor expectations.' Since her meaning was unmistakable, Lizzie was silenced, though inwardly she fumed.

'Which is why, Aunt, I wish to urge caution in your dealings with Baron Blackstone. I assure you that my wishes are as your own – solely for Anne's happiness – and I am by no means certain that marrying a man so many years her senior is the best way to secure that.'

'Stuff and nonsense, Darcy. Who would be more caring for the happiness of a young girl than a man with so much experience? And we all know that happiness sought by means other than of comfort and compatibility are fleeting indeed. I am sure you, above all, will understand my meaning.'

'I understand your meaning, madam, but I entirely disagree with the sentiment.' Darcy's manner hardened. 'And, I wonder, might we have the pleasure of Anne's company, since it is her future which is being discussed.'

'Anne has remained in her room with a slight fever.'

'Oh…' Lizzie could not contain her distress. 'We had so hoped to see her. A slight fever… Yet she was so well when she left Pemberley.'

'She may have picked up some infection on the way. That is the worst of travel: it is much healthier to remain at home.'

'Let us not bandy words, Aunt. But, before Mrs Darcy and I leave Rosings, I mean to have a word with Anne to ascertain her true feelings. If she truly agrees to this marriage, then I shall accept it, though with the most profound misgivings for her future. But, for the moment, I would appreciate hearing from you once more what you find so advantageous in the connection.'

'Well, he is an undoubted gentleman with an established place in the best society. His title goes back to the Stuarts, and he has large estates in the West Country as well as in Kent, so I shall never be long parted from my daughter.' She sat back, her usual air of challenge lending an aura of arrogance but also a curious vulnerability, something which touched Elizabeth, who had never thought to have tender feelings for this woman.

'Aunt, for that we respect you. I know how much Anne has always meant to you. You have been a most devoted mother; she a loving and dutiful daughter. But, if she cannot enter into this plan, I beg you, excuse her. Especially excuse her since she has never before defied you in anything you have asked of her.'

For the first time, Lady Catherine looked slightly frail and shaken. 'Pray, do not go on so, Darcy. I am trying to secure her future, do you not see? It is a mother's duty to do so, and I know in time she will thank me for it.'

'But, should she not, what then?'

'Then she may not marry at all.'

'And would that be such a bad thing, Lady Catherine?' Lizzie interrupted in a tone of kindliness. 'Marriage in itself solves nothing. In truth, where a young woman of fortune is concerned, then it might be a positive handicap.'

'That is easy for you to say, miss,' Lady Catherine answered, with all her normal confidence and a touch of venom. 'But my daughter has not the means to ensnare—' Here she broke off, perhaps knowing she had gone far enough. 'She is an innocent child who needs the protection of an older man.'

'She needs the protection of a good, kind man, Lady Catherine,' Darcy resumed the discussion. 'And I am by no means certain that this Baron Blackstone is the one for such a task as caring for my cousin, much less of making her happy.'

'Happy!' She responded in a note of scorn. 'No one has the right to be happy.'

'But when it happens, it is a very pleasant state indeed, I assure you. And, to return to the gentleman, I suggest that he is not of an age—'

'That I see as one of his advantages.'

'A few years, perhaps. Perhaps even more than a few, but this man is old enough to be her grandfather. How can any young woman, particularly one who has led such a… a sheltered life as your daughter, ma'am, feel anything but distaste for such a union. And that is not all, Aunt: Baron Blackstone has an unenviable reputation.'

'Idle gossip!' She spoke in her old tart, dominating manner. 'You spend too much time in those London clubs, Darcy. You should look to it, Miss Eliza Bennet that was: if your husband is content, he will stay close to home. My own husband rarely left my side.'

'Indeed, ma'am.' Inwardly amused, Lizzie's tone was sympathetic.

'Idle gossip it is not, Aunt.' As he spoke, Darcy extracted from a pocket the package which had been delivered to Longbourn the previous evening, placing it on the table in front of him. 'The Baron is well known in the London clubs for his rakish behaviour. The proof is contained in this communication from an impeccable source. Also, it is being whispered that his estates are by no means as secure as his excessive expenditure suggests. According to my information, even before he inherited, his finances were shaky, and he married his first wife for her fortune, ruining her within a twelvemonth. His second fared almost as badly, and now, with some desperation, he seeks another alliance which will keep the wolf from the door for a few more years.'

Lizzie, who had watched Lady Catherine's countenance throughout this recital, had seen the colour drain from her face, her lips tremble, and when it seemed she might fall forward in her seat Lizzie rose and hurried forward to support her.

'A glass of wine,' she suggested to her husband, who rose to ring for some refreshment. Such was instantly brought, but not before the lady, with her usual spirit, had rallied.

'I am perfectly well.' She straightened her back and glared at both her visitors while accepting the glass of Madeira offered, sipping with apparent relief before placing the glass on the table in front of her. 'Perfectly well,' she repeated in her normal strong voice. Then, after a moment, she looked at her nephew. 'What you have told me is the truth, Fitzwilliam?'

'Only the truth, Aunt.'

There was a long silence as she considered. Then, 'I thank you for it.' Another period of contemplation before she rose. 'I must go to my daughter. You will excuse me.'

Darcy rose and escorted her to the door, where she paused. 'I have allowed myself to be misled. A new attorney, who came to replace my old Dawes, who died, has been assiduous in pressing the Blackstone case and I have been...' With that she turned and crossed the hallway, leaving the two visitors to consider matters before either spoke.

'I...' That Lizzie had been affected by the scene, was apparent in her unsteady tone. 'I wish it had not come to this. I feel sad to see your aunt so shaken.'

'It has been hard, Elizabeth, but... it was necessary. I should have been failing in my family duty if I had hidden from my aunt what I know to be true. It seems clear that she has been the victim of some scheme, but I shall leave this letter so she can read the full extent of the problems facing this man.' He shook his head sadly. 'It is hard to understand how a woman such as she, strong and not unversed in the ways of the world, could have been so easily duped.'

'She wanted to secure her daughter's future close at hand, Darcy. She must have dreaded the loneliness of her possibly moving further afield, though...' Her voice drifted away.

'You were about to say... Let me guess, Lizzie: you were going to say that my cousin would not attract attention for the force of her personality and so would have few chances of marriage.'

'I might once have thought so.' His wife smiled wearily. 'But now I have changed my idea and still entertain hopes that she may marry to please herself. Darcy, do you think your aunt might be persuaded to allow us to take Anne north with us? Is it impossible, do you suppose?' As ideas began to float into her head, her imagination took off. 'We could stay a few days in London to enable Anne to regain her strength and—'

'Do not run on so, Lizzie. I dearly wish to return to Pemberley as soon as may be, and I think Anne may not be well enough to undertake another journey so soon. Unless the news her mother is even now imparting to her has such restorative effects that—'

'I doubt that will be so, Darcy. Clearly the past days have been a setback to her. In truth, I feel sorry for the child.' There was a momentary hesitation before she continued, rather more slowly. 'And I feel sorry for her mother, which is not an emotion I ever thought to feel for Lady Catherine de Bourgh.'

'We all have our weaknesses, Lizzie, even my aunt,' he smiled at her. Then, as the sound of footsteps approached across the hall, both turned their faces to the door, which opened to reveal the tall, gaunt figure of the chatelaine.

'Aunt,' Darcy rose and accompanied his relative across the room; he waited until she had settled in her chair. 'You have seen Anne.'

'I have seen my daughter, yes. She begs you will excuse her, but she still suffers from weakness.'

'And have you told her of the changed situation, Aunt?'

'I have, nephew.' The words were spoken slowly, and to Elizabeth it seemed Lady Catherine had shrunk before their eyes. 'I have not told her the entire truth but have explained that since

she is so much against the plan then I shall not force her and…
And she was much relieved and seized my hand and kissed it in
her gratitude.'

At these words, Lizzie released a great sigh. Instinctively she
rose and crossed to where Lady Catherine sat, placing a hand on
her shoulder. 'It cannot have been easy for you, ma'am, and I
respect your courage.'

'Indeed. It does take courage to do the right thing when it is
against your instincts to do so. I would wish to see her wed, but if
it is not to be…'

'Hush now. Do you recall my mama?' Elizabeth did not know
if she were doing right with such a reference but felt it might raise
the lady's spirits. 'She was quite in despair, but then,' at this
moment she darted a quick and playful glance towards her
husband, 'three of her daughters were wed within a few months.
We cannot foresee what may soon happen to raise our spirits.
Lady Catherine, Mr Darcy and I would be so very happy if you
and Anne could return with us to Pemberley. You are both
wearied over the past days and a change of air would refresh you.'

'No, Mrs Darcy.' Some of Lady Catherine's vigour appeared
to have flowed back into her veins. 'It is out of the question. Anne
is not well enough for a further journey and my spirits are too
low.'

'Your nephew would do his best to raise your spirits, and dear
Anne would have the companionship of Georgiana, which would
surely speed her recovery. Besides, would it not be more comfortable if you were from the district for a time?'

'No. I think not, Mrs Darcy. Both Anne and I are too fatigued
and we should be more comfortable at home. But your thoughts
are kindly and I thank you for them.'

'Then,' Lizzie rose, 'since my husband is anxious to be off,
would it be possible for us to see Anne before we depart? It need
be for only a few moments.'

'I do not think I can refuse you.'

Reaching out, she rang a bell for a maid, who soon appeared
and was instructed to take the visitors up to Miss Anne's sitting
room, an order which was soon accomplished.

There was a warm reunion during which Anne, looking

slightly weary, shed a few tears, though on the whole she looked better than her cousins had feared she might.

'I could not marry him, cousin.' She spoke fervently to Darcy. 'You see, since I have spent time with you and Mrs Darcy, I have seen what is most to be valued in marriage. And this man who has offered for me...' Again, tears seemed imminent but were avoided. 'For him I could have felt neither respect nor admiration, but only fear and distaste. I thank you both for what you have done.'

They were taking their departure when Lizzie glanced back at the slight figure reclining on the chaise and, on impulse, bent down to embrace the girl warmly. 'And soon, when you are well enough, you must return to Pemberley. Georgiana pines without you and we, too, miss the company of younger people.'

'And,' the girl's voice was a mere thread, 'the friends who visited? There is news of them?'

'We shall hear more of that when we return, and I shall write and tell you.' Mr Fife's name was not mentioned, and Lizzie dared not do so for fear of raising hopes. 'But you must continue your practice on the pianoforte so you can continue to give a good account of yourself when you do come north. I leave it to you to persuade your mama.'

And with that, she followed her husband from the room and soon they were on their way north, the following day reaching Pemberley, where they found Georgiana much restored by the application of cloves and ginger, together with the solace of a wool bag filled with hot salt, which greatly eased the pain. The story her brother had to relate shocked her greatly, and she at once set about writing a letter to her cousin, promising she would make no reference to recent events. Instead, she concentrated on plans for their future meeting and one or two tiny pieces of information, which had interest only to those most closely concerned. And so, life at Pemberley was restored, affording Mr Darcy the peace to complete the disrupted alterations to the park.

The improvements had been much reported and discussed in the north, leading to an increase in the number of visitors who came by appointment, thence to a celebration for all those who had contributed to the success of the undertaking. Sunshine blessed that special day, which Mr and Mrs Darcy spent among neighbours and workers, discussing past such occasions, as well as future plans, and ensuring a plentiful supply of refreshments and diversions which all could enjoy.

That evening, Lizzie wrote a long letter to her sister, describing the happy event and pressing Jane once more to bring her family to spend some time at Pemberley.

'It is a month since we were together, Jane,' she concluded, 'but it might be a year, I so long to see you all again. Please write and tell me you will travel north to Derbyshire. Charles will be delighted to see the remodelled lake; the aspect from the house is indeed fine and we have a little bower where Emily and Catherine may sit safely and watch the swans glide among the water lilies.'

So it was with much pleasure that, no more than two weeks later, Mr and Mrs Darcy stood together as two carriages swept along the drive at Pemberley, from the first of which emerged Bingley, then Jane, both of whom were warmly welcomed on this first visit since their marriage. The children and their nurses had travelled in the second carriage, and all were much relieved to be released from the confines of the journey and were soon settled in the nurseries, where Georgiana appeared to find them objects of the greatest fascination and delight.

'She is a charming young lady, Lizzie.' From the window, Jane observed Miss Darcy pushing the children along a path in one of the ancient baby carriages, retrieved from the attics and carefully restored for the visitors. She sighed deeply. 'You are so fortunate, Elizabeth.'

'Am I?' Elizabeth, who was sad for an entirely different reason, resurrected by the proximity of her two little nieces, was less wholehearted. 'Are you again saying you are less fortunate than I, Jane?'

'No,' her sister smiled. 'I think we should both agree that we have been equally fortunate, Lizzie. But I do, very slightly, envy you such a young and pretty sister by your marriage, while I...' And here there was another deep sigh, which gave the lead for which Mrs Darcy was waiting.

'So... is Caroline Bingley being very difficult, Jane? I do confess that I prefer my own situation to yours – in that respect, at least,' she said hurriedly, but by no means wholly honestly.

'Yes. She is being difficult, and I agree that I was truly glad to escape her presence, since she appears still to consider herself her brother's housekeeper. In fact, Bingley and I came to the very edge of our first real disagreement since our marriage.' The beautiful face was marred by an expression of deep discontent. 'He began to write to your husband, Lizzie, to enquire if it would be in order to ask Caroline to join us here at Pemberley, an invitation which, I hasten to add, would have been accepted instantly, since she is,' and here Jane affected a not unsuccessful mimicry of her sister-in-law, 'utterly devoted to dear Pemberley.' Her voice returned to its natural tone. 'And naturally to its dear master.'

Here, the two young women dissolved into helpless laughter, which would doubtless have shocked Miss Bingley, Mrs Hurst, Lady Catherine de Bourgh and many more of the relatives inherited by their two marriages, but it was some moments before equanimity was restored.

'I am sorry, Lizzie,' Jane touched a kerchief to her eyes. 'I ought to behave with more decorum, but you have no idea how much relief it gives me to talk with you.

'That, alas, is what is missing from my life. But, to return to my tale, I assured Charles that I would prefer to visit you without the additional presence of his sister. This did not please him greatly, since he avoids conflict at all costs, and when he remonstrated, I told him that I did not unduly inflict my own sisters on him and that perhaps he ought to be equally discerning in his invitations. Such an opinion caused a little awkwardness between us, but now all is well. He assured me that he understood my concerns and that he, too, would welcome some time alone with you and Mr Darcy. But in truth, Lizzie, Charles is such an obliging man that anyone can take advantage of him. Whenever Caroline or the Hursts wish to do so, they simply invite themselves to Netherfield. But now I think the time has come to indicate that it is not always entirely convenient.'

'Bravo, Jane.' Elizabeth leaned forward and kissed her sister. 'I think a spell to meditate on these matters will do Miss Bingley a deal of good. The change of climate will also help you, my dear. You looked a little wan when you arrived, but now there is some colour in your cheeks and—'

'As to that…' Blushing more noticeably now, Jane studied the piece of linen she held in her hand, then, swiftly, looked straight at her sister. 'There is another reason for my ill looks, Lizzie. I am again with child.'

'Jane!' Elizabeth ignored the stab in her breast and put an arm around her sister. 'What splendid news! I am delighted for you and for Mr Bingley.'

'You are?' An expression of relief passed Jane's countenance. 'Then I, too, am pleased. I confess, I did have some concern for your feelings in the matter.'

'Mine?' Her sister maintained her steady smile. 'Why should you doubt my pleasure, Jane?'

'I simply wondered. I feel…'

'You feel that since I have not yet achieved what you have, that I should be envious of you. Jane, for shame. You must not think in that way and, believe me, I have every hope that before long…'

At that very moment, there were footsteps from outside and both men entered the parlour, their faces warm from the sun and their hair lightly dishevelled from the strong breeze blowing outside.

'Well, Mrs Darcy.' Bingley threw himself into the chair facing his sister-in-law and smiled. 'We have ridden round the park and I congratulate your husband, ma'am, on all the changes since I was last here. That was the time,' and his frank expression showed he felt no embarrassment at the behaviour of his sisters to the person who was now mistress of Pemberley, 'when we were both unmarried, Darcy, was it not? And you,' he said, turning towards his wife, 'were not here, Jane, but Darcy and I were able to persuade your sister–' here a slight bow acknowledged his hostess, 'now Mrs Darcy – to come along with her aunt and uncle to spend some time with us. Happy days,' he said with some lack of feeling. 'And how are Mr and Mrs Gardiner, Mrs Darcy? They are well, I hope.'

'They are well, sir, I thank you, and I hope to see them next time they travel north.'

'Yes, I recall that, of us all, Mr Gardiner was the most successful with the rod. His perch quite broke all records and I think he meant to have it mounted. Did he proceed with that plan, think you, Darcy?'

While the two men continued to discourse on the subject of

fishing, Lizzie smiled quietly at her sister, who almost, but not quite, shook her head in silent amusement at her husband, while at the same time Elizabeth was reflecting on the kindly ways of providence, which had seen fit to prevent their roles being reversed. It was possible to convince herself that had she now been Mrs Bingley rather than Mrs Darcy, she would have found much to cause dissension, possibly even as much as had previously existed at Longbourn. There was in the simple goodness of Charles Bingley a deal which could be trying, such lack of stimulation in his conversation and... She would not confess that her present judgement was perhaps coloured by the news so recently imparted by her sister. Never.

The remainder of the visit passed quickly enough, with the children a frequent diversion, especially for Georgiana, who was wholly taken up with them, intrigued by their babbling attempts at language, and laughing as they propelled themselves across the nursery floor, determined to snatch at something which had caught their attention.

One or two excursions through the countryside were arranged, and one evening Mr and Mrs Arbuthnot, along with their son, John, came to dine, which was a great success, made still more pleasurable by the musical entertainment. Georgiana took her place at the pianoforte without any persuasion and, glancing across from time to time as the young couple discussed the challenges of various pieces, Elizabeth was more than happy to observe the ease with which they deferred to each other; his protective manner and her shy smile appeared to proclaim their continuing attraction.

It was while she was involved in these thoughts that her husband caught her eye, and in his she read a warning message and nodded submissively, though she knew he was having difficulty in disguising his own interest.

'And have you heard,' he enquired of *père* Arbuthnot, 'any news of your young friend, Mr Fife?'

And Elizabeth sensed that Darcy, as well as she, was more than anxious to hear the answer.

Chapter Nine

*T*he Bingleys and their entourage had been gone a week when Elizabeth sat down to reply to a letter which had been received from Anne de Bourgh, addressed to Mr and Mrs Darcy, the duty of reply falling to the wife, as is so usual in these things. Before starting to write, she refreshed her memory of the detail, which was not unduly onerous in such a short letter, and then took up her pen.

My dear Anne,

Mr Darcy and I were delighted to have your letter and especially happy to know that you feel so much better and have plans for travelling north to Pemberley in the near future. Fitzwilliam and I shall be more than happy to welcome you and Lady Catherine, and, if the weather remains fine, it may be possible to plan a few excursions. Georgiana has been informed of the possibility of such a visit and is practising some more advanced pianoforte pieces in a determination to impress you.

You may know that my sister and her husband, Mr and Mrs Bingley, have recently been with us, along with their twin daughters, all of which was extremely diverting. The girls are at a most attractive age and received much attention from both family and servants.

Towards the end of their stay, we received a visit from the Arbuthnot family, a considerable pleasure during which Georgiana was persuaded to perform to the admiration of all. Your cousin enquired about Mr Fife, but there is little news from Scotland, so I cannot say if there is a possibility that we may see him in the immediate future. From what his friend, Mr John Arbuthnot, reports, Mr Fife has been deeply immersed in all the legal complexities of inheritance. I am uncertain if you are aware that his relative died shortly after he reached Scotland. I have no idea how this will affect our friend's prospects.

I am so happy, dear Anne, to know that your spirits have revived sufficiently to contemplate the long journey to Pemberley. I am instructed to inform you that Georgiana will write soon.

Please pass to your mama my kindest good wishes.

Yours affectionately,

Elizabeth Darcy

That duty done, Elizabeth further wrote to her family, firstly to her father and next to Jane, before taking out, with some reluctance, Lydia's last communication to which a response was long overdue. Sighing, she took a sheet of writing paper from the shelf and stared out through the window, determined to resist a treacherous inclination to forget the George Wickhams and their problems and instead walk through the park where she might meet her husband, at this very moment supervising some improvements to the gardeners' cottages. But she decided to be rigorous with herself, sighed once more and began to write.

My dear Lydia,

I thank you for your letter received recently. I send my congratulations to you and Mr Wickham. As you say, if this time you follow Jane's example and have a daughter, your family will be complete. As you may know, the Bingleys visited us recently and their twin girls are quite bewitching.

While pondering her next words, Lizzie wondered if the last sentence might be seen as a provocation. She could easily imagine poor Lydia feeling outcast that her sisters had the privilege of being welcomed at Pemberley, a privilege which was denied her own family. On the other hand, she must not forget her youngest sister's nature and invest her with sensitivities which she did not possess. Having decided on that point, she was able to abandon thoughts of tearing up the page and starting again, and continued.

I am sorry that the house in Lincoln did not meet your requirements on your recent journey south. Mr Darcy has issued instructions that you are all to be welcomed and made as comfortable as possible. At this distance, it is not practical for us to supervise things ourselves but provided you give the caretaker due notice – which, I understand, this time you did not – I am certain the house will be adequately warm and comfortable for you. Shall we see how the arrangement goes in future…

Again Lizzie contemplated, wondering if she dare say that the Wickhams would be free to make their own arrangements should they choose to do so, but, in the end, family ties were too strong for such a bald statement, and she proceeded in a soothing vein.

and hope that your next visit will be a pleasure for you all.

Returning to the original topic, you would know that Charlotte Collins now has three daughters, which must augur well for your hopes. I observe that you and Mr Wickham continue to enjoy life in Newcastle and that my nephews are well and happy.

With my love,

Your affectionate sister,

Elizabeth

Her correspondence addressed, Elizabeth felt free to indulge her pleasure of walking through the park and, as she had hoped, she reached the spot where the main carriage drive crossed a minor pathway, known for no obvious reason as Dog Lane, when she saw, some way ahead of her, a horseman approaching and smiled her greeting as her husband came level, sliding easily from his mount.

'I thought you were decided to spend the afternoon answering your correspondence, Mrs Darcy.'

'I have completed that duty, praise be, and am now walking through your park, Fitzwilliam. Even now I can scarce believe that I might almost say "our" park.'

'Yes.' Lightly he put his hand about her waist, allowing the horse to walk placidly behind. 'I, too, experience such feelings of amazement. But have you written all your letters? To Anne, and to your sister, Mrs Wickham?'

'And also one to my father. I have been prodigious busy, my dear, and thought I deserved a little turn about your estates. How do the cottage plans go?'

'When they are completed, they will be very comfortable, I think. Already Mrs Armstrong – you know, that kindly woman who comes to help in the laundry – is quite excited at the prospect of water from the stream being piped into her kitchen.'

'Well, it is a great step forward.' Elizabeth had experience enough of the inconvenience of water drawn from a well to understand the woman's feelings.

'And what did you say to Cousin Anne?'

'I told her you would soon write to her yourself.'

'Did you indeed.' He sighed. 'Am I to have no peace when I have finished my duties on the estate?'

'You need not worry: I said nothing of that sort. Although, to be fair, her letter was addressed to you as much as to me.'

'But you have answered for both of us and I doubt if I could add anything to what you have written. Did you mention Mr Fife?'

'I hesitated to do so for fear of accusations of meddling but…'

'Lizzie!'

'But I did just report what had been told us by our neighbours. The news was not what the poor girl would be hoping for, I am sure.'

'You are right, of course – with all your vast experience in such matters.'

'Thank you, Fitzwilliam.'

'On a similar point, I encountered John Arbuthnot when he was riding on the stretch of land which adjoins theirs, and he has sought my permission to invite Georgiana to a musical entertainment in town, and I have said I can think of no reason why she should not decide for herself whether she wishes to accept.'

'Oh, Fitzwilliam!' His wife seized his hand and turned towards him, her face alight with pleasure. 'How kind you are!'

'And not proud?' With one finger he twisted a strand of her hair into a curl, then released it. 'Nor haughty?'

'None of these things. You are the kindest of husbands and the best of brothers. Now, do not tease me further with all the foolish things I have said in the past but tell me more of the invitation to Georgiana.'

'He has asked if he may approach Georgiana direct with the suggestion, and, since it is rather a long drive, wonders if she may be permitted to spend that evening at Astley Abbey rather than return to Pemberley. Oh, his parents will accompany them throughout, and if she prefers to come home then that will be her choice. So, what do you think, Lizzie? I believe he is even now on the way to seek her answer. Do you think she will agree?'

'I dare not express an opinion.'

'So, you are in your provocative mood! Well, in that case we must simply wait until we hear what has happened.'

'But if you were to insist on a reply, then I shall say that Georgiana will accept the invitation, but whether she will choose to spend a night at the Abbey, that I cannot say. It may be that she needs some time to contemplate such a departure; the veneer of ease which she wears is very thin. I sense she is still nervous of strange situations without the support of those close to her, but she must be encouraged to decide for herself: it is the only way to gain confidence.'

'You are right, my dear. And if she does decide to stay the night at the Abbey, then of course she will take her maid with her, who may be just the support she needs in this first venture.'

'It is a pity though.' They had almost reached the house when Elizabeth spoke again. 'A pity that Mr Fife and Miss de Bourgh are not here, for then the problem would be much eased.' They walked through the courtyard where the ostler led the horse to the stable. As Elizabeth climbed the steps ahead of her husband, she added, 'But perhaps that would be too much to expect.'

Inside the house, they found Georgiana and Mr John Arbuthnot seated in the family drawing room, more than adequately supervised by Mrs Annesley, who was quietly stitching away at the chair seat which Elizabeth had long since abandoned.

'Mr Arbuthnot.' Lizzie put a hand to her hair, which she all at once feared was disordered, but since it was too late to do anything she at once dismissed the concern from her mind, smiling as she took a seat opposite the young couple. 'I hope you have been offered some refreshment after your journey.'

'Yes, indeed, Mrs Darcy.' Having risen and bowed, the young man sat down. 'But I must soon return to the Abbey, since my father has some plans for me.' He glanced at Darcy, who had silently taken up a place at the far side of the room, sitting with his back to the window. 'I have put my plan to Miss Darcy as you, sir, suggested, and I hope that she will agree to what has been proposed.'

Though Georgiana had her head slightly bowed, Lizzie could still see the warm glow in her cheeks which lent her an air of such innocent pleasure. She was much improved in looks, and Lizzie flattered herself that it was thanks to her own lightness of manner and also her advice regarding more becoming gowns, the present one being in shades of soft rose, a purchase made during their spell in Paris, which had a style that unmistakably proclaimed its provenance. It was more than likely that Mr Arbuthnot, with his experience of travel on the continent, was not unaware of that fact.

Since Georgiana showed no sign of an immediate reply, it was left to her brother to nudge her with his usual self-indulgent concern. 'And you, Georgiana: have you decided on what your answer might be to such an invitation?'

'Oh yes, Fitzwilliam.' The young woman raised her head and smiled, something which Lizzie thought she would have shrunk from doing a few short months ago. 'I would very much enjoy going to the musical event. Did Mr Arbuthnot tell you there is to be a performance of Beethoven sonatas, which will surely inspire me – as well as works by Mozart, whose music we all love? But...' She hesitated.

'But?' Lizzie encouraged. 'You have some reservation, Georgiana?'

'Only that I am uncertain as to the end of the evening. My feelings are that I should return to Pemberley, but I do not wish to cause undue trouble to my hosts.'

'As to that,' Mr Arbuthnot said, with a note of relief in his voice, 'it would be no trouble I assure you, if that is what you prefer.'

'But...' Georgiana began and stopped.

'If that is your only objection, Georgiana, then I would bring the carriage myself over to Astley Abbey and so save Mr Arbuthnot an additional journey.' As he spoke, Darcy rose from his seat and walked towards his sister. 'There is no need for any concern on that point, and the main objective would be served: that you had enjoyed an evening of music in the company of friends.'

'Then may we leave that final decision until nearer the time?'

'Of course. That is something you can choose at the last possible moment.'

And Mr John Arbuthnot, looking extremely content at the outcome of his visit, rose, made his farewells and departed, leaving the residents of Pemberley, each in their own way, equally satisfied with the outcome – especially, it must be said, Mrs Elizabeth Darcy, who could not help but congratulate herself that her influence on her young sister-in-law was proving to be very beneficial to her chances in the field of, if not matrimony, at least friendship. Not that she would allow a whiff of her self-satisfaction to be picked up by her husband's keen senses, naturally!

When the great evening arrived and Elizabeth was left alone with her husband (Mrs Annesley having availed herself of the chance to visit her sister for a few days), she greatly appreciated the opportunity to discuss affairs of the sort which occupy most married people: matters of great moment, such as whom they ought to invite to the reception planned for the near future, what colour might be chosen for one of the bed chambers about to be repainted, and which of the two young women on the housekeeper's staff should be trained to replace her if she ever decided that the time had come to retire.

But, in this, she found herself thwarted, since her husband exhibited a restlessness that was unlike him, appearing unable to concentrate and so much at odds with his normally attentive style that she found it distracting and, in the end, irritating.

'So.' She put aside the swatch of curtain materials in which she had been endeavouring to excite his interest. 'You cannot address these important matters, Fitzwilliam.' Even as she spoke, he sighed and rose from his chair. 'Should we then perhaps play a hand of cards? Would that settle your mind to the fact of your sister being in perfectly safe company and most likely enjoying this opportunity to stretch her wings?'

At that, he turned and gave her the sudden charming smile which had such an unsettling effect on her emotions, so that she, too, lost all concern for the shades in her new drapes. He came forward to sit with her on the sofa.

'How well you read me, Elizabeth: I am all admiration. Of course Georgiana is in the care of a sensible family, who will without doubt show her great consideration, and I am proud that in the end she decided to spend the night with the Arbuthnots. Despite what has happened, I know she must move out into the world without her family always guarding her like a queen bee. But she and I were both deeply affected by past events. Perhaps I was more conscious of the dangers than she was herself, since I was so much the older and it was... Well, it was I alone who had arranged her time in Brighton in the belief that she would be safe. If... anything had happened to her, I could scarce have borne it, since I was, after the death of our parents, her sole guardian.'

'But that which you feared did not happen, Fitzwilliam. Thanks to your swift action, you saved her from what would have been a most unhappy attachment to an unprincipled man. And we cannot always keep safe those whom we love: I know that. Do you think I do not daily regret that my own sister, despite her foolish, ill-judged behaviour, is tied to a man who is certain in the end to bring her low with sorrow?'

'I do realise that, Lizzie.' But she suspected he was considering that which they all knew: that it was Lydia's unbridled actions which had in large part brought about her downfall, and that the marriage itself was simply a veneer to protect her own and, even more important to Darcy, her family's respectability. 'And I promise you that I will progress from this anxious and fraught spell with each step Georgiana takes towards the normal life of a young woman of her station. Now, you said something about cards; shall we have a hand or two before we decide that it is time to retire?'

In the event, Georgiana, escorted by Mr Arbuthnot, returned from Astley Abbey the following day, full of animation and excitement as each reflected on the pleasures of the previous evening, describing at length how well the musicians had performed and the elegance of the audience. This led to Mr Arbuthnot interrupting with a complimentary remark about Georgiana's gown – another bought in Paris – assuring her smiling brother that she had been greatly admired.

It was as he was about to depart that he mentioned he had

heard the previous day from his friend in Scotland. There were hopes that Mr Fife might soon spend a few days with them, as he was required to travel to London in connection with the estate which he was to inherit from his relative.

'Really?' Mr Darcy raised a surprised eyebrow. 'So, are we to understand that his cousin also had property in the south?'

'Considerable, so I understand, which is very pleasing for him since his means were limited all the time we were at Oxford. No, I think my friend will find his position in society much improved.'

When the young man had departed amid much appreciation on both sides, they listened once more to an account from Georgiana of the previous evening's affair, which had included a most delicious selection of sweetmeats and – something rarely encountered – dishes of some iced confection, a mix she imagined of cream, eggs and sugar, with the addition of fruit.

'Then,' said her brother, beaming at this freely described and entertaining discourse, 'we must check the ice house and see if we can produce something of the kind at our reception. I think you are about to write out the invitation list, are you not, my dear?'

'Yes, Fitzwilliam, it is already complete, and… it has just occurred to me that perhaps it might be arranged to coincide with the visit of your aunt and cousin.'

She ignored her husband's raised eyebrow, which could speak such volumes, allowing her mind to roam over all kinds of intriguing prospects.

And so Elizabeth's attention for the following weeks was almost wholly engaged in busy discourses with the housekeeper, with whom she had had a warm connection since her arrival at Pemberley. (Mrs Reynolds, she always felt, considered she had had a hand in bringing her master and his wife together.) There were long discussions of food and table decorations, which Lizzie knew would mean much extra work for the servants, but when she spoke of this she was assured that all the staff were excited by the prospect and, despite the extra duties, they looked forward to such a celebration, the like of which had not been seen at Pemberley since the days of the old master and mistress. Thus, much in harmony, together they made lists for the supper, deciding where in the ballroom the musicians might be most advantageously placed so arrangements for a small dais could be planned and other matters of moment.

There were also meetings with the head gardener, who promised a display of flowers and plants the like of which had not been seen in the area for a generation. When she reported the latter conversation to her husband, he shook his head and laughed lightly, explaining that Pemberley was by no means the only great house in the district with famous gardens and hothouses, where tender flowers and fruits were grown.

'But,' she reminded him gently, 'it is right that he should think it is. I confess I have never seen anywhere such a wonderful display as he and his men produce throughout the year. You will remember to tell him so, Fitzwilliam.'

At his wife's tone of mild reproof, Darcy laid down the papers he was studying and surveyed her severely. 'I always remember to do so, Elizabeth; have no fears.' Then he raised his papers and carried on as before, a reminder to his wife that she must not assume too much, and also that gentlemen do not wish to be thrust into every domestic detail of entertaining. All they expect is that whatever arrangements are made, they should proceed faultlessly, without the least disturbance of their own lives.

Since Georgiana was involved in much of the planning, Elizabeth encouraged her to express her views on how the occasion could be made more adventurous, and it was her suggestion that a treasure hunt might take place in the orangery and along the lower gallery, with a few small prizes for the most successful participants.

All this planning went on apace, but sadly, the following week, there came a letter from Lady Catherine, written in a hand which looked surprisingly shaky and infirm for one as confident as she, and which caused Fitzwilliam to exclaim as he scanned the first few lines. His wife raised her eyes from her breakfast coffee.

'My dear, what is the matter?'

'Oh... nothing much, I suppose, Lizzie, except... that it begins to appear that there will be no guests from Rosings to our reception.'

'Oh, no, Fitzwilliam! I was so hoping—'

'I know exactly what you were hoping, my dear, but it appears my aunt is by no means well and that she must decline, since she cannot at the moment contemplate such a long journey.'

'How very vexing.' Though she replied in moderation, Elizabeth allowed the question of the lady's motives to drift into her mind, causing her to wonder if she could have any inkling of her daughter's feelings, or of the designs of her niece-by-marriage. 'I suppose... there is no chance that Anne may be allowed to come alone.'

'That is something I very much doubt.' Her husband finished reading and passed the letter across the table. 'It is not an idea which would readily present itself to my aunt.'

Quickly, Elizabeth read through the letter, concluding, in spite of herself, that indeed Lady Catherine appeared out of spirits and there was little to be gained by ascribing that to a depression caused by her disappointment over the lost connection with Baron Blackstone. 'Yes, she appears far from well and is clearly unable to make such an uncomfortable journey. I wonder...'

'That particular tone of voice makes me exceedingly nervous, Lizzie.'

'I cannot think why it should do so.'

'Because it tells me you have some plan, which will not immediately be revealed lest I disapprove.'

His wife smiled at once and surrendered. 'You know me almost too well.'

'So... are you ready to confess what you have in mind?'

'Well, it occurred to me that, since we know Mr Fife may be at the Abbey at that time, it would be a great pity if he and Anne should not have the chance of meeting. A pity for Georgiana as well, since I am convinced each girl lends the other some confidence, but... What do you say to this suggestion, Fitzwilliam? You know my father and sisters are journeying north for the occasion: how would it be if he were to arrange to bring Anne in his party?'

'Mmm.' Her husband clearly was less enthusiastic than she was. 'It will be a crowded carriage: four people, three of them young ladies with all the luggage they must have before they can stir. I doubt that your father would agree. Indeed, I think he is a brave man to venture so far with his own two daughters. No, I think we ought to leave it, my dear. The Rosings party cannot be with us; let us accept that fact. If there is any strong attachment between young Fife and Anne, then they do not require us to engineer their meetings.'

'You are probably right,' his wife replied meekly; too meekly, perhaps, for his reply was immediate.

'You continue to make me nervous, madam.'

'I?' Her indignation was feigned. 'I cannot imagine why.'

'Because it is so unlike you to be submissive when one of your plots has been denied.'

'You are so suspicious,' she retorted in a bright tone. 'I cannot think why.' The dissimulation only made him laugh as he rose from the table.

'You are even more devious than I thought when we married! But consider: if all your plotting should bring my cousin and Mr Fife together – and I am by no means convinced it will – then what will your feelings be if, in a few years' time, it turns out to have been a grievous mistake for both parties?'

'I do not think that would happen. I feel they are destined for each other.'

'If they are destined, then they need no help from you. Surely that is the implication of the word.'

'We had help, had we not?'

'No, we had nothing but hindrance. And from every quarter, including my own dear aunt. That, I suggest to you, is why our marriage is so precious to us: that we came together in spite of all the handicaps.'

'You are not saying that those who have a more straightforward courtship cannot have an equally happy marriage.'

'No, not that,' he sighed. 'But I cannot agree that too much meddling is helpful. In truth, I think it is up to Mr Fife to make his own opportunities should he have sufficient interest to do so. Most men do not like to think they are being pursued; I thought that was generally recognised. And certainly there is nothing to prevent him, when he goes to London, from taking a journey into Kent to visit Rosings. If he should express such a wish, then I would be perfectly happy to give him an introduction to Lady

Catherine. But now, I shall leave you to your plotting, and I daresay, in the fullness of time, you will be prepared to share with me whatever scheme you are brewing.'

And with that, he dropped a kiss on the crown of her head and departed, leaving her to her thoughts.

When she was alone, Elizabeth took time to reappraise the situation in light of what her husband had said. And, perhaps more importantly, what he had not said. And she felt her skin grow quite warm with embarrassment for was she not – and certainly not in any way she wished – was she not once more taking on some of her mother's more extreme characteristics? On this point she had examined herself before and had decided that, unless she was positively invited to do so, she would leave her young relatives to find their own happiness by whichever route was appropriate.

Think, Lizzie, she ordered herself. Your mama would have chosen Mr Collins as the perfect match for you, so even one's dearest and closest family can be wildly wrong. Dear Mama, whom they still mourned, had been so misguided in many ways. She must not grow into her mama. Indeed she must not.

Such decisions are simple to reach but somewhat difficult to achieve, as she found out. But she conquered her weakness by concentrating her mind hard on the coming party, which had the additional benefit of keeping Georgiana's relationship with Mr John Arbuthnot to the fore of her mind. It was a pity, she thought, that, since they were not to dine at one large table, she would be unable to oblige them to sit together. But as it had already been decided that their guests would choose their supper partners to join them, as was the modem style, at a series of smaller tables, then she must leave that decision to chance, or at least to their own inclinations, and thereafter she tried to forget the subject altogether. She was successful to the extent that her husband quizzed her obliquely once or twice on the matter and it gave her some amusement to appear unaware of his teasing.

The day before the party, her father arrived with Kitty and Mary, who were making their first visit to Pemberley. When Lizzie saw how many boxes were being unloaded from the coach after they themselves had descended, she realised exactly how impractical her suggestion had been concerning Anne. There could scarce have been another ribbon or furbelow tucked inside, or even outside, since further boxes were strapped on there as well.

Her father looked as well as she had ever seen him and more genial than she recalled from the past. He greeted her warmly and shook hands with his son-in-law, who then turned his attention towards the 'two remaining Bennet girls', as he occasionally called them when he was alone with his wife. But he did not remark to her his first opinion that they were much improved in both manner and appearance, since he thought that might be considered tactless in view of past statements on the subject.

Kitty, he thought, was very near pretty, and even if she would never be as handsome as her two elder sisters she would be a welcome addition to their soirée, since there were sure to be one or two young men without especial partners. While Mary… Well, she would never be a beauty, but she was more agreeable than he had once considered, and now he was close to deciding that what he had seen as over-confidence might be an attempt to conceal a retiring nature. He had little doubt that, when his wife had done a little more polishing, they would not stand out too much from the great and the good of Derbyshire. For their own sakes, he hoped it would be so.

And, since he was in the habit of having his desires translated into reality, he welcomed the two young ladies who, accompanied by their father, descended the grand staircase at Pemberley on the day of the party, much to their delight addressing them in turn – 'Miss Mary. Miss Kitty.' – each accompanied by a courteous bow, which was reciprocated by demure curtsies.

Kitty was in a pale silk gown of a becoming shade of lemon, while Mary wore pink, which lightened her rather dull complexion. Both were decked with pieces of jewellery which Darcy recognised as belonging to their sister, and he immediately decided that before they left he would ask Lizzie to take them into town and allow each to choose an especially pretty piece to remind them of their first visit north.

His own sister could not help but outshine them, of course, since she was wearing one of her Paris gowns and looking extremely pretty, her hair dressed with a few curls about the ears from which dangled crystal earrings formerly belonging to their mother. Lizzie, as always, looked stylish and confident in a deep rose shade which became her greatly, giving her an exotic glow, and she had chosen the silver filigree necklace presented to her on her last birthday, very striking against her handsome neck and shoulders. He made certain that she was aware of his approval, though he said nothing which could detract from his appreciation of the others.

But before there was time to comment at any length, there came the sound of wheels crunching on gravel as the first of the guests arrived and were announced to Mr and Mrs Darcy and their party. Elizabeth, who had been slightly nervous at the prospect of such an occasion, found that all she had to do was smile and say a few kind words to each party, and then allow the atmosphere of the house and the pleasure of the guests to carry the evening along.

It was interesting to see Mr John Arbuthnot, having had a few words with his host and hostess, detach himself from his parents and drift towards where Georgiana, along with Kitty and Mary, was observing all that was happening. Elizabeth was also happy to see that Georgiana was enjoying her role as leader of the younger set, and before half an hour had passed was escorting quite a bevy of people her own age into the orangery, instructing them on the names of plants, as well as explaining some of the rules of the treasure hunt which she, with some help from her brother, had devised. Elizabeth smiled happily as she moved among and spoke with their guests, receiving compliments on all sides.

When the musicians took their places on the dais at the end of the ballroom, she and her husband led off the set, and as they returned to their places she found herself quite entranced by the spectacle, which was indeed a fine one. Since the evening was still pleasantly warm, open doors at the far end of the room caused the candles to flutter in the faintest of breezes, their flames reflecting in the mirrors and in the jewels worn by the ladies.

Then, a light-hearted dance was chosen with the young in mind, and she watched as Georgiana was led on to the floor by John Arbuthnot, their second dance together that evening. She was happy, too, to see that Kitty and Mary both had partners and gave every sign of enjoying themselves.

'You have done well, my dear Lizzie.' She looked round as her father joined her on the sofa. 'It is a most elegant gathering, and my two girls are seeming less and less foolish with every day.'

'Papa!' she mildly remonstrated. 'You must remember that they are being what young women have always been: a little giddy sometimes and—'

'Mary? Giddy?' he questioned with a little laugh. 'She has never known the meaning of the word. But that is perhaps a pity, since it would be refreshing to hear her laugh from time to time.'

'You are right, Papa.' As she spoke, she smiled. 'Giddy is not a word that applies to Mary. I was thinking of Lydia and Kitty, but at least Kitty is being more sensible, and it is very pleasant to see they are enjoying themselves.'

'Oh, I have heard of nothing else for weeks but the great ball at Pemberley. I am certain Mrs Castlemain was tired of the very sound of it.'

'She is still attending to the music lessons, I gather,' remarked Lizzie with circumspection. 'We hope to hear some of the results later.'

'Oh, yes; she is a very dependable sort of woman, Lizzie, and I think the girls value her advice.'

'Mmm.' There appeared little more to be said on the subject and it was only moments later that, while the musicians were having a respite, Georgiana sat down at the pianoforte and played most felicitously with Mr John Arbuthnot turning the music for her. Something about their manner brought an ache to Elizabeth's chest and she wondered if her husband were equally moved by the memories evoked, but since he was sitting with others of their guests in a corner behind a large urn of flowers it was impossible to know. Then, immediately before the dancing was about to recommence, Kitty and Mary were persuaded to join John Arbuthnot, Georgiana accompanying them, in a round, which, being very light and engaging, was greeted with some applause and calls of encore that were dismissed with smiles and head shaking from the performers.

At the end of the evening, when all the guests had departed, the house was once more secured and most of the candles extinguished, Lizzie took it on herself to seek out Mrs Reynolds, expressing her gratitude for the devotion the servants had shown, thus ensuring success for the evening. The housekeeper was pleased and assured her mistress that all her comments would be passed on to those concerned and that the surplus food would be distributed, as was the custom.

'I shall attend to all that, Mrs Darcy.' She escorted her mistress to the door of her room. 'But I am sorry I shall not be able to send any of the iced pudding, as all was eaten. It was to everyone's taste, I trust.'

'It was much talked of, and I am certain every cook in the district will be calling for your recipe.'

'Well, it was quite special, madam. Some years ago I learned the secret from a Frenchman, and Cook has been trying out the method for the past week in order to get it just right.'

'It was quite perfect, Mrs Reynolds, as I shall tell Cook myself in the morning. But I am certain you must be tired, and so I shall bid you goodnight.'

Thus, when Elizabeth went upstairs to bed that night, she was filled with a sense of achievement that such a hurdle had been successfully overcome. Not even to herself had she confessed to any nervousness, not until this present moment, but she was confident that from now on she would face any such challenge with complete equanimity.

But even after she was in bed, listening to the soft, regular breathing of her husband, her mind still too lively for sleep to come easily, she returned inevitably to the events of the evening, thinking how happily her family mingled with other more distinguished ones, before progressing to the growing easiness between Georgiana and John Arbuthnot; which thought took her mind in the direction of Anne de Bourgh. It struck her that Lady Catherine's indisposition might have been a hidden blessing, since Mr Fife had not yet returned to the area and it was unlikely that the young woman would have attracted other attention. She and the young Scotsman had something in common, in that his very small stature might have caused difficulties much as Anne's slight build and lack of height were bound to do, though this was perhaps more acceptable in the female than in the male. However – carefully she moved to a more comfortable position in the deeply voluptuous feather bed – now that Mr Fife looked to be on the high road to financial improvement, doubtless his lack of inches might be overlooked by the more ambitious, which would be a pity, since she was convinced that the two young people had many interests in common, as well as a genuine appreciation of each other.

Chapter Ten

*L*ife at Pemberley swiftly returned to normal after the departure of Mr Bennet and his daughters, Elizabeth finding herself pleased that their lives had resumed their usual routine. And she scarcely required even to give thought to Georgiana's future: Mr John Arbuthnot was spending so much time in her company, his intentions hardly needed a query. But it was a great pleasure when, having ascertained her brother's feelings on the matter, he offered marriage to Miss Darcy and was at once accepted.

Both families were delighted with the wholly agreeable match, and Lizzie, scarce having recovered from the reception, found herself thrown headlong into the preparations for the marriage, which was to take place without delay. The reason for such haste was that Mr John Arbuthnot was engaged to travel to New York on his father's business and wished to take his bride with him. At first, Lizzie had had some concern over such a proposal, thinking it might be too much for Georgiana, but that fear was dismissed by the bride herself, who assured a sceptical sister-in-law that she had long harboured an interest in the native people of the New World. Elizabeth could not but suspect that the young woman's interest in such things was of shorter standing than she admitted, and that indeed it had only been awakened during her talks with Mr Arbuthnot, who had previously travelled widely in the Americas.

Another of Georgiana's wishes was that her cousin, Anne, should attend her marriage. And so messages were sent with that invitation to the young lady herself, as well as a special plea to her mother, who, though improved in health, had by no means fully recovered. Replies were swift and generally positive, for while Lady Catherine emphasised her own frail condition she did, to her credit, state that she would try to ensure that her daughter would be present on the great day.

Anne's own reply was enthusiastic and much more certain than anyone might have expected. Lizzie did wonder if she had had some means of knowing that Mr Fife had eventually been contacted and had agreed to stand as usher, but then she decided that Anne might simply have been hoping, assuming that since the men had been friends since boyhood the chances were that Mr Fife would at least be present.

In the event, Lady Catherine decided she was sufficiently fit to make the journey and was able to accompany her daughter, arriving with her two days in advance of the ceremony and looking, at least to Elizabeth, much as she always had done, showing little sign of the weakness which had afflicted her so grievously. Once again it occurred to her that perhaps it had been more to do with disappointment over the Blackstone affair, and possibly even the Darcys' involvement in it, that had made her refuse the last invitation. But at least on the day before the wedding, when the two young ladies were much engaged with dressmakers and the trio sat down together to drink a glass of wine, Lady Catherine was gracious enough to thank them for their intervention.

'I am indeed much obliged to you, Darcy.' Lizzie, suspecting the brightness of Lady Catherine's eyes, felt her own heart soften. 'I have recently discovered that matters in that family are even worse than you suggested. Blackstone is quite without a penny in the world and has for years been living on his wits.'

'So I have heard, Aunt,' her nephew confirmed gravely. 'I believe you have saved your daughter from the worst kind of fortune hunter and that she will be eternally grateful to you.'

'But still...' her voice shook, 'without your intervention, Darcy... Anyway, Anne is much improved since that unhappy time. She has gone out into society a little more and I think shows some spirit.'

This remark Lizzie heard with some amusement, since she could never forget how Lady Catherine was inclined to crush any spirit and stamp on any opinion which conflicted with her own, but she agreed kindly.

'She is looking much more lively, Lady Catherine, and I shall do all in my power to see that she enjoys the company of some young people during your stay here. The Arbuthnots are a numerous clan and there are to be several cousins of that age attending the wedding, I am sure there will be music and dancing which will please all.' Then, changing the subject she added, 'It is such a pity that Colonel Fitzwilliam is still abroad and cannot be with us for such an occasion. Darcy had a letter from him last week. Are you going to pass on his news to your aunt, my dear?'

'I was about to do so, Lizzie. Fitzwilliam wrote in his letter that he has made the acquaintance of a very wealthy French family. They have large sugar plantations and the additional blessing of a very pretty daughter, much younger than my cousin, but I fear he is smitten. I expect to hear of another marriage before too many months have passed.'

'Well!' The lady appeared disconcerted and, for the moment, almost speechless, such a notable event in itself that Elizabeth toyed once more with the idea that perhaps her ladyship, having failed to net one cousin for her daughter, had fixed her hopes on the other. For though in purely advantageous terms, the alliance would have been less impressive, still the Colonel was a gentleman, and the connection might have had some attraction – though Lizzie could not believe that it ever would have happened. One cousin would have found the proposition as unacceptable as the other, as Darcy had so firmly stated.

'Well,' Lady Catherine repeated. 'I hope he will choose with discernment.' Her eye fell on Elizabeth as she spoke, before moving quickly towards her nephew, continuing in a less positive manner than was her habit. 'So many alliances remind me that I shall not always be here to look after the interests of my dear Anne. Who will protect her when I am gone?' she asked mournfully. 'This is now my main concern in life.'

'My dear aunt.' Darcy rose from his seat opposite and sat down beside her on the sofa. 'You must know that I shall always care for my cousin. Lizzie and I shall, if need be, look after her and guide her so.'

Lady Catherine regarded Mrs Darcy with something of her old hauteur, then sighed, as if giving in to fate, her shoulders slumping. 'She will need some strong influence, since I fear she may be easily led.'

'As to that, Lady Catherine,' Elizabeth said, with some temerity, 'I see increasing signs that Anne is taking on some of your strength of character. She is altogether more lively and positive than when first I knew her, and I believe she is more aware of the ways of the world, which, as we know, are not always honourable. I think perhaps you should not worry unduly.'

'I thank you for that, Mrs Darcy. And I am grateful to you, nephew, for your support. There are so many who give false assurances, but I know I can depend on you and...' she sighed deeply, 'from what you say, it is unlikely that Colonel Fitzwilliam will soon return to the country, so I shall not be able to look to him.'

This melancholy little interlude gave Lizzie an insight into the fears and anxieties that were afflicting her old adversary, and she found it became easier still to forget past offences and so put herself out to be courteous, and even affectionate, from time to time – something which amazed her when she considered it afterwards.

But soon the wedding morning itself dawned, driving all else from her thoughts as she sat in church beside her husband, watching Georgiana and John Arbuthnot being joined together. The bride, though serious, looked amazingly pretty and happy as they made their vows before walking together from the church into a day of blue skies and sunshine. Georgiana, Lizzie stated firmly to her husband, had never looked prettier. She wore a delicate white silk gown trimmed with blue, and matching flowers twisted into her hair. Her hand was slipped confidently through her husband's arm, and the tender exchanges between the pair were affecting to those present, suggesting they were oblivious of all else. Which was not true of Mr Fife, who kept scanning the assembly, relaxing only when he caught sight of the figure he sought, sitting close to her formidable mater, who was unaware of what was happening. And during a break in the formalities, he could be seen approaching Anne, bowing to both ladies, while Lizzie, being close by, was comfortably placed to overhear.

'Miss de Bourgh, I hope I find you well.'

'Oh, Mr Fife. Yes, very well, thank you,' the girl replied,

almost overcome, but eventually finding her voice. 'And you? You are well?'

'Very well indeed.'

'May I,' a tiny quiver in Anne's voice betrayed her nervousness, 'present Lady Catherine de Bourgh? Mama, this is Mr Peter Fife, a friend of Mr John Arbuthnot.'

'Mr Peter Fife?' Lady de Bourgh stared for a moment before inclining her head in a faint bow, then, raising her lorgnette, she surveyed him at some length.

'Lady Catherine.' His salutation was brief and confident. 'I had the pleasure of meeting Miss de Bourgh and Miss Darcy, as she then was, during the time they spent in Paris.'

'In Paris?' Clearly this required explanation, and the lady was something of an expert in direct interrogation techniques. 'You were in Paris studying, I presume.'

'Not entirely, ma'am. Mr Arbuthnot and I, having finished university, embarked on a tour of the continent and quite by chance found ourselves in Paris at the same time as Mr and Mrs Darcy and their party.'

'Which university, may I ask, Mr Fife?'

'The University of Oxford, ma'am.'

'I see.' That at least was acceptable, and a slight pause was followed by the young man requesting Anne's mother's permission to take a stroll round the lake where some of the younger guests could already be seen relaxing.

'I think the air is a little chilly for my daughter, sir. She is by no means strong and must be protected from the vagaries of the weather here in the north. From your accent, I judge you to be a Scotsman, but we are used to a gentler climate and I cannot have my daughter at the mercy of the elements.'

'I understand perfectly, ma'am, but then perhaps you will permit me to take her into the orangery, where we can both take some exercise. I have much to tell her since last we met.'

'Indeed, sir?' Just as it appeared inevitable that Lady Catherine would utterly reject such a proposal, Elizabeth broke into the overheard conversation with some soothing words.

'I am sure, Lady Catherine, that Anne will come to no harm in the orangery; it is quite warm, and if you have any concern then she may go upstairs and find my maid, who will bring her a shawl. Tell her the cream wool one, Anne: it is very warm and comfortable. Then we shall know there is no danger of her catching a chill.'

Rather surprisingly, Lady Catherine acceded, albeit reluctantly, and together she and Elizabeth watched the two diminutive figures, animated in conversation, walk away from them in the direction of the hall and disappear.

'What a very odd little man.' Lady Catherine gave the impression of continuing to fix her gaze on them even when they had quite vanished from view.

'He is small,' Lizzie replied, sitting down beside the older woman, 'but there is nothing odd about him. In fact, I believe him to be gifted and clever, as well as being an engaging companion.'

'It is strange that my daughter did not mention him to me.'

'Well, she may simply have forgot. Doubtless she had much to relate after her journey through France.'

'Hmm.' That expression was sufficient to convey a considerable degree of scepticism before the lady continued in equally disapproving tones, 'He is a Scotsman.'

'Indeed.' There was little to add.

'And what do you know of his circumstances, Mrs Darcy?'

'Little enough, ma'am: simply that he and Mr John Arbuthnot have been lifelong friends and that he gives the impression of being a likeable, open young man.'

'I am by no means certain that I want my daughter to go to live in Scotland and—'

'Who is going to live in Scotland?' Darcy appeared by his wife's side, smiling down at both of them. 'I have not heard of any such plan.'

'Do not provoke me, Darcy.'

'I would not dream of it, Aunt.'

'I am surprised that no one thought to tell me of this Scotsman who met my daughter in Paris.'

'And here, Aunt. They also met here in Pemberley.'

'Here, sir? I am astonished that this has been kept from me.'

'Well,' Darcy pursed his lips, 'I imagine it was kept because it appeared of little importance.'

'But now,' his aunt retorted, in a tone of outrage, 'he is walking with my daughter in the orangery.'

'Indeed? It seems an innocent enough way to pass some time. They are both young and—'

'That is the point, Darcy. I do not wish my daughter to go walking with a strange young man without the protection of a chaperone.'

'If that is how you feel, madam, let us set matters right. If you will do me the honour, Aunt.' He held out his hand to assist as she rose to her feet. 'We shall take a turn about the orangery now, along with many others of our guests, including, I believe, my sister Georgiana and her new husband, and, if we spoil their pleasure, at least we shall have the satisfaction of knowing they are chaperoned.'

I see.' The lady subsided into her seat. 'I see, Darcy.' She looked despondent and slightly shrunken. 'You mock me when all I want is to protect my daughter.'

'That is what I want, too, Aunt, and indeed I may have teased a little, but truly I did not mean to mock. But do you not see? The young must have a little freedom, and since Anne and this young man are both sensible, then they deserve our trust.'

'Lady Catherine.' Elizabeth took up the issue. 'You need have no concerns about Mr Fife, and certainly you need have none about your daughter's propriety. They are simply young people taking pleasure in each other's company.'

'What do we know of him, Darcy? Who is he? What of his family?'

'About these I know little, Aunt, but I understand his circumstances have recently improved, following the death of an aged relative. For other information you must enquire of the Arbuthnots – not today, I beg. Perhaps it might be more circumspect if you were to wait a little longer but...'

At that moment, there was a sign from the butler, the young couple returned to the room and there began the round of feasting and speeches, followed by dancing. And then, when the sun began to fade from the sky, Georgiana, having changed into her travelling dress, came down the curving staircase to where her husband was waiting and, before anyone knew what was happening, she was being helped into the carriage and they were escaping down the drive in a shower of rose leaves and even some rice.

And Lizzie, feeling quite as emotional, as a girl's mother might feel at such a time, turned her head into her husband's shoulder as his arm came about her waist. 'Oh, Fitzwilliam, I do so hope she will be happy!'

'I think they will be, Lizzie, and if they are half as content as we are, then everyone will envy them.' Words which his wife acknowledged to be undeniable. For, when she had been upstairs with Georgiana, checking that she had all the necessities for her long journey, the bride had held her for a moment and, with her face hidden from sight, had murmured words of thanks.

'You have been such a blessing to us, Elizabeth. You have made my brother the happiest of men, and I mean to follow your good example with John. Thank you for all you have done. I am so glad that we shall be living close by, and when I am in need of advice then I shall call upon you at my old home.'

'This will always be your home, Georgiana: you know that. And thank you for being the perfect sister. Our friendship can only grow stronger over the years.'

Soon all the guests began to leave and the family was once again alone. The following days, though busy, were something of an anticlimax after so much excitement. The only ripple of excitement was caused when Mr Fife appeared two days after the wedding to make his goodbyes and to ask Lady Catherine de Bourgh and Miss Anne if he might call at Rosings when he had finished his business in London.

'It is a pity you did not come yesterday, Mr Fife, since then you would have had the opportunity to make your request in person,' Lizzie reprimanded him slightly, knowing that Anne had gone off disappointed that he had made no further approach since the wedding.

'I did mean to do so, Mrs Darcy, but, as I told Miss de Bourgh, I had some business I had to attend to in Yorkshire; then, since matters were more complicated than I had been led to believe, I was delayed. You do know that I have come into a considerable inheritance from my late cousin, but since his financial affairs were left largely in the hands of those who were not competent, there is much sorting out to be effected.'

'I see. Well, I am sure when you explain matters, those at Rosings will understand.'

Her tone caused Mr Fife to smile, his rather homely countenance illuminated. 'I do hope so, ma'am. You must know something of my intentions where Miss de Bourgh is concerned, and while I may not measure up to her mother's plans for her – I am unlikely to have any great title or distinctions – I think we should suit each other very well. She reminds me so strongly of one who was very dear to me.'

'I do understand, Mr Fife.' At the sound of the door opening, she turned to her husband with some relief. 'And I am sure Mr Darcy will have more understanding than I of Lady Catherine's likely attitude, but, for myself, I wish you well in your hopes.'

So it was that no more than two weeks later, Darcy had a letter from his aunt telling him that Mr Fife had offered for her daughter and that, after considerable anxiety and heart searching, she had agreed that her daughter might decide for herself such an important matter.

'Since above all, I seek her happiness and safety,' the lady concluded, 'I feel it is all I can do. Mr Fife is an amiable enough young man and, as I was reminded by Mrs Darcy, it is not his fault that he is a Scotsman. Indeed, when I ventured that I was most reluctant to see my only child settled so far away, he countered this objection with the information that his recent change of fortune includes a London house with one of the finest addresses. From what I gather, he will spend much of his time there, and so I shall not be entirely cut off from Anne.'

Having read the letter and passed it across to his wife, who quickly scanned the pages, Darcy looked across the table with a challenging expression. 'So Elizabeth, you have told my aunt that Mr Fife could not help himself in his choice of nationality.'

'I do not recall using those exact words,' she replied calmly, folding the pages and putting them aside, 'but I think no one could disagree with them.'

'My aunt, I think, would have liked to challenge you on that, and the fact that she has not done so inclines me to think she is indeed losing some of her old vigour.'

'Well, at least she must be happy that when she is no longer here, Anne will have a husband who will care for her, someone who is not attracted by thoughts of her fortune.'

'I fear she dreads the loss of her daughter as much as she wishes for the other. But at least Mr Fife has been diplomatic and has said she may stay in London with them as often as she wishes to do so.'

'Mmm,' Lizzie considered, contemplating with apprehension the idea of Lady Catherine as a mother-in-law. 'But I do hope she will have the courtesy not to avail herself of that invitation too often.'

That was a hope with which her husband showed himself to be in agreement, but both parties were considerably satisfied at the outcome of events, and it was not long before they were on their way down to Kent to attend the wedding of their cousin to Mr Fife, with, as was always a great pleasure to both Mr and Mrs Darcy, the opportunity to spend a few days at Longbourn. The additional bonus on this occasion was being able to visit the Netherfield family, recently augmented by the addition of a son to join the two little girls.

When Lizzie went to visit her sister, still lying in after the birth, she felt the familiar pang when she looked into the tiny cradle at the baby, who was, as was the family custom, to be named Charles. As she observed the screwed-up features and the tiny, waving hands, she wondered when it would be her turn to experience the same kind of happiness enjoyed by almost every other female in her acquaintance.

'My dear Jane.' Leaning forward, she kissed her sister's soft cheek. 'I congratulate you and Mr Bingley with all my heart. He is a beautiful boy: you must be proud.'

'Of course I am, Lizzie.' But as she spoke, Jane's mouth trembled. 'I am so pleased he is a boy, so I may—' Here she broke off, seeming to struggle against tears.

'Dearest?' At once her sister was all anxiety. 'What is the matter? Surely… there is nothing amiss with the child.'

'No, Lizzie, not that. He is perfect. But… you do not know. I do not think childbearing suits me. I find it so… agonising is the word which comes to mind. If I were to know that Charles would be my last, then I should be happy, but I fear this will not be the case and… I dread it so, Lizzie.' She held out her hand to her sister, and this time the tears would not be stopped.

'Oh, my dear.' Elizabeth did not know how to reply. 'I am so sorry that is how you feel but…' She knew she must tread with care. 'Perhaps Charles will indeed be your last child. It might be—' She broke off, knowing she was the last person to offer advice.

'It is all right, Lizzie.' Jane squeezed her sister's hand as if she were the comforter. 'It is much to do with weakness after a difficult half year, but I shall be all right when I build up my strength again. Besides, seeing you is the great tonic I need more than anything…'

'Jane, my dear,' Elizabeth smiled and brushed a strand of hair back from her sister's brow, bringing up a matter which she thought might prove a diversion. 'You recall how, once, you and Mr Bingley expressed an inclination to come north to live in Derbyshire?'

'But then we had to cancel because of Emily and Kate…'

'Yes. You were not well enough to make that decision, dear Jane, and you must remember how disappointed I was then.'

'We were all disappointed, Lizzie. Not over the girls, of course, but… to have been closer to you.'

'Then how would this cheer you, Jane? Fitzwilliam has heard of a house that is about to become available and not above ten miles from Pemberley. I have not seen it, but he says it would suit you and the family perfectly, and I believe he is talking of it with your husband at this moment. Is that not something to think about, my dear, to cheer you a little? The only thing is, you may not wish to desert Papa and our sisters.'

'Oh, that is another thing, Lizzie.' Jane wrinkled her forehead. 'I have not had the opportunity of writing to you on this matter, but I am afraid that I have some distressing news. Our father has been observed visiting Mrs Castlemain at her cottage and leaving in the early hours. It was such a delicate matter that I did not wish to put it on paper.' She lay back, her eyes fixed on her sister's stricken face. 'I am so sorry, Lizzie, to repeat such things about Papa, but it is better that you should know.'

'I can scarce believe it, Jane.' Lizzie bit fiercely at her lip. 'That our father should, for whatever reason, put himself in a position which will undoubtedly cause speculation – when he has two unmarried daughters at home! How could he and this woman—'

'Hush, Lizzie. You know as well as I that Mrs Castlemain is a thoroughly good woman.'

'If he feels like this, then why does he not do the honourable thing and marry her?' The words spilled from her lips before she could control them, but the instant they were spoken she looked at her sister in dismay. 'Jane! Forgive me! I do not mean to insult our mother's memory. How could I have spoken these words?'

'Lizzie, do not distress yourself. While I have been thinking of the matter, the very same thought has come into my mind. And that shows, does it not, Lizzie, that our feelings have changed in the time since our mother died. Then we could not bear to think of it, but now it does not seem so very unreasonable. Mrs Castlemain is a very good sort of woman; Mary and Kitty like and admire her, and who knows? Perhaps Papa is lonely and would welcome the chance of some domestic happiness. After all, Lizzie, we cannot pretend even to ourselves that our parents were sensibly connected; in fact, they were as ill matched a couple as ever you would find. And, to tell the truth, Lizzie, Papa is a much better man since Mama died; not so sharp in his opinions nor so severe in his judgements.'

'Yes, I had noticed that, Jane. His attitude to Mary was positively indulgent last evening, and Mary herself has mellowed because of it. At least Mrs Castlemain would be better—' Abruptly she broke off, realising where her wandering thoughts were taking her.

'Yes? You were about to say, Lizzie?'

'I was about to say, better than some of the ladies of our acquaintance.'

'Such as Caroline Bingley, were you about to say, Lizzie?'

'Jane, you shame me. I had not thought to speak of that, but since you have done so… I did at one time think she might have set her sights on…'

'I, too, had that feeling, Lizzie, and was most anxious. But I am certain Papa was aware of the danger, and that may be why

Mrs Castlemain was brought into the household.'

'Poor Miss Bingley. Is she still visiting Bath?' enquired Mrs Darcy in a skittish way.

'She is at present in London, Lizzie, but I fear she will descend upon us at any time.'

'I have just had the most wonderful idea, Jane!' Elizabeth was determined to raise her sister's spirits. 'You recall I told you the tale of a certain relative and a Baron Blackstone?'

'Lizzie!' Jane spoke in a warning, but amused, tone.

'Well, as far as I can tell, he is still looking for a lady of means, which of course we know Miss Bingley to be. And imagine how it would be to have a baroness in the family. How we should be patronised, Jane!'

'Lizzie, Lizzie!' When they had finished laughing, Jane wiped the tears from her cheeks. 'You are incorrigible. Just like Mama.'

'Oh dear, Jane! But with more discretion, I trust.' Which set them giggling again, and it was only when their husbands came into the room that they were able to compose themselves.

Chapter Eleven

*T*he betrothal of Anne de Bourgh and Mr Peter Fife was a quiet affair with fewer guests than had witnessed the wedding of Georgiana and John Arbuthnot at Pemberley, the latter pair much missed, since their travels in America continued. But there was a respectable number of Mr Fife's university friends present, as well as, from Scotland, his parents and his brother, who acted as groomsman. The bride, who, though pale and nervous, looked pretty in a delicate way, was given in marriage by her cousin, Mr Fitzwilliam Darcy.

After the ceremony had been completed, the Darcys, along with a rather gloomy Lady Catherine and others guests, were watching the happy couple walk from the church when Fitzwilliam spoke to his wife in the droll fashion which she was still finding such an unexpected, but welcome, facet of his character.

'Soon, my dear, you will run out of available candidates for your schemes.'

'I cannot think what you mean, Darcy. What schemes are these?'

'You know perfectly well what schemes, Lizzie.'

'In any event, I still have two more... schemes... before I can relax.'

'Oh?' The note of anxiety in his voice was loud and clear.

'Only my two unwed sisters, my dear. And they may prove the greatest challenge of all.'

'Well, let us get it over quickly, for I am sure my nerves will not survive much longer.'

'Nonsense, Darcy, your nerves are in perfect condition and you cannot pretend that such schemes as have been accomplished have had much to do with me, though we may have been part of the background...' Catching sight of her friend, Mrs Collins, who had been providing music for the ceremony, Elizabeth put a hand on her husband's arm. 'But hush! Here comes Charlotte.' Then, in an undertone, 'Soon you will be accusing me of arranging her situation, but I had no hand in it! Only, I have not spoken to her for some time and... My dear Charlotte! How well you look. I was so pleased to see you in church and to hear you play; it was quite like old times.'

After some friendly words with Mrs Collins and an exchange of a few civilities with Mr Collins, who had conducted the marriage service with his customary air of self-importance, Darcy excused himself, leaving the two friends sharing felicities while he went to support the bride and groom, now beginning to receive greetings from their guests. Some time later, Elizabeth followed, adding her own good wishes and receiving a few private words with the bridegroom.

'Mrs Darcy, I have much to thank you for – you and Mr Darcy. Had it not been for meeting my wife in Paris and then at Pemberley, I should not have been the happy man I am today.'

'I hope you will always be so. And Anne...' As the shy young bride came smiling towards them, Lizzie bent her head to kiss her cheek. 'You look so pretty! My only regret is that Georgiana and Mr Arbuthnot were not able to be with us. But perhaps, when they return, you may all be able to visit us at Pemberley and we can celebrate again.'

'We shall look forward to it, ma'am,' said the bridegroom, speaking for both of them. And a moment later, when Anne's attention was distracted, he again spoke softly in Elizabeth's ear. 'You are the first, apart from Lady Catherine, to know, but this evening we set out for the Channel and shall spend a week in Paris to remind us of how things began, going on to Brussels for a few days before returning to England. Our plan then is to spend some time in London, setting our home to rights, and later to journey north to Scotland.'

'And...' Lizzie hesitated, one eyebrow slightly raised. 'Lady Catherine approves of all this?'

'She does not approve of Scotland: that much was made clear to me. But it is impossible to alter facts. If Anne is ever homesick, then of course I shall bring her to visit Rosings and her mama, but there are times when it will be necessary for me to be in Scotland. I think the lady understands and will act reasonably.'

'I am certain she will.' Lizzie spoke with more compassion than truth. To her it was scarce possible to imagine a more dire fate than inheriting Lady Catherine de Bourgh along with a wife. 'And perhaps you will both come to visit us in Derbyshire from time to time.'

'You are very kind, Mrs Darcy.' He bowed and smiled as to a fellow conspirator. 'But now I see we are about to return to the house, so, if you will excuse me…'

The rest of the day followed the usual pattern of such things, and in the evening Darcy and Elizabeth were left in the large house, alone with Lady Catherine, whose melancholy manner Elizabeth tried to raise, despite that lady's determined resistance. The ceremony was discussed at some length before moving on to the reception, at which the bridegroom had sung some Scottish airs accompanied by the bride herself. But since none of her diversions could raise the lady's spirits, Elizabeth surrendered completely and mentioned that her sister, Jane, and Mr Bingley thought of moving with their family and household to Derbyshire.

'Derbyshire? So far north? And what, pray, is the purpose of such a move, Mrs Darcy? It seems to me an exceedingly wayward choice.'

'Be careful, Aunt: you know we are very defensive about our situation in those distant parts.'

'That is different, Darcy: that is where you were born and raised. But for people to choose such an out-of-the-way situation is nothing short of perverse.'

'It will be very pleasant for me to have my sister nearby, and I hope for her, too. You know we have been very close for all of our lives, and I shall enjoy indulging my nieces and nephew.'

'Yes.' Here Lady Catherine subjected her guest to a long, slow observation, which went from her head to her toes. 'Your nieces and nephews. Yes, I dare say.' And obviously satisfied with her deliberate snub, Lady Catherine rose grandly, again pronounced herself wearied with such a long day and begged they would excuse her.

It was a moment before a word was spoken when they were alone, but at last Fitzwilliam rose from his seat and joined his wife on the sofa. 'You must not allow her to goad you, Lizzie.'

'I try not to, Fitzwilliam. I promise, I do try.' Her voice was pain-filled and not entirely steady.

'I do not suppose she meant what you imagine she—'

'Yes, she did. And you know it, too. You knew instantly her words were meant as a reproach.'

'Well, that is solely because I am sensitive to your worries, Lizzie. What hurts you, also wounds me. I know what my aunt is like, and because she is my aunt I forgive things I would find difficult to excuse in others. Besides, she herself is unhappy, since she feels she has lost her only daughter and so is alone. She has few friends and now...' He smiled at her in the most tender way. 'Now she must depend still more on the company of Mr Collins. Pity her, Lizzie. Pity such a fate.'

His words made her smile, then laugh, and she found his arms were about her, his mouth against her hair and he was saying something else, words she could not quite distinguish until she had loosed herself and was looking into his face. 'You will find sometime, my dear Lizzie, just how painful it is to hand your daughter over to someone else. We shall both find it so, but we shall be able to comfort each other.' And she blessed him for his kindness to her. And for his understanding.

Within a few months, Elizabeth had the happy news that the Bingleys were quite decided to take the house close to Pemberley, and for several weeks all that was discussed was this or that aspect of Seton Manor, how it compared with Netherfield or Long-bourn, how the aspect from the drawing room might be improved by raising a terrace on one side to catch the afternoon sun, and other important problems. But, at last, as the move was being accomplished, the family spent a few days with the Darcys to allow time for the servants to put everything into place at the manor, thus providing a pleasant interlude for the two sisters to indulge each other with all the snippets of gossip which one is inclined to miss from letters and, for Elizabeth, the special pleasure of much time with her nieces and nephew.

Since Georgiana and her husband were recently returned from their wedding journey and settled happily at one of the houses on the Astley estate, the young bride made frequent visits to her old home. Their American journey had been very successful, affording travel outside the cities, so she was able to keep the sisters entertained with descriptions of what they had seen and done, and all with such humour and pleasure that Elizabeth was quite astonished at how marriage to such a kindly husband had changed the shy Miss Darcy into the more confident young matron.

Together, the three ladies spent many happy hours in the parlour at Pemberley, entertaining the children, whom Lizzie found especially diverting, until their mama at last had had enough and hustled them off to the nursery. Then the tales of the New World would begin. They would be astonished by all they learned of the city of New York, amazed to hear of the thunderous noise of the great Niagara Falls, the droll wooden Indians, which stood outside stores advertising tobacco, and a thousand other unusual aspects of that amazing land.

But at last it was time for the Bingleys to leave Pemberley and move to their new home and, while Georgiana still called frequently, often with her husband but more usually alone, life for the Darcys returned to its normal calm and orderly state.

Letter writing, which had always been one of Mrs Darcy's principal interests, came back into its own, but sadly neither Kitty nor Mary were as accomplished in the art as their elder sisters, and much of their news consisted of mild complaints, one against the other, and since they themselves were now deprived of visits to Netherfield, previously a rich source of interest and gossip, their news tended to be of a mundane nature: what Cook had produced for last night's supper was of major importance, and how the new kitchen maid stirred sugar into the leeks by mistake and no one realised until it was served on the day the new curate came to dine with them.

Mr Bennet naturally continued to write regularly, communicating nothing very much, and it seemed to Lizzie, who had not entirely forgot Jane's concern, that his omission of anything to do with Mrs Castlemain was disturbing, especially when she recalled his enthusiasm when first the lady had appeared on the scene at Meryton. Jane, too, expressed her own misgivings on the subject, though, by mutual consent, they did not dwell on the gossip they had heard of their father's visits to Mrs Castlemain's cottage.

Nonetheless, their lives were more seriously disturbed by a letter from Kitty, incoherent and with a suggestion of panic, which spoke of their father having some grave problem but without explaining, or indeed knowing, what it might be. There was also a worrying reference to a visit from Mr Collins, of raised voices coming from the library, followed by the clergyman's departure from Longbourn in what could only be described as high dudgeon, but further explanation was not forthcoming. It was enough to send Lizzie into a spin, and she relieved her feelings by sitting down to write, asking for more information, begging her sister for an immediate reply. But before that letter could be despatched, another arrived, written in her father's hand. She tore the envelope open and read distractedly.

'What is it, Elizabeth?' Her husband, aware of the situation and watching anxiously, could restrain himself no longer when he heard her weary sigh and saw her bite her lips. 'Is there any explanation?'

Miserably, his wife shook her head. 'He sounds… strange.' She passed the letter across the table for his opinion. 'Almost as if… I do not know what it is all about.'

'But you should know quite soon, my dear, since he says he is coming north immediately.'

'Coming north?' With a feeling of relief she looked up and took the page that was being held out to her.

'Yes. If you read to the end, you will see he has written a postscript. Not in his usual clear hand, I confess.' And he waited as his wife read aloud in a thoughtful voice.

'"Since it is impossible to write an explanation, Lizzie, I have decided the best I can do is to travel to Derbyshire forthwith and I shall be able to relate all the news when I see you. I shall be glad to be relieved of this burden…"' And the last words trailed away as if he had been interrupted.

'What has happened, Fitzwilliam?' she besought her husband as if he might have the answer. 'I shall not rest until I know! Rising from her seat she paced the floor until he blocked her path and led her back to her seat.

'Come, Lizzie. Sit down and calm yourself. Your father is a sensible man and will have done nothing so very terrible. In any event, he may be with us this very day so we shall soon know what has caused so much... concern.'

'My family!' The words burst from her. 'They seem to dedicate their lives to causing concern.'

'Like most other families, Lizzie. And I have confidence that your father will not have behaved in an ungentlemanly fashion.'

His use of words caused her to blush, then to smile a little wanly before she allowed herself to be led to her seat.

'Now,' he continued, 'would you have me ride over to Seton Manor to fetch Mrs Bingley? I know she, too, has been concerned over what has been happening at Longbourn. This is what comes of the Bingleys' moving north; we now have no sensible reporter to tell us what is happening at Meryton. And I am not criticising your younger sisters, who are coping with things as they best know how. I wonder if Mrs Castlemain is on hand to help them resolve things. It must be so hard, dealing with matters in such a crisis.'

'They make no mention of that, Fitzwilliam. But no, I do not think you should fetch Jane immediately. There is nothing to be gained by us sitting here stoking each other's anxieties, so let us... let me try to remain calm until my father arrives. I do not know what we can do otherwise.'

It was at the end of a long day before Mr Bennet's carriage pulled into the drive of Pemberley and a tired and weary figure emerged to be greeted by his daughter, who ran down the steps before the horses had come fully to a halt.

'Papa!' With a cry, she threw herself into his arms and sobbed once against his chest, before he patted her with a comforting gesture and dried her eyes with his kerchief.

'Hush, my dear Lizzie. Your father has behaved foolishly in times past, but I hope this time you will agree he has been very sensible.'

'Papa?' she repeated in a note of enquiry, before turning to her husband for support. But he, Mr Darcy, was distracted, his eyes being fixed on the carriage door. And even as his wife stared, he was advancing to assist the lady who was descending through the opening.

For one prolonged moment, Elizabeth Darcy stared, unable to adjust her mind to what was obviously happening in front of her eyes and then…

'Mrs Castlemain.' Releasing herself from her father's arms, she took a step forward, bestowing a light greeting on the cheek of the woman who had been kind enough to accompany her father all the way from Hertfordshire. 'Please come in. You must be wearied after such a long drive.'

And in no time at all, the visitors, having been given a short time to refresh themselves, were sitting in the parlour sipping glasses of Madeira, dinner having been put back while arrangements for a slightly extended meal were keeping the kitchen staff busy.

'Papa.' Lizzie quickly tiring of small talk, rose from her chair and addressed matters head on. 'Papa, I have been so concerned: first Kitty's letter with a reference to Mr Collins, and then yours, which was so different from your usual calm report…' She looked towards the outsider with a hint of apology in her manner. 'I am sorry, Mrs Castlemain, to force your attention on what is so tedious but…'

'Lizzie.' Her father stopped her in mid-flow as he rose from his seat. 'My dear, I beg your indulgence on this.' He looked so crestfallen that his daughter was filled with still more dire foreboding. 'I am afraid I have long been a penance to my children, but it is your concern, my dear Elizabeth, which grieves me most. So I hope you will find it in your heart to forgive me when I say Roberta – Mrs Castlemain – and I were married some time ago, and so she is now your stepmother.'

For a long moment, Elizabeth stood staring, not moving even when her father held out his hand to the pleasant, elegant woman who had been sitting silently in the chair by the fire, and who now rose to stand beside him.

'Papa?' She frowned as if his words had been spoken in some strange tongue, but even when Mr Darcy came closer and put his arm round her she did not take in the meaning of her father's words. 'Fitzwilliam?' Still the dark eyebrows were drawn together. 'What did Papa say?'

'Sit down, my dear.' With his guidance, she reached her chair and sat down, looking at the others, who had also retaken their seats. 'Lizzie.' Her husband was very close and supportive. 'Mr and Mrs Bennet have come to tell us of their marriage and we must congratulate them.'

'But...' It was as if the cry was ripped from her throat. '...it cannot be! Why were we, your family, not informed of this? Why such secrecy?'

Her husband's hand was very tight on hers, conveying some of his own strength. 'That need not signify, my dear. Indeed, some illustrious names choose that very route. And for mature people who do not require permission or advice, then it is a choice they make and not so very unusual.' For a moment he left her and refilled their glasses. 'And I think, in the circumstances, we must wish them joy. Come, my dear: to Mr and Mrs Bennet we give our warmest wishes for many long and happy years together.'

And, scarce knowing what she was about, Lizzie raised the glass to her mouth and drank, surprised to realise how quickly these strange events were finding acceptance.

'You see, my dear,' said Mr Bennet, 'I was very conscious that you and Jane and the others were devoted to your mama. Roberta, hearing all the chatter from Kitty and Mary – you know how they rattle on – also had the idea that no one could ever replace her. And... when I proposed to her,' here he reached out a hand towards his wife, who sat quietly beside him on the sofa, 'she could not agree with me that it would be a good thing for the whole family.'

'Mrs Darcy,' said the lady whom Lizzie still could only think of as Mrs Castlemain. 'I would not for the world attempt to take the place of your mother. I know that would be impossible, and for some time I would not even consider the idea, though by then I had become attached to your father and to Mary and Kitty. But I did not wish to cause any estrangement between you and your father.'

'No, she was difficult to persuade.' Mr Bennet spoke ruefully though fondly. 'But at last, we decided to be married secretly and hoped that the time might come when we could be wholly open about our situation.'

'And, since my first marriage was entirely happy, the temptation was great: we have so many interests in common. You, Mrs Darcy, Mr Darcy, will understand the blessing of a truly happy marriage.' Mrs Bennet spoke so gently and thoughtfully that Lizzie felt her resistance begin to fade.

'That is certainly so, Mrs... Bennet,' Fitzwilliam responded with a smile. 'And I for one do not begrudge others who seek the same pleasure in each other's company. Only... it has been a shock to my wife and she may take some time...'

At this moment, one of the servants entered to let them know that dinner was ready to be served, and so the small party adjourned to the family dining room, where naturally conversation was limited in the presence of the butler and others, a welcome spell of normality in which Lizzie found herself adapting still more to the notion that would have been so entirely foreign to her just an hour or so earlier.

The conversation became more general, with the new Mrs Bennet showing herself to be knowledgeable about many aspects of music and literature, and suggesting gently that it was a pity Mrs Darcy had not been able to able to travel as far as Rome.

'You are right, Mrs Bennet,' Darcy quickly found he had no reservations about the woman who had so unexpectedly become his mother-in-law. 'We have been thinking of such a journey for some time; there is so much to see in that city.' He smiled engagingly across at the older pair. 'But recently, we have been much involved with weddings and have scarce had time to make plans for ourselves. But since I doubt there will be any more weddings in the immediate future, we may be able to do so before long.'

'I am less certain than you of that, Mr Darcy,' Mrs Bennet said, returning his smile and then turning to her husband. 'Do you mean to mention to Mrs Darcy anything about the young Methodist preacher who has come to reside near Meryton?'

'My dear!' Mr Bennet rolled his eyes in a droll manner before becoming more serious. 'We have this young man, Mr Matthews, who has taken over the Methodist church at Staveley and, since they were lacking an organist, poor Mary has been drawn into their worship. Nothing I can say or do will divert her from what she sees as her calling.'

'Do not be too hard on Mary, Mr Bennet,' his wife persuaded. 'The position of organist is one she will fill with dedication. You know church music is one of her interests.'

'Aye, maybe so. But I never thought to see her turn Dissenter. And it does concern me how often his name intrudes into our conversations.'

'Papa, you cannot mean... Is Mary? But no, that is not to be thought of.'

'Your sister Mary is much concerned about that young man's well-being, taking dishes of food from Longbourn kitchen to ensure that he has a decent meal and suchlike. I have heard he has expressed a great liking for Cook's pickled walnuts, so my own partiality is forgotten. Oh, he did come to visit us recently, and I must say he is not an unlikeable man: a mite preachy, and plain, but that is to be expected.'

'Only remember,' his wife added, 'there is something about the eye of the beholder.'

'You are perfectly right, my dear. And, if there were to be a sincere attachment, then I should not stand in Mary's way. And all things considered, she might make a perfectly proper wife for a minister. They would suit each other, I dare say.'

'Indeed,' his son-in-law agreed with him. 'Besides, Methodism has a large following throughout the country and is a great power for good, no one can deny. None should be able to dictate how the rest think or worship: I should resent it mightily if it were directed towards me. But now, if we have all finished, shall we go into the parlour and have a hand of cards perhaps? Or Lizzie might play for us...' He looked expectantly towards his wife, who shook her head.

'Not now, if you will all excuse me. Perhaps tomorrow. And I have just thought that we might ask Jane and Charles over to dine with us, if they are free. I think they ought to be... told what has happened. I know my sister will be anxious.'

'I am aware of that, my love.' Her father patted her shoulder comfortingly as he passed to sit beside his wife on a sofa. 'We are both more than conscious that our actions have caused something of a stir and wish to set things to rights as soon as may be. I wonder, Darcy, would it be possible for me to borrow a horse and ride over to the Bingleys tomorrow morning?'

'Of course. And if you do not object, I shall come with you as guide, since you do not yet know the way. And then we shall hope to have them come for dinner tomorrow. Will that suit you, Elizabeth?'

'Yes.' His wife essayed a smile. 'Of course. I shall look forward to it.' And to sharing with her sister the latest eruption in the Bennet family history, though, on the whole, she found herself less dismayed than might have been considered possible. Since the rumour of her father's night-time visits to Mrs Castlemain's cottage, she had been beset by anxieties about the dangers to his reputation, so the knowledge that they were in fact married was almost a relief when compared with other dire possibilities. And, as they did look singularly happy in each other's company, it would be most unfair to deny her father his share of happiness and the right to live his own life. Naturally, she did still think of her mama, and, had she been the survivor of the marriage, surely it would not have been too difficult to accept if she had found a pleasant, mannerly companion to share her latter days. Thus, looking across at the two opposite, seeing their mutual devotion and admiration, she was amazed at how natural it all seemed. And her mind was at peace.

That night, since the visitors were exhausted by the events and stresses of the long day, they were not late out of bed, and it was not until her husband was brushing out her hair that Elizabeth exclaimed and put her hand to her mouth.

'Lizzie?' He regarded her through the glass. 'You are still very concerned?'

'No, I feel almost… very nearly happy that nothing more dire has befallen my family than a secret marriage – certainly a happier one than poor Lydia's.'

'Do not compare the two,' her husband replied, since he could scarcely bear to think of that matter. 'But still, you were about to say?'

'Just… I forgot to ask my papa about Mr Collins's visit. I cannot think why he should come all the way from Kent on any business which concerned Papa.'

'You surprise me, Lizzie.' Darcy laid down the brushes and sat close to his wife, still regarding her through the glass. 'You can think of no reason why your cousin might find the marriage of your father and Mrs Castlemain something of a threat?'

'Truly, I cannot think...' Then, abruptly, she stopped and pressed her hands to her suddenly hot cheeks. 'Oh, no! Surely no. You cannot mean what—'

'I think it unlikely, Lizzie: extremely so. But not impossible. At least, that is how the mind of Mr William Collins is proceeding.' His lips curved upwards and his eyes were alight with merriment. 'Think, my dear Elizabeth, of what the poor man is enduring at this moment. He sees a chance, however faint, of his inheritance slipping away from him.'

'Oh, poor Mr Collins.' Then, into her mind came the picture of her cousin on the very day of her mother's funeral, how she had come upon him testing the glasses for quality, looking round the room with satisfaction as he saw himself move a step closer to his ambition, and she began to smile. Then, to her own shame, she laughed aloud. 'Oh, Darcy! How awful and how wonderful.' Slipping from her seat, she deposited herself on his knee and raised her mouth for his embrace. 'How awful,' she whispered, 'but... how wonderful.'

The next few days passed in a blur of happiness that dismissed all the concerns of recent times. Mr and Mrs Bennet were given the freedom of Pemberley since they, too, were glad to relax after all the worries, and it was clear that now they both saw that things might have been ordered in a different, more formal, way if they had taken the chance of confiding at least in the two elder daughters. However, all recognised that the past could not be recalled and, on reflection, it pleased Lizzie and Jane to pretend that having a parent sufficiently unconventional to do something so out of line with his nature might be no bad thing.

And when Elizabeth confided to her sister the possible reason for Mr Collins's anxiety, both young women, while slightly shocked at their own reactions, nevertheless thought it a sufficient riposte to Mr Collins, who had patronised them to such an extent on his visit following Lydia's elopement.

'But I do not think it will happen,' the elder sister admitted when their laughter had subsided. 'After all, Mrs Bennet must be over forty.'

'She is thirty-eight, Jane, and we all know that women can breed well beyond that age.'

'But, Lizzie, since she never had children from her first marriage... perhaps it is unlikely,' sighed Jane. 'Only... another girl! Imagine!' There was a long moment of contemplation before she could continue. 'But poor, *poor* Papa. And one truly would feel equally for Mrs Bennet, especially since none can influence these matters.'

'Indeed, Jane, as you say, it is hard; I can imagine Mama often felt it so, especially when the spectre of eviction by Mr Collins was brought to her attention. No, it would be too much... for the second Mrs Bennet to disappoint in the same fashion.' Elizabeth sighed deeply. 'And I fear our father would hide his feelings with difficulty. Yes, in such circumstances, poor Mrs Bennet, indeed.'

'I think she would not sit about complaining: she is much too sensible and lively for that,' Jane replied. 'And I understand that a woman such as she may wish for a child of her own—' Abruptly she stopped and bit her lip. 'Lizzie, I am sorry. I did not mean to distress you.'

'My dear.' Lizzie, with her head averted, smiled a tiny, secret smile. 'You have not. Besides, I have your three beautiful children to borrow when I may. You cannot know what having you so close has done for me.'

Shortly afterwards, Mr and Mrs Bennet, rather reluctantly it seemed to Elizabeth, decided they must return to Hertfordshire where, for the first time, they would set up home together. And on the morning of their departure, Mrs Bennet confided to her stepdaughter that she was looking forward to setting matters to rights and moving into Longbourn.

'It has been a great concern for me, Elizabeth, since I have had some strange sidelong glances, which have made me think your father and I have been less discreet than we believed in keeping our secret.'

It was hard for Lizzie, knowing that others had heard rumours, to find a suitable reply, so she merely nodded and smiled as the lady continued.

'I know it has been hard for him to keep it from you, Mrs Darcy, since you are closest to him of all his family, and we both now regret our course of action. Oh, do not mistake me, my dear: nothing shall make us regret our present happiness. But we ought to have been bolder and trusted all of you to support us. Will you forgive my part in this? It is most important to me that you and Mrs Bingley should not feel that we have behaved badly.'

'Dear Mrs Bennet.' Elizabeth leaned forward and kissed the woman warmly. 'Now that I see Papa content in a way which I have never before seen, I can find nothing to forgive. And no one who knows you could ever believe you would behave badly. I do, most warmly, wish happiness to you both and trust now that you have been to Pemberley you will feel able to make the journey from time to time.'

And so it was a slightly emotional, but contented, family who took leave of each other, leaving life in Derbyshire to return to its usual tranquillity. Though not entirely, since Elizabeth's secret, which she now felt sufficiently confident to share with her husband, caused both great delight. And naturally he had to claim credit for his many assurances that things would turn out well for them, though eventually he also gave his wife due recognition for her part in the matter.

The news from Longbourn continued to be harmonious, and since the Darcys had been apprised of the way of things with Mary it was not any great surprise when they heard that Mr Matthews had made an offer for her, one which had been accepted with alacrity, and that the wedding would take place as soon as could be arranged.

Lizzie regretted but one thing of the present situation, in that she dared not risk such a long journey, but in this her husband surprised her by suggesting that they might travel down in easy stages, spending a few days en route. But, still feeling anxious and protective after her long wait, she felt even this might pose too much of a risk and declined, while being touched by his consideration.

Happily, though, Jane and Mr Bingley were able to attend, and their report was avidly listened to on their return.

'Mary looked very pleased,' Jane assured her sister. 'As much, I suspect, at not being the last Miss Bennet as for the more usual reason. As did our new brother-in-law, who is a pleasant enough man. But I fear he will be somewhat dominated by Mary, who now begins to show a rather masterful streak.'

This, coming from Jane, who had also found a husband who could be strongly influenced by his wife, caused Elizabeth to smile a little, but when she spoke of this later to Darcy he regarded her with a raised eyebrow.

'But don't you realise, my dear, that you come from a family of dominating women? Certainly your mother was set in that mould, and so it is scarcely surprising that it should be in the blood.' He raised the papers he had been studying so his face was hidden, leaving her to digest his words in silent thought. Then…

'I hope you are not suggesting, Fitzwilliam, that I am following that same path.'

'You, my dear Lizzie?' As he spoke he rose from the table where they were sitting, removing his papers to a small desk and depositing them before turning to face her. 'I would not dare make any such suggestion.'

Suspiciously she scrutinised his bland countenance but, seeing nothing untoward, returned to her original remark.

'I was referring more to Mr Bingley than to his wife. He is an amiable man, but he constantly defers to Jane on every matter. Such lack of spirit is something that does not recommend him to me wholly.'

'Thank you for that warning, Lizzie. Then I must try to cultivate a more forceful personality.' Reaching the door, he stood for a moment with his fingers on the handle and a frown upon his face. 'I should hate to be a disappointment to my own wife by being too complaisant.'

With this, he whisked out of the door, but not before she had caught a glimpse of the mischievous expression on his face. Resisting the temptation to stamp her foot, she chose instead to sit down, reaching out for one of the delicious peaches which had just been picked from the tree in the orangery, biting into the wonderfully sweet flesh, the expression on her face suggesting she had arrived in Paradise.

Chapter Twelve

M y dear Lizzie,

It is strange to think that four months have passed since, with Roberta, I spent those few happy days with you and Mr Darcy at Pemberley. I particularly enjoyed the day of fishing in the lake, despite the fact that my success was limited.

I was pleased to read in your last letter that you were keeping well, and I hope you will take great care in the coming months. I can understand how you both must feel about the prospect of an heir to such a great estate, and I am sure your family will bring increasing happiness to you both.

I know my own daughters have brought me much contentment; yes, even poor Mary, who looks set to become the best wife of all of you. Do not scoff, my dear Mrs Darcy: I shall not be mocked by you of all people. We – Roberta, Kitty and I – were invited to dinner at the little cottage which is now Mr and Mrs Matthews' home and were all quite amazed at how cosy and comfortable she has made it. I did visit the bachelor establishment before their marriage, finding it indeed drab, but Mary, with the help of one young girl, has quite transformed the place.

The furnishings gleamed with polish, a fine fire blazed in the grate, there were flowers in abundance and the meal provided for us was well cooked. For that, much of the credit must go to our own dear Annie, who gave her so much instruction in the kitchen before she left Longbourn, but she has indeed perfected the art of pastry making, and we had a delightful fruit pie after the beef. I must say we were impressed and, although Mr Matthews does not approve of wine, he made no protest at the bottle of claret I had taken with me, and I observed that he even partook of a little himself – well thinned down with water and accompanied with much grimacing, of course.

Reading this, Lizzie laughed aloud, which caused her husband to look at her enquiringly.

'It is from Papa, Fitzwilliam. They have been over to dinner with Mary and Mr Matthews, and he goes into ecstasies about, of all things, Mary's light hand with pastry. Isn't that remarkable?'

'If you say so. It is a subject upon which I have never speculated. Most remiss of me.'

'You may laugh, but it is diverting to hear how she has changed – and for the better. I imagine she will be in her element, playing the organ for all the hymn singing. No eyebrows will be raised when she is preaching. And along with the new interest of making pastry, she may have found her true purpose in life. But hush! I have only just begun on Papa's letter.' Again she concentrated on the pages in her hand, throwing out a few details from time to time.

'Oh, and Kitty has met a new young man, although… Not so young, it appears: a widower with a son of four. An artist… He has taken the manor house at Meryton. Mrs Bennet had previously met him somewhere, hence an invitation to Longbourn, which was reciprocated…'

'An artist?' Mr Darcy queried. 'Did Mr Bennet mention a name?'

'No, I think not.' Lizzie riffled the sheets and shook her head. 'He must have forgotten but… Oh, here: it says he is very successful and that he also has private means. Of course, he could not take the manor house if he were not solvent. Oh, he has travelled abroad a great deal, but now he is determined to settle for the sake of his son.' For some time, Lizzie read silently with murmurs of approval, before setting the letter aside with a sigh of satisfaction. 'Hmm. I wonder… He comes by Longbourn when he takes a morning ride, and Papa thinks it is not for the pleasure of his company but rather that he looks at Kitty more than might be considered polite. Now, that is the kind of letter I like to read, Fitzwilliam.'

'I am sure,' he retorted dryly. 'You will not be happy till you have married her off.'

'I simply want everyone to be as happy as we are.'

Her husband smiled at her. 'You set yourself challenging targets, my dear. It is impossible for everyone to be as happy as we are.'

'And after Kitty,' she frowned in a teasing mood, 'I think the very last one I wish to see married is Miss Caroline Bingley.'

'That I absolutely forbid, Elizabeth. Our own family, that is one thing – and I confess so far you have chosen with discretion – but, no further. And without being ungallant, I cannot think of anyone in our acquaintance who would suit.'

'No,' she sighed sorrowfully. 'I shall never be free of the feelings of guilt.'

'Guilt?' Her husband frowned. 'If this is the conversation we had some time ago, Lizzie…'

'Well… I did marry the man she had most set her sights on.'

There was a moment's silence and Elizabeth thought she might have gone too far, but then Darcy threw back his head and laughed. 'What nonsense you speak, Lizzie! There was never the least chance that Caroline and I would marry.'

'I am convinced that is what she wanted.'

'You recall, when we last spoke on a similar matter, I told you that there was never the least chance that I would marry my cousin, Anne; then the same applies in equal measure to Caroline Bingley. You must know that.'

She did know, but it was undeniably pleasant to hear him repeat it each time he was provoked, and she was reluctant to let the matter rest. 'She must have considered it a possibility.'

'You told me yourself that she had designs on your father.'

'Yes.' She shuddered theatrically. 'And because of her pursuit, my father assured us he would never, never marry again. And then, it seems, forgot that promise.'

'Then let us be truly thankful for Roberta and leave Miss Bingley's matrimonial arrangements to her sister-in-law. She is no concern of yours, my dear, and I daresay Jane has inherited that same talent should she wish to exercise it. But, for your next essay into the business of arranged marriages, you must wait until we have a daughter of that age.' He rose and dropped a kiss on her cheek. 'Now go and rest, and then you can plan her wedding, select the dress and the flowers if you must.' Gently he touched her thickened waist. 'But do not choose a husband for her. Let her choose for herself. Let *them* choose!' And, when she was left alone, Elizabeth Darcy brushed away a sentimental tear, reflecting that she was indeed a very fortunate woman.

It was two months later that the Darcys received a visit from Lady Catherine de Bourgh, who was on her way to Scotland to pay her first visit to her daughter and her husband, who had decided to spend some months on their small estate a few miles south of Edinburgh. Elizabeth, who at one time would have dreaded the visit, found herself looking forward to it, if not with enthusiasm, at least with equanimity.

'Lady Catherine.' Having been forbidden by her husband to descend to the drive, Elizabeth remained by the door while the visitor was assisted by her nephew on one side and her maid on the other up the flight of steps to a hall chair, where she subsided with a sigh of relief. 'I hope you are well after your long journey.'

'I am very well, Mrs Darcy.' Then she turned to her maid, who was offering a phial of sal volatile, which she sniffed. 'Just a little giddy. The last few miles have been full of bends and corners.' She spoke in her usual accusing manner, then, quite abruptly, she stood up. 'And you are looking well.' Quickly she appraised the other's altered figure. 'I am glad to see it, at last. Well, shall we go into the parlour? And, if I may be offered a dish of tea.'

And when the lady's immediate needs had been served and she was enjoying the comfort of a warm fire, she grew more relaxed and began to talk of the trials of her journey, wondering if, after all, she ought to have remained at home in Kent rather than risking the dangers lurking in the depths of Scotland.

'I am certain, Lady Catherine, you will wish to give Anne the pleasure of your visit. I had a letter from her recently and she was feeling the want of company, especially since she had made some friends in London. But Mr Fife's brother is about to be married and that will add to their circle. But your company will, I understand, be especially welcome.'

'Besides, Aunt,' said her nephew, adding his own encouragement, 'Edinburgh is an exceptional city, which you will admire. I have often heard you speak of the works of Scott and other leading figures of the Enlightenment. Doubtless Mr Fife will be able to tell you more on that subject than I can, since he has spent most of his life there.'

'Yes, yes, Darcy!' the lady broke in impatiently. 'I am sure I shall have my head well stuffed with radical nonsense, but it is the journey that troubles me. I am wearied though I am not yet halfway there, and still I have to come back again.'

'Well, Aunt.' Darcy gave his wife a sidelong glance, reminding her of a matter they had discussed recently. 'The pity is that we are not all living twenty or thirty years hence, when it will be possible to travel the length and breadth of the country by rail.'

'By rail, indeed! I cannot think what the world is coming to. Stuff and nonsense.'

'It is no nonsense, Aunt. I am in the process of selling land to a group which has the most ambitious plans for direct links between all the major cities and beyond.'

'You ought to be more prudent, Darcy. There are many rogues about, who would separate a man from his estates and—'

'I think I am dealing with honourable men, but, I agree: there are many scoundrels about. Only, I hope to live long enough to enjoy the opportunity of travelling about the country quickly and in comfort.'

'Mrs Darcy.' It was almost a command. 'I trust you agree with me that such things are the work of the devil.'

'I can see the advantages if they prove to be possible,' was the tactful reply.

'Well,' retorted Lady Catherine with her usual finality, 'it is a matter I shall never reconsider. Never.'

But after that pronouncement, she appeared to mellow slightly, perhaps confident that she had won the argument, and went on to mention a letter she had received from Colonel Fitzwilliam, who had married within the last month and was planning to bring his wife to Europe to visit her relatives in France, as well as to make the acquaintance of her new family in England. Darcy, too, was able to add to that with the hope that they might spend some time at Pemberley and, since he understood the new Mrs Fitzwilliam had some Scottish connection, they might then go north.

On the morning that her ladyship was due to depart, Elizabeth received a letter from her father, which caused her great dismay and some consternation, reactions she was unable to conceal from her husband, who found her pacing the floor of her boudoir when he came to see what was delaying her.

'My dear Lizzie, what is the matter? You must not distress yourself.' Then, seeing the letter in her hand and recognising the writing, he asked, 'Is there some bad news from Longbourn?'

Her answer was to thrust the letter towards him and stand while he read it, watching his changing expression.

'So?' He was frowning. 'News, indeed. But not, I think, news which ought to distress you unduly, my dear.'

'Oh, Fitzwilliam! It is so... ridiculous! A man of Papa's age, and a woman of hers.'

'I cannot agree. In fact... it might be very good news. Indeed it might.'

'Well, I confess I cannot look at it in that light, Fitzwilliam.'

'And if it is a boy, my dear, will you still hold to that?'

She shrugged her shoulders, for the moment fixed firmly in her own opinion, but then she turned to the door. 'We must go. Lady Catherine will be waiting. '

'Shall you tell her the news, then, Elizabeth? I confess I would find it interesting to note her reaction.'

Lizzie smiled faintly and shrugged. 'As you say, it might provide some diversion – if you care to introduce the subject. I fear I do not have the heart for it.'

'So...' Lady Catherine's features grew still more grim when the news was relayed. 'I would have thought better of Mr Bennet. I had always thought him a sensible sort of man. But, at his age!' Sipping her tea, she replaced her cup with a clatter. Then, 'Poor Mr Collins.'

But her introduction of the odious name caused Lizzie to raise her head proudly. 'I beg your pardon, ma'am.'

'Poor Mr Collins. For who would not pity him that his inheritance is in danger of being snatched from his grasp?'

'And yet, ma'am,' Lizzie said with deceptive forbearance, 'I believe you do not approve of estates being entailed away from the female line.'

'You are very forceful in your opinions, Mrs Darcy. Indeed, you have always been so.'

'I was merely expressing surprise, Lady Catherine, that you appear to have altered your opinion since we discussed the matter on our first meeting at Rosings. But perhaps you do not mind if my father's family are to be disinherited whereas—'

'Elizabeth.' Her husband's voice had a warning edge. 'I suppose we may all feel for Mr Collins's disappointment while congratulating Mr and Mrs Bennet.'

'I myself warned Mr Collins of the danger when we first heard rumours of Mr Bennet's behaviour, and I advised him to spare no time in going to Longbourn to settle matters...' She shook her head with grim disapproval.

'Then I think that was a pity. There was little chance of Mr Collins persuading my father against marrying, if that was his wish. Rather the reverse, in fact, since his voice was scarcely a disinterested one.'

'And poor Mrs Collins,' was Lady Catherine's response to that. 'You and she have long been friends, I think.'

'And I hope ever shall be. I consider Mr Collins is singularly blessed in his choice of wife and,' encountering a certain weary expression in her husband's eyes, she altered her choice of words as well as the tone in which they were uttered, 'he is assuredly fortunate to have your patronage, ma'am. By no means could anyone say he was other than specially blessed, even without the certainty of inheriting Longbourn.'

'Indeed.' Mr Darcy agreed with his wife, but was also aware of his loyalty to his aunt, at present a guest in their home. 'Indeed, Mr Collins has much to be thankful for in both of these. And similarly, Mr Bennet has the right to find happiness where he may and also, Aunt, the right to try to preserve his own direct line at Longbourn. It is, surely, what all men of property seek.'

'Well, I daresay you may be right, Darcy.' Lady Catherine, having eaten and drunk enough, rose majestically to her feet. 'Though I still have regrets on behalf of the Collins family. Consideration for others has always been my weakness and I am too old to adopt other habits now.'

'But you must not give up, ma'am,' said Elizabeth, unable to resist this last thrust. 'It may be that my father will add to the clutch of girls whom he will be obliged to try to place advantageously, and Mr Collins will be saved. Pray reassure him with that idea when you return to Rosings. Though I do not doubt that such a thought has already buoyed up his spirits.'

Mrs Darcy was subjected to a long, intimidating scrutiny, which she bore with courage, before Lady Catherine turned away. Walking through to the hall, where final goodbyes were said, she departed amid all the usual platitudes. And, as she returned to the breakfast room, Lizzie was already feeling slightly insecure about her husband's reaction to the unseemly exchange.

'Well, madam.' He sat opposite her and passed his cup across for refilling. 'I see you have lost none of your waspish ways.'

'I was forced to defend my family.'

'She is old and lonely and—'

'And she, too, has a waspish tongue. I should never have attacked her family in such a way had the situation been reversed.'

'In fact… I was rather impressed to see that you had not lost your spirit, Lizzie, that you are still willing to defend a principle so long as… so long as that is what it was and not simply an opportunity to settle old scores.'

'Principles?' For the moment she could not follow his argument. 'We were talking of principles?'

'The principle – or the right might be a more accurate word – that a man, in this case your father, has the right to marry if he is free to do so and has the right to have a child if that is what he wishes. And without interference or criticism. From any quarter.'

'Yes, I see what you mean, Fitzwilliam. Earlier I was thinking only of myself I was wrong and shall at once write to my father and his wife to congratulate them in the warmest tone.'

'I knew you would eventually see things in that light, my dear; you are too honest not to do so. And I was proud of the way you stood up to my aunt. Despite what I said earlier, you were right to do so. I imagine even she, on her way north, will be mulling it over and will, with some reluctance, come to the conclusion that your words have some relevance.'

'No,' his wife returned sadly, 'I do not think she will ever harbour kind thoughts about me. She thinks me forward, self-opinionated and thoroughly undeserving of the honour my husband has bestowed on me.'

'Lizzie,' he laughed, 'is that not exactly my point? What outsiders think of this or that does not matter if those most closely concerned are confident that it is right.'

'But I am uncertain that my father is so confident. His words were distracted, it seemed to me.'

'But do you not see, my dear? That is because he is as uncertain of your feelings on this as on the subject of his marriage. When you write as you suggested, all their worries will be resolved. Go and do it, Lizzie. Set their minds at rest.'

And that she did, like any good obedient little wife and not at all like the former rebellious Miss Elizabeth Bennet. She was all happiness and congratulation, and by the time she finished her long epistle her earlier attitude was wholly transformed, and she was filled with admiration, not untinged by a touch of melancholy since her mother's memory would never be entirely expunged, and with a profound wish, one she dared not challenge fate with expressing even in a whisper: that this time her father might have a son.

Chapter Thirteen

*D*ear Mr Bennet,

   I am writing to you in some haste to inform you that Elizabeth gave birth this morning to a boy. She and the child are both well and I find it difficult to express the joy we both feel.

   My wife was brought to bed late last night after a restless day, during which she walked from one end of the house to the other and then back again. For part of this time, Mrs Bingley was with her, but she was obliged to return to Seton Manor, where I have just sent a messenger with the news.

   When Elizabeth is sufficiently recovered, she will be writing to you and Mrs Bennet to let you have all the details of eyes and hair and weight and name – the latter so far undecided – which are so important to ladies, but meantime, rest assured that all is well, that we are very content.

   I send to you and Mrs Bennet our best wishes, in particular that your wife continues to keep as well as your recent assurances declared.

Yours sincerely,

Fitzwilliam Darcy

'Lizzie.'

Mrs Bingley, who by this time was almost as much at home at Pemberley as at Seton Manor, came into the morning room, followed by her two small daughters, Emily and Kate, who immediately rushed to their aunt and threw their arms about her legs, babbling in their childish way and demanding her attention.

'Jane.' When the needs of the children had been met and they were seated on cushions, playing with the tiny dolls which were kept especially for such occasions, Mrs Darcy gave her full attention to her sister. 'This is an unexpected call, my dear; you did not mention yesterday that you would be coming today. Let me ring for some hot chocolate, and might Emily and Kate have some?'

'No. Please, Lizzie, do not let them hear the word or they will forget the toys and demand what you mentioned. So I, too, must do without. No, I was merely passing close by and decided to call and let you know that I have heard from Lydia. She proposes to come and stay with us, and there is something in the tone of her letter which gives me cause for anxiety.'

Lizzie sighed. 'It appears to be her role in life, to cause anxiety whenever possible.'

'She has not written to you, Lizzie?'

'No. As I mentioned last week, she writes but infrequently now. Since she was displeased about the house in Lincoln, I think she has taken it upon herself to punish me by not corresponding. But tell me: what is causing you concern, Jane? Apart from the prospect of her visit of course,' she could not help adding wryly.

'For the first time, she appears discontented with Wickham. You recall how she frequently remarks on him as the kindest and most loving of men; well, things have now taken on a slightly different colour, and she speaks of him being out late at nights and of money being in short supply.'

'Oh dear,' Elizabeth sighed, 'I did so hope that the arrival of Lucy would have made them all more contented.'

'Well, Lizzie, you know as well as I do that another child does mean increased expense, and since there was a shortage of money from the first...'

'They ought not to be so very poor, Jane.' The words were out before Elizabeth had time to consider and, aware of her sister's knowing look, she was scarce surprised by her response.

'So... I have always suspected, Lizzie, that you and Mr Darcy, despite his feelings for Wickham, have been generous to them.'

'That was remiss of me, Jane. I did not mean anyone to know. They have their pride, after all.'

'You are too kind to them, Lizzie. To Lydia, as well as to her husband! Neither has shown much pride. I do not know what Wickham did to offend Mr Darcy so, but I do know Fitzwilliam and understand it must have been something of a very serious nature.'

'Jane, you are my dearest friend as well as my sister, but still I cannot tell you what happened: the secret is not mine. You must believe me that it puts George Wickham in the most dastardly light, and I very much regret that our sister is married to such a man. I truly pity Lydia and fear for her future.'

'As I do, Lizzie, for I feel she is as giddy as ever; experience has not increased her sensibility. Only, this time, I believe I must indulge her and have her to stay for a time.'

'Yes.' Lizzie sighed, less than excited at the prospect of the Wickham family, even without the husband, being in the area for a prolonged spell. All of the servants at Pemberley knew of his reputation for wild living. 'I do not think it is avoidable.'

'Well, that is all I came to say, Lizzie. And now, I left the nursemaid with Mrs Reynolds, so I shall collect her and return home. But not before I have paid a visit to my nephew, if I may, of course.'

'Naturally,' Elizabeth smiled. 'You know how I love to show him off.'

And when the two little girls were collected by their nurse-maid and despatched to the carriage, they reached the nursery and hung over the cot, admiring the heir to Pemberley. Jane stroked his soft cheek, smiling as he reached for the tip of her finger with his searching mouth.

'He is the most beautiful child.'

'Yes. We are both so fortunate that each of us has the most beautiful son in the world. And in addition, you have the loveliest of daughters.'

'Indeed.' They both laughed. 'And you have finally decided that the family tradition is to be broken, that he will be called Benedict?'

'Yes. I think two Fitzwilliams in the house would be too much. I am pleased that my husband agrees with me.'

'When does he not, Lizzie?'

When her sister and the children had returned home, Mrs Darcy sat for a time in the nursery, looking up when the nursery maid hurried out and in with piles of newly ironed clothes, then resuming what was now her greatest self-indulgence. And not hers alone, for several times she had found her husband following the selfsame path into the nursery, had glimpsed through the open door the tall figure simply standing there, gazing down at the small sleeping form. She would scarcely have believed it possible to feel such a level of happiness. There were times, indeed, when it seemed as if her heart would escape from her bosom, such was the power of her love for this helpless child. Smiling down at him, she tiptoed from the room and went down to greet her husband.

Benedict Darcy was but three months old when, far away at Longbourn, his uncle arrived prematurely into the world, though naturally neither was aware of these facts at that time. Elizabeth received the joyful news when she opened what appeared to be her usual letter from her papa and read, with relief and with great excitement, 'Dear Roberta this morning gave birth to a son, almost seven pounds and very lusty, if his lungs are to be believed. Understand, my dear Elizabeth and Mr Darcy, I am the happiest man in Hertfordshire.'

'So, Lizzie,' said Darcy, when she ran over the leaf-strewn autumn lawn in her rush to pass on the incredibly wonderful news and they turned to walk back to the house, 'does this compensate for all the ups and downs of the last year?'

'Much, much more,' she said happily, as she rested her head on his shoulder. 'I would not have believed it possible to be happier than I was this morning. Yet, I find I am.'

'Your father having a son at last? Is this what has made the difference, Lizzie? Or would you have been equally pleased if you had another sister?'

'Yes, Fitzwilliam, you were right; I am happy to confess it. Of course you were. The child being a boy makes much difference. In a way, it grieves me to make such a confession, but I am glad for my father and for Roberta, and I am glad for Longbourn and all who live there.'

'So...' With his arm about her waist, they walked slowly back towards the house. 'Now you have everything you can possibly want.'

'Yes,' she said, although without total conviction. 'And soon, it seems, Kitty will marry her artist and Papa and Roberta will have the house to themselves.'

'Yes.' Now it was Darcy who sounded less than wholehearted.

'So long as Lydia and her children do not decide to return to Longbourn.'

'But they must not. Fitzwilliam, they must not. Papa and his wife must not have that visited on them: it would quite spoil their happiness. Are they not happy at Seton Manor? Have you seen Mr Bingley? What does he say?'

'The Bingleys…' Darcy's manner became suddenly more thoughtful, as if he were mulling over concerns of great moment and almost – it came to her in a flash – almost as if these were matters he was reluctant to share with his wife. That very suspicion was wounding. 'The Bingleys, my dear, are finding the situation as trying as you might imagine, and we know how tolerant they are, but still…' Again he paused, as if loath to continue, before guiding her in the direction of the summer house. They sat quietly, momentarily soothed both by the pleasing aspect and the late sunshine.

'Fitzwilliam…' At length, the realities of their problems intruded and his wife could no longer contain herself. 'You… they… so many uncertainties are making me more anxious.'

'Yes.' He gave a great sigh, smiled somewhat ruefully, and rested his cheek against her brow for a moment. 'I can see that, and now I feel I must confide that which I hoped you would never have to hear: something which, because it concerns the Wickhams, involves all of us.'

'Pray go on.' The tremor in her voice was barely controlled.

'You recall when we were about to leave Paris.' His mention of that day aroused all the anxieties she had since forced to the back of her mind, determined that no word from her would ever reveal her apprehension. Whatever might have happened long before they met was, so she had resolved a thousand times, his concern alone, and even if she had not been wholly successful in blotting the scene from her mind, she— 'Elizabeth.' Tenderly he ran a finger down her cheek. 'You cannot have forgotten. I had unexpected business which required my attention.'

'Of course I have not forgotten.' Her voice, despite the inner turmoil, was calm, almost detached. 'I remember it very well indeed.'

'I am sorry to say that was not the whole truth, my dear. I had a cry for help from an old friend of this family, one who was in sore need of advice.'

Linking her trembling fingers together, Mrs Darcy sat up straight. 'Go on.'

'A close connection on my mother's side, one who deserves my support, a young woman exiled to France these several years and who now longs to return to where she spent part of her childhood…'

'Exiled, you say? A strange word to use in these times.'

'Well…' Darcy's manner stiffened, increasing his wife's forebodings. That he now seemed to avoid looking at her was in itself unusual, his eyes fixed on a distant avenue of trees. 'Well, this young woman also has a son: a boy of five years.'

'I cannot understand.' The knuckles of her clasped hands gleamed white. 'What is it you are trying to say, Darcy?'

'This… person has no wish to return to the country when there is the slightest chance that she might encounter anyone with the name of… Wickham.'

Whatever Mrs Darcy had expected in the way of revelation, it had not been this. She turned in her seat, showing surprise and total lack of comprehension, heard the heavy sigh, saw him rise, walk to the open door of the summer house, where he stood for a moment, absorbing the aspect, before coming back to her and placing a hand on her shoulder. Then he spoke.

'Elizabeth, my dear, the last thing in the world I want is to cause you further distress; there has been more than enough of that over him. Over George Wickham!' The name was spoken with contempt. 'It is a matter I have longed to keep from you, you above all! Which is why I have not spoken of it before. But now I must explain, confide in you, appeal to you and your good sense; ask for, indeed beg for, your help and guidance. Helen Franks, the young woman I mentioned and who sought my help that day, is the granddaughter of a distant cousin of our family. In fact, her grandfather was the sole incumbent at the parish of Littledean. Her parents had both died young and, when she was adopted by an aunt, they used to travel north together to spend holidays at the rectory, and from there the whole family visited Pemberley from time to time. It must have been on the last of these visits that she caught the eye of George Wickham, though it was not until very much later that I learned the truth of the situation and of his involvement. The family were anxious, when her condition was discovered, to cover up what they saw as a disgrace, and she was despatched to Paris on the pretext of a governess post. It was here, often alone and certainly lonely, that she had her son, and, despite persuasions, refused to give him up for adoption.'

'How... how very sad.' Rising, Elizabeth put her arms about her husband, scarce recognising the sense of release which, tragic story notwithstanding, flooded through her. Relief, quickly followed by realisation and shame that she had ever imagined... Anguish, too, as the character of the man married to her youngest sister was being so clearly demonstrated once again.

'When we were in Paris, my dear, I saw Helen at her pressing request when she sought my advice on the possibility of her return. At that time, I advised caution, but now she has written, telling me she has been offered a position as governess with a family who have lost their mother and where her own son can be accommodated. It sounds as if it might be a perfect solution, except for one thing. The problem is that the post would be located little more than twenty miles from Pemberley, and she seeks assurance that there will be no risk of encountering the man, or any connection of his, who betrayed her so basely. Until I can give her such a commitment, then she cannot accept the offer.'

'The poor young woman.' Even as she spoke, Elizabeth's mind was connecting the history with that of her own family, imagining how they might all so easily, but for Darcy's intervention, have been brought to disgrace. And yet she, knowing him so well, she who loved him so much, who owed all her present life and happiness so entirely to him, she, Elizabeth Darcy, had still been sufficiently base as to imagine... Oh, she would not, could not torture herself for ever by reliving such thoughts! Rather she would try for the rest of her life to make amends by— But her husband was continuing.

'Indeed,' he sighed deeply. 'She was a mere child herself when the boy was born. Anyway...' After a moment, Darcy went on. 'Even before Helen's letter reached me, and hearing so much of

191

the situation at Seton Lodge, with Lydia constantly showing her boredom and discontent, thinking of the problems which could possibly arise at Longbourn should Lydia decide to move on there, the strain she would place on Mr and Mrs Bennet...'

'Oh, I feel for them all and—'

'Now, Lizzie, I can imagine how your mind is working, but on this one thing I shall not concede: I am quite determined that Lydia and her family shall never come to live at Pemberley.'

'Oh, my dear!' She knew he had already done more than could ever have been expected of him for the family of a man who had behaved as Wickham had done. 'I would never ask that of you.'

'Well, think carefully of this, Lizzie. Over recent weeks I have been talking things over with Bingley and have come up with an idea, but I shall not take it any further unless you agree. There has been word from a reliable source that Wickham's resignation would, if offered, be very readily accepted by his regiment.' He paused for a moment before continuing. 'And you know of my interest in rail stock?'

'Yes, of course I do, my dear, but...'

'Well, I have also invested in American rail stocks and, having some influence with the directors, I am confident I could secure Wickham a position out there. He could set out with his family, knowing nothing of my part in this. The most likely arrangement would be that Lydia and the children would remain in one of the towns and that he would go ahead with the engineers. He is not an unintelligent man and, if his interest were to be engaged, he could pick up many skills and might even, if he were sufficiently determined, make his fortune. Who knows? So, what is your opinion of my plan, Lizzie? Of course, I should also have to apply to Mr Bennet for his permission.'

'Oh...' For a moment, the proposal being so entirely unforeseen, his wife knew not what to think. She leaned back onto the bench, Darcy beside her, holding her hand, looking into her concerned face. And so her first reaction was ill-judged. 'But... poor, poor Lydia. Is she to be sent away like a common criminal?'

'No. Not like that,' he frowned, his voice betraying a touch of impatience. 'Of course not. They would travel out in some comfort and a house would be secured for them in New York where the company has its offices. There she could live well, and I can readily imagine your youngest sister setting herself up in a salon and patronising those around her. I think it might well be the making of her, if not of her husband. You will think about it, Lizzie?'

'Yes.' As all the advantages of the proposal became obvious, her expression began to lighten. 'Yes, Fitzwilliam, I do see that it might answer very well. Thank you. And forgive me.' Raising her face to his, she kissed his mouth. 'Thank you for taking so much trouble, my dear, dear husband. It is so much more than either Lydia or Wickham deserve. And I do think my father and Mrs Bennet might be very relieved to avoid the prospect of invasion by Lydia and her children. But... you will ask him first.'

'Of course. But not a word to anyone else, Lizzie. I will not have my name mentioned to Wickham in this regard.'

And as they walked slowly back across the park to the great house, Fitzwilliam Darcy felt as if a great weight was falling from his shoulders. He almost dared to hope that he might be about to hear the last of the man who had cast such a long shadow over the House of Darcy.

Epilogue

*D*ear Mrs Darcy,

You may have heard from our father that I, along with Mr Wickham and our family, am about to sail for New York and, despite your recent coldness to me and to my children (who surely have done nothing to offend you), I could not leave my home and country for ever without a word of goodbye to you.

My husband, Mr George Wickham, was recently approached by a large rail company in North America, offering him a post, which he has been very happy to accept. At first he thought the regiment would be unwilling to release him, but, after due persuasion, they agreed to part with him and he immediately resigned his commission.

I cannot tell you how proud I am that his reputation has been such that he has been sought out in this way, thus proving that the petty jealousies of some of our relations have been so wholly undeserved. I hope that those who have these actions on their consciences will, in due time, repent their behaviour.

George encountered some of the rail representatives through a mutual friend and, having spent many evenings in their company, they recognised that his qualities were what they wanted in this new venture.

We sail within the week for New York, and, though I do not feel entirely happy at the prospect of so many days on the ocean, I know that our fortune lies in the New World. So, Mrs Darcy (although to me you will always be plain Lizzie Bennet), we may not meet again – if ever – but I am sure I shall be happy with my dear Wickham and our three children. I hope your own Master Benedict Darcy will give you as much joy and happiness as our children do us. And that he will not be too proud.

I am,

Your loving sister,

Lydia

(Mrs George Wickham, soon of New York)

'So,' said Elizabeth, having read the letter aloud to her husband. She placed it face down on the table and rested her chin on her hand. 'That,' and her voice trembled slightly, 'is my youngest sister saying goodbye.'

'Do not be too upset, Elizabeth. Besides,' he said wryly, 'she – they – may all be back before long, if things do not please them.'

'I am not upset, Fitzwilliam,' his wife replied with a faint smile. 'I am furious that she does not even mention your name when but for you… If you had not obliged Wickham to marry her, I dare not think where she might have been.'

'Well, that is of no account; it is best that she considers Wickham chose her for herself. Certainly I do not wish at some time in the future to be accused of pushing her into an unhappy marriage – though that seems far from the case at the moment.' He held out a hand towards his wife. 'May I glance through it, Lizzie?'

'I would rather you did not, Fitzwilliam. It is scarce legible and with so many misspellings and scorings out…' But even as she spoke, she was giving him the two blotchy pages, watching his impassive face as his eyes scanned the lines.

'There is no date, but I suppose they should now be almost ready to sail. Mr Bennet has gone to see them off, has he not?'

'Yes.' Mrs Darcy sighed. 'I hope he does not feel too despondent.'

'I think he will survive. After all, he must be enjoying peace and quiet at Longbourn such as he has never known for many years. The past few weeks, with all the Wickhams descended upon him, would have tried him sorely.'

Elizabeth laughed. 'Indeed. I am certain that he and Roberta will be very happy to have their home returned to them.'

In fact, Elizabeth mused, as she climbed the stairs and walked along the corridor towards the nursery, she suspected the entire Bennet family would be glad of a respite from the constant anxiety of the Wickhams and their demands. And with them bound for America, with Mary and Kitty apparently happily settled in life and with her father's altogether unexpected change of circumstance, perhaps they were moving forward into a more placid period of their lives.

She stood for a moment, looking down into the cot where her

son lay, sweet smelling and drowsy, blinking once or twice, grimacing then closing his eyes. Lizzie held her breath, looking round only as an arm came about her waist.

'Fitzwilliam! He smiled at me! Did you see?'

Without replying, he shook his head indulgently, simply holding her a little tighter as they stood for a moment longer, looking down at the recent addition to the Darcy family, before, slowly, they turned and left the room. And Elizabeth, for the first time in her life, or so it seemed to her, realised what bliss it was to be the most fortunate woman in the world.

Printed in the United States
104396LV00003B/22/A